YANG HAO was born in Shanxi and grew up in Beijing. She studied film and art history and is now pursuing a PhD in comparative literature at Trinity College Dublin. In Chinese, she has published an essay collection, *Into Renaissance*, and two novels, *Novel Noir* and *Diablo's Boys*. Her debut novel, *Novel Noir*, was shortlisted for the Blancpain-Imaginist Literary Award in 2019. She currently lives in Dublin. *Diablo's Boys* is her first work to be translated.

NICKY HARMAN lives in the UK. She has won several awards for Chinese literary translation, including the 2020 Special Book Award, China, the 2015 Mao Tai Cup People's Literature Chinese-English translation prize, and the 2013 China International Translation Contest, Chinese-to-English section. When not translating, she promotes contemporary Chinese fiction through teaching, blogs, talks and her work on Paper-Republic.org.

MICHAEL DAY is a traveller, translator, and writer who lives in Los Angeles and Mexico City. His awards include the 2015 Bai Meigui Translation Prize and the 2020 Jules Chametzky Translation Prize. His work has appeared in *Georgia Review*, *Massachusetts Review*, *Words Without Borders*, and *Chicago Quarterly Review*, among other publications.

Yang Hao

DIABLO'S BOYS

A Novel

Translated from the Chinese by
Nicky Harman and Michael Day

BALESTIER PRESS
LONDON · SINGAPORE

Balestier Press
Centurion House, London TW18 4AX
www.balestier.com

Diablo's Boys
Original title: 男孩们
Copyright © Yang Hao, 2021
English translation copyright © Nicky Harman and Michael Day, 2025

First published by Balestier Press in 2025

A CIP catalogue record for this book is available from the British Library.

ISBN 978 1 913891 52 7

Cover art © Pu Yingwei

This book is a work of fiction. The literary perceptions and
insights are based on experience, all names, characters, places,
and incidents either are products of the author's imagination
or are used fictitiously.

DIABLO'S BOYS

1

HE did his best to keep staring as he unleashed his Gospel of Heaven skill, the way Suwei did. The glare of the screen left him nowhere to hide, isolated as he was in his room. He found himself screwing up his eyes, like the monster stunned by the green glare of the Gospel of Heaven. The creature was called Nightmare, according to Suwei. He was Diablo's loyal sidekick. Defeating him and finding the Worldstone in his green heart would be equivalent to destroying Diablo's spirit of terror.

Although he didn't know what this spirit of terror was, it sounded malevolent – he agreed with Suwei on that. What he actually wanted to ask him was, *Without the spirit of terror, is Diablo still the Lord of Terror?*

Just now, when he gave the housekeeper Mrs Zhao his new thermos and asked her to rinse it out, Mrs Zhao's lips curled, and she held his eyes for two seconds. He could not tell whether her expression meant astonishment or mockery. Would she put it in the cupboard that only the guests used, or next to the white porcelain cup with a band of gold that belonged to Mrs Luo, Suwei's mother? Uncertainty nagged at him. Mrs Zhao categorised everything in this villa: cups and crockery, clothes, rubbish and dust. Anyway, from the very start he began to drink mineral water, like Mrs Zhao did; every time they finished a bottle, it seemed to mark the completion of a particular task.

Today was the day when Mrs Luo would have her photorejuvenation treatment. He did not need to drive her or go with her. He had to leave before she came back in the evening and then return three days later. In those three days, Mrs Luo would be like a cocooned moth, tightly wrapped in a waterproof web until she emerged into the bright light of day. The people in this house all had their own time systems, the units of measurement of which could be money, youth, vanity or just boredom, which allowed them to claim that they were not bound by gravity.

The first time that he and Suwei launched an attack on Diablo together, he couldn't have imagined that he would end up here.

They had winkled the Worldstone out of Nightmare. He was well aware that his own character, the Priest of Light, had no power to do harm and was only an assistant. He could only cast healing spells or blessings over the Necromancer that Suwei controlled. Although he did possess one power: when he was pumped full of blood and Suwei was defeated, he could restore him to life. But most of the time, Suwei did not need anyone to give him a second life. He was able to summon the brightest and darkest of spirits to decimate all enemies in the Lord of Terror's world.

Diablo roared, then roared again. The Lord of Terror had bled so much that his blood swept Li Wen into a tunnel. It was narrow, and echoed with crashes and bangs that seemed to come from nowhere and go on forever, but always stayed on the same frequency. This frequency made Li Wen feel nauseous, as if he were looking at a swarm of blue-bottles buzzing over a piece of rotten meat. Where and when had he seen this before? Perhaps in the recent past, or perhaps when he was projecting into the future. Grief overwhelmed him, and he dropped into a blind void. He squatted on the ground, scrabbling at the soil in the tunnel with his hands. It was hard and it was filthy. Nothing stirred. He remembered playing in the reservoir behind his grandfather's house when he was a child, squatting on the edge and soaking his hands in the cold water, convinced that this was a surefire way of catching fish. But he never caught one. Every time, he felt that if he waited another fifteen minutes a fish would appear, but then he would feel his mother's footsteps approaching. He never heard her, she was always so silent, as if she had squirrelled herself away in some corner of his body and was spying on his every move.

His phone vibrated. It was a text from Mrs Luo, asking what they were doing. Since the day he told her he knew Suwei's secret, she always made a point of asking them what they were doing. Only a lioness who felt that her cub was threatened would behave like that. He typed a few words, then deleted them. He was not being completely honest, but neither was he lying. Propping himself against the memory foam cushion, he bent down, took a real-time photo of Suwei playing the game and forwarded it to Mrs Luo. He knew that she did not believe his words, only the evidence of her own eyes, and her female instincts. Suwei's short-sleeved white shirt was overexposed, causing Diablo to dissolve in a blur of light on the screen. The blood on the Lord's body was suddenly endowed with a bizarre purity, as if Death had given it a carapace it had never had before, as if any species could wrest immortality from the nauseating process of putrefaction before it died.

The spell he chanted in response and the roar of the Lord of Terror melded together, giving him the illusion of a tragic drama. He saw all the humans, other living creatures and angels that Diablo had devoured erupting from his enormous red body as his power weakened, surrounding the Lord of Terror with a miasma of even greater terror. He began to suspect that even if Diablo was killed, the world's fear would not disappear, and everything would be thrown back into the cycle of life.

He screwed up his eyes, trying to see more clearly.

'Do we have to kill Diablo?' he asked.

Suwei's hands kept moving, and he did not look at Li Wen.

'Yeah. Every time.'

'Because he's evil?'

'No, because he's the Lord of Terror. That's how his mother Lilith made him.'

Before he could lay the second blessing on Suwei, Diablo let out a final roar as the brilliance of Suwei's Holy Light Summoning fell upon him, and all the blood and befouled ashes disappeared in a plume of smoke. The screen in front of him became bright and soft, and the Promised Land, once dominated by fear, was resurrected. Suwei took a long breath. When faced with the prompt to enter the name of the warrior who had beaten the game, Suwei thought for a while and turned to look at him. 'This is your first time. I'll write yours.'

He hesitated, watching as Suwei typed his name on the screen: Li Wen. And it was as if the blocky characters cast a spell over both of them.

2

THE Luo home was like an oasis hidden in the heart of Beijing. The pale-yellow houses looked snug and warm, but each kept itself a little apart, as if they did not want their shadows to overlap. Back where he came from, people loved sharing secrets, which spread about them like randomly shaped scraps of knitting. But here, in this oasis, was the silence he craved. He saw himself reflected in Mrs Luo's glittering crystal ceiling: a young man wearing a shirt with the top button fastened too tight, hands folded in front of him, very formal.

Before he first set eyes on Suwei, Li Wen had not spent much time imagining what the boy looked like. He had already had a year's experience of being greeted at the door by the mistress of the house. These women always opened the door with an impenetrable smile as they let him in. Behind them stood the master of the house, ready to give a final nod of approval, as well as the children, somewhere in the background, or sometimes made to line up to greet him with their cat or dog. Li Wen had been accustomed to women being in charge of the home since he was a child himself – they controlled the opening and closing of doors, monitoring the delicate internal balance of the home. This could be the reason why male tutors had become more popular than females in recent years: young women reminded the mistress of the house how she had arrived at her present state, while young men were more likely to become their allies.

But Li Wen had always been careful not to allow himself to

take sides, although he knew that if he wanted to stay with the family long-term, he would have to choose whether to come under the mistress's or the master's influence. And this, in turn, meant that he needed to make apparently trivial but visible choices: for example, when the kids were doing well, he had to choose who to tell first. Or if they had a secret that they did not want their mum or dad to know, whether he should reveal it. Or if the kids excitedly told him what they wanted to do when they grew up, whether he should lobby for one choice or another. With every choice he made, Li Wen felt that he was trapped on an infinite chessboard. Every time he took a step, no matter whether it improved or weakened his position, he still had no way of knowing whether it would eventually bring victory within his grasp.

He had really looked forward to his job with Mrs Luo and Suwei. Their appearance seemed like a sudden cold light shed upon this chess game, finally turning the tables in his favour. Besides, he knew that this time around, his graduation certificate improved the odds for him. Quite apart from his English degree, all the women who managed these pale-yellow houses were very taken by the fact that he supposedly had a degree in sports management as well. It was crucial to nurture their children's life force, so naturally they counted physical fitness as an indicator of their children's future competitiveness. As far as Mrs Luo was concerned, his sports experience was exactly what she was looking for. Not so much to enable Suwei to compete in the future, but to ensure that he would glow with vitality.

If Li Wen had had a choice, he would have classed what was, in their eyes, his most marketable skill as an absurd fantasy. He was quite unlike the kids he taught, including Suwei, and yet there were surprising similarities. Once, one of his pupils had just started senior middle school and was getting ready for his SAT exams. His name was Tao, and he was skinny with narrow eyes and a face covered in pimples. He wobbled any time he moved, as if unable to support the weight of his head. Tao was a good student who threw himself into his work, and there was little that Li Wen, as his tutor, could do for him. He gave Tao English dictation, and made him stop every hour to do some press-ups. Tao's mother seemed very satisfied with Li Wen's arrangement, especially the press-ups. She was always complaining to Li Wen that Tao was too skinny. At first, Tao couldn't manage even one press-up. His arms shook as if they were about to give way and land him on the ground. There were no miracles. Tao never learned to do press-ups properly, but he liked to try, and did his best to copy Li Wen's movements. Li Wen sensed that Tao was responding to him in a polite, grown-up way. The kid had a puritanical guilt about any game, or any other break from studying. He told Li Wen that he was going to Harvard to study law and wanted to get a job at the United Nations. He had ambitions to work on the principles of justice.

'Do you know what justice is?' Li Wen had asked.

'Sure,' Tao said. 'It means that both good and bad people get their just desserts.'

'And how do you define good and bad?'

'People who do good things are good, and those who do bad things are bad.'

'What if good people do bad things and bad people do good things?'

'Then the good are bad, and the bad are good,' said Tao.

Tao was due to take his SATs this year. Li Wen hoped he would get what he wanted in life. He wondered if Tao would come back from Harvard one day, holding the banner of justice aloft, and make revolution on his lawyer father.

Li Wen never kept in touch with the children he no longer taught. He had group chats on his mobile – with Tao, Qingming, and Wuqi – but once he was no longer their tutor, the groups fell silent. He did not believe it was deliberate. People just chose to forget and bury unimportant memories. When he was in junior middle school, he wanted a Samsung flip phone. Even though he only got the red phone that his mother's company gave her on her retirement, he was still delighted. His mobile was full of his classmates' numbers. Back then, he had asked them for their numbers and entered them in, but he only ever took his mother's calls – she called all the time, and he couldn't avoid answering. Probably for that reason, he started to dislike phone messages. To Li Wen, messages were to be received, not answered, and should be deleted after he had read them.

At some point in his life, he began to hear a manikin jumping up and down in his ear, frantic as he shouted at Li Wen, 'Don't get too close to them! Don't get too close to them! It could be disastrous!'

Li Wen could almost see the manikin, with his cupped hands and his eyes staring.

Mrs Luo opened the dark wooden door to him, and he breathed in the aroma of figs. Her face was quite unlined, her skin clear and bright. Her first words were, 'Mr Li, we've been waiting so long for you.'

*

Li Wen stamped hard on the brakes. In the centre of the narrow road, he could see something dark – a blue cat with pupils that shone gold. He wondered whose it was. It was obviously shy, because it fled like a silent shadow. Maybe it had come out of one of the nearby houses. He thought no more of it and carried on driving. This evening, he would give her back the car key.

Later, when he thought back to that moment, he was still unsure how the car key had triggered subsequent events. Mrs Luo could not drive. Apparently not long after she first joined the Beijing Ballet, Old Chen had taken a fancy to her and used to send his car to pick her up and deliver her home, so she never had a chance to learn. Li Wen was aware that Mrs Luo's car key was a token of her regard, a unique privilege awarded to her current man. But she could also, arbitrarily, take it back. No problem, he thought. When she gave it to you, she trusted you absolutely. Her life was in your hands. As for when she took it back, it would be a clean break, but not something he could prepare for in advance.

For the moment, Li Wen played the perfect secretary to Mrs Luo, but the closer he drew to her, the more frightened he became. This was completely different from the first day, the day he met Suwei. He had been warned that Suwei was a special child, but in fact Suwei's silence pleased him. He was afraid of children's careless curiosity about him (even if that curiosity was short-lived), but Suwei did not have that problem at all. Suwei had no interest in who he was. The boy lived entirely in a world of dark spirits, and all that Li Wen needed to do was keep an eye on him.

The tutors formed a particular community in the city. They belonged to other families; they were itinerant bystanders. They were attached to a hitherto unknown sort of home, constantly going in and out, and the family who employed them had to trust them one hundred percent before flinging the door wide and welcoming them in. They, the tutors, only needed to show a sheet of paper with their CV. Could anyone verify the claims in it, their antecedents? He did not know. And none of the tutors believed in themselves. In this city, everyone lived in the present; the past was forgotten, and the future was unknown. All was uncertainty.

That day, Li Wen had arrived home with a mixture of trepidation and pride. He read his name on the new card on the door over and over, until his unsmiling face in the photo began to seem like a stranger's. He was a jerk, a deserter gone AWOL, but he was also brave. Once he was sure about this (he had a feeling he was merely going with the flow), he moved out of the house he had been sharing and into a newly developed housing complex on the Fourth Ring Road. When he first came to Beijing the year before, he had been here to look around. It was a convenient distance from the centre, not too near, and from what he could see through conveniently-placed windows, the rooms looked cosy. The best thing was that the fancy villas occupied by Mrs Luo and her ilk fell in the same zone, but were physically separated by a network of new roads. Beijing was the same as his hometown, in that when spring arrived, it brought wind squalls and sand storms that dried up his face, scouring away all traces of tears. That was fine for Li Wen. He didn't mind what Beijing was like. All he wanted to do was escape. His goal was to live comfortably in this Fourth Ring Road housing estate hidden behind rows of identical grey buildings, and to be completely anonymous.

To start with, Suwei and his mother were the perfect clients. 'Please call me Mrs Luo,' she had said, and that was fine by him, he had no reason to refuse. He discovered afterwards that everyone called her that, from the housekeeper to the family doctor, though he assumed that Suwei was the exception to that rule. Li Wen had to admit that from the get-go, he had an inexplicable sense of connection with Suwei. Not sympathy exactly, but a feeling that he wanted to make things right for this kid. He felt envy too, especially when the curtains in Suwei's room were drawn, and all that could be heard in the darkness was Suwei's breathing, and everything was neat and in its place.

Li Wen went forward and reversed four times, the rubber flooring under the tires wheezing as he did so. He tried to park the car so that it was perfectly level. He glanced at the phone. It was just ten o'clock at night. Suwei might be asleep or wide awake. While living with his own mother, Li Wen had needed to be sneaky at night – sneaking up to the bathroom, burrowing inside the quilt to listen to music. Even his dreams were furtive, and if they made him smile, that was furtive too. His mother's bedroom had been next door to his, and her senses were as keen as a civet cat at night. She could hear and see everything, and occasionally he was startled awake when he heard her cough or clear her throat. If there was anyone else in the house, he was always on the alert, afraid that his mother might suddenly burst through the wall.

Mrs Luo always teased him when he tiptoed around.

'Suwei won't hear. His room is soundproof.'

'I still don't think he's asleep.'

At night, the house was divided into two restricted zones. Half belonged to Suwei, and the rest belonged to Mrs Luo. Li Wen was never sure that Suwei was asleep. He could sense the boy's eyes staring at him like two black holes boring through his mother's magnificent wallpaper. Suwei had, he knew, listened to the message he had left for him on the portable recorder. It was the last communication between the two of them. For a few nights now, Li Wen had dreamed of Suwei curled up naked, like a baby.

He was even more convinced that Mrs Luo and he were locked into a promise that neither could break. He had never met anyone as decisive as she was. That night, after agreeing to his conditions, she had brought him to her bedroom without a shadow of hesitation. Every time he woke up in her bed, his head felt heavy – the skin of this woman had the aridity of the north, as well as a life force that was intimidating. Her obstinacy felt familiar, yet alarming.

A ravenous hyena will devour the corpse of its own kind. Li Wen could see that he was turning into a hyena, having swiftly bartered Suwei's secret for the opportunity to join the mother's camp. He had asked Suwei who Diablo was, and Suwei said that he was the Lord of Terror. He saw the secret fear that enveloped Suwei getting closer and closer to him, until he had nowhere to hide. He began to monitor his own actions meticulously, avoiding touching Suwei's hair, even casually, or brushing Suwei's hands, but Suwei did not seem to notice anything, as if the owner of the overwhelming secret was Li Wen, not Suwei. It was as if Suwei's voice message was buried deep in a tree hollow within the portable recorder from which it could not escape. Li Wen had only entered this sealed-off world once, staying there for a day: it was pitch black, and jammed into some wormhole in the universe, where there was no such thing as time or space. He knew that Suwei floated in such a world. He was not apathetic, just unresponsive.

Anyone who knew the secret might be beheaded. He had never been able to keep secrets from his mother, and he could not keep a secret now.

'Is an apartment enough?'

Mrs Luo's voice floated in the stagnant air. With her, it was probably not worth exchanging a house for silence; a despicable person like him was worthless, Li Wen thought. But he was absolutely not as determined as the other young men around Mrs Luo. He had no clear-cut goals. The apartment was a hiding place for him. He had become more cautious, but not because he and Mrs Luo were getting closer. He increasingly felt that this woman was manipulating him; he had made a demand which he almost immediately regretted and which made him feel oddly guilty. It also reminded him of Suwei's secret. Everything rolled around in her hands; he might be swallowed up too.

It was despicable the way he had threatened her, he thought. He defined it thus: although they came after he had issued his demands, both his vileness and his threats transported him back to the day when the results of his college entrance examination results came out, and he had to face his mother's long silence and his own helpless panic. Before Li Wen had time to say, 'Yes, it's enough!' (of course, Mrs Luo knew there was no other answer he could give), she began to tell him how talented a ballet dancer Suwei had been, as if she had prepared herself to tell only Suwei's story this evening. Others could only remember rhythms after listening to the music several times over, but the boy's body kept time with the music from the first moment he heard it. She also told him that when Suwei was young, he was afraid of the dark, and could only sleep with a nightlight. She no longer had to plan what Suwei needed to do the next day. This house was moving backwards through time. There were no arrangements for tomorrow, only constant, suspicious (he could see that now) memories connecting the mother and son whose house this was. Li Wen began to understand that both he and Doctor Zhong had only one real task, and that was to ensure Suwei's safety. There was no need to treat him or teach him. The more Mrs Luo talked to him, the more panicked Li Wen became. He was afraid of disrupting that feather-light balance, of discounting the dark world that Suwei had so carefully created. He was afraid that one day Suwei would fall into the world of Diablo and vanish. But what would happen if he were to snatch Suwei out of that world? He could not even be sure whether the things that Suwei had witnessed came from the real world, but he knew that Suwei had not forgotten them, had only closed his eyes to them. And he, Li Wen, could neither save the child Suwei who loved ballet, nor the adult he would become. He could only be a bloody executioner, driving everything towards a trap in the name of truth.

Mrs Luo never drank or smoked. In fact, she was almost robotically self-disciplined, and regularly practised turtle-breathing qigong exercises to stave off the ravages of age. Fully dressed, she smelled like a just-ripened fig. When she took her clothes off and he possessed her, there was a whiff of something pungently astringent underneath the figs. No matter how smooth and clean she was on the surface, the fermentation that came with age could not be concealed. The more often he went to her room, the more persistently the smell spread and clung, almost suffocating him. The smell reminded him that everything would fade away, reminded him of pretence and deceit, reminded him of his mother.

'Damn it, women stink. Why do I keep sniffing them?' Li Wen muttered, accidentally biting his tongue with his back teeth as he chewed on his chewing gum. It hurt like hell.

Li Wen was disgusted at his own inability to use bad language when he shouted at people. He laid the blame for his cowardice in this respect with his mother, there was no doubt about it. Even Dr Pei swore. He had heard him effing and blinding at the other doctors and nurses through the wall that divided the clinic from Mrs Luo's office.

'Swearing is a strategy, it's very strange,' said Mrs Luo, ever keen to instruct him. 'When people see you spewing out bad language, they're afraid of you.'

Mrs Luo was always like this with him. She was never open about her desires, only hinting at what she wanted him to do. Li Wen wondered if it might actually have been worse if that stuff hadn't happened to Suwei and the boy really had become a ballet dancer. To be honest, Li Wen could not bear the sight of men in leggings. He thought of the organs and muscles wrapped in sheer white fabric, and it made his skin crawl to see them so proudly on display. He could not understand how the minds of ballet lovers worked. The extreme limits to which the dancers pushed themselves came at the price of misshapen, even deformed, bodies. The way they developed and used their bodies inevitably led to injuries. At university he had studied exercise theory and followed the athletes' training routines, and was constantly sick. Although, in the end, his muscles never lost the memories of their training, in Li Wen's view, it was just the brain using inertia to deceive the body over and over again. He had seen Mrs Luo's feet, and her two big toes were grotesquely enlarged even though she had never once had the chance to perform on stage.

'We never got opportunities back then. No matter how good your English was, you could only get a job locally as a teacher.'

His mother's words had been echoing in his ears recently, whenever he got the lift from the garage and went upstairs. Sometimes the lift light shorted out. Mrs Luo had said today that she would ask Mrs Zhao to get someone to repair it. The lift was slow and cramped. He always looked up whenever the light inside went off. This time he seemed to see a dance stage, and he realised that he was no different from Suwei. Below the stage, his mother was looking up at him with a smile. His whole body was covered in pale fishing lines. His mother moved her finger and he took a step. When she raised her finger, his limbs hung suspended in the air, ridiculous and hollow.

'I've decided, I've definitely decided,' Li Wen muttered to himself. Cowardice bred resentment. He knew that Mrs Luo was waiting for him, standing silently on the soft floor, feigning delight at being conquered by him. Another ten minutes. He could make her wait another ten minutes. He could tell her that the lift stopped suddenly and he was waiting for it to start again. Just like back then, as soon as he opened his mouth, she would know that he was panicking. The minute it was uttered, the secret bound the person who knew it, but bolstered the confidence of the teller. He wanted to see Mrs Luo's fortress crumble with his own eyes, but he had by now begun to fear for the mangled remains of Suwei in the ruins, because these women were so tenacious in their vitality.

What he faced now must be a farewell, not a confession. No one had told Mrs Luo and Suwei his story, which was a pity. He would stand before her, a despicable specimen who had used the naked truth to scam a place to live in Beijing, but was too timid to hide himself. He, that man, was scared again, and was about to go cap in hand to beg for a bolt hole. Mrs Luo might respond to a story like that. She had probably never found herself needing to take back something she had given. For women like her, once she had taken it back, the thread that bound them together would be broken. The next day she would not even remember his name.

Li Wen had insisted on working out for himself the layout of the house. Strictly speaking, these residential developments were supposed to be sealed from the outside world. If the regulations were lax, then the place would be full of family friends and acquaintances swiping themselves in and out. But for anyone with a grudge against the inhabitants, a barrel of oil and a lighter would be enough to burn them in their beds. Their houses were not impregnable, it would take no time at all. There would be no point in the attacker trying to grab hold of their victim, who would have died instantly. Li Wen knew he couldn't do anything like that because he was a coward. Suwei would crow if he ever found that out. Though he might not find out, or care if he did. Suwei had tried to teach Li Wen to play as the Necromancer, who he maintained was his favourite character, but Li Wen failed every time. Unable to wait for the souls to be summoned, he was always being beaten to death by the emissary of terror. Suwei would often laugh out loud. Li Wen did not tell Suwei that this was the first time he had played *Diablo*, and this was why he was afraid.

Mrs Luo opened the door, wearing a fuchsia-pink dress which clung softly to her body. He saw the flame alight on her, and felt the urge to get one last taste of that musky astringency, that damned smell, and then leave the key, and flee.

He must move forwards. He must not be devoured by Diablo. A greater terror awaited him.

3

AFTER puberty, Chen Suwei stopped developing. It was not until those two huge black holes appeared in his eyes that he felt the rigid world around him begin to turn clear and bright. Like spending fifteen minutes in the dazzling noontime sun: a brief spell of dizziness followed by an even shorter period of ecstasy.

Mum was still downstairs.

Their house was at the western end of the housing development, the fifth from the left in the third row. Like the villas around it, it was a pale-yellow rectangular building with a red tiled roof, and a crabapple tree by the door. They had not planted it themselves; there was one at every door on the estate, all more or less of the same height. Here, standardisation was approved of, as if standardisation equalled style. The message was, we provide everything you might need. And you cannot refuse it.

Mum had stayed home all morning. She sat at the long table in the dining room downstairs, silently watching Mrs Zhao wipe every inch of the floor. She performed this task scrupulously, day after day, until the floor was spotless. He did not understand why anyone these days would make people squat down and scrub their floors with a rag. In his opinion, this activity was both meaningless and pernickety, just like all the useless decorations in their home. For four years, he had watched Mrs Zhao spend her days wiping away every particle of dust, leaving silently after cooking dinner at night. He had no idea where Mrs Zhao spent the nights. Maybe in the squat, grey hostel not far from their estate, or perhaps another grey hostel much, much further away. As for himself, he could not be sure because he had stayed in the same pale-yellow cuboid of a house for four years.

To be perfectly honest, Suwei detested the colours in their home. They were too bright and dazzling. In Diablo's world, everything was perfect: dark red body, dark red gems, black air . . . only Suwei gleamed with light. It was not dazzling at all. He always drew the curtains and locked his room door so that the screen in front of him could devour him, leaving nothing behind.

Mum would knock at his door three times at one o'clock in the afternoon and say she was going out. Sometimes he looked around and the door was closed. Other times, he did not look around, and the door was open. Then, having waited a quarter of an hour (he could judge the interval with increasing accuracy), Suwei opened up, slipped downstairs and gobbled down the lunch that Mrs Zhao had prepared. Occasionally, when Mrs Zhao was doing the washing-up, they would exchange glances. He would give a quick nod which, in his mind, expressed his thanks to her for saving him from dying from malnutrition – of course, that was a nonsensical proposition. Some days, it occurred to him that his mother might not actually be afraid of him dying, that perhaps she had mentally prepared herself for it. He could not see into her mind. After all, it was not her who had shut him in the house.

He went back to his room again and fired up his computer. It was exactly half as old as he was. He did not immediately turn on the screen, he wanted to wait and see.

Suwei's room was neither as messy as a typical eighteen-year-old boy's, nor as silent as the equipment of that era should have been: a computer with a separate tower from the noughties, a huge LCD TV, a black PlayStation 2 console, and game discs neatly arranged in a dignified white box. These things embodied a complex network of time, belonging neither to the present nor to the past.

Suwei wondered if Li Wen would ever come back.

It had been three days, and Suwei sensed that once again he was in a world where nothing but Diablo existed. Diablo was huge and amorphous. He had never seen Diablo's face. Although the voice had said that Diablo was the Lord of Terror, he had never felt afraid. He turned on his screen: there were trees, pools, churches, and dead bodies littered everywhere, all of the same degree of brightness as his room. This was his world. It was easy for him to forget his face in an instant, because the only thing that could represent him were the blue and red liquids in the spherical cups. When the liquids were there, he was there. When they departed, he would die. It was as simple as that.

He might have died a long time ago, but for the fact that in these last two days he had finally succeeded in seeing his surroundings only through the black holes in his eyes without panicking. Everything was poked through those holes. He just had to open his eyes and the black holes attached themselves to the trees, pools, churches, and littered dead bodies, while warning him that he could only eliminate them by closing his eyes. The curse of the Lord of Terror.

Li Wen did not come.

He had wanted to be the first to tell Li Wen about all this. Recently, it had seemed to him that he could communicate with his mother through Li Wen. They all thought he was sick because he didn't speak. They didn't know that he was just exhausted. He did not much like Li Wen, but he was in no doubt that he felt more at ease with him than any of the other young men who turned up randomly at home. It was not that he felt comforted by Li Wen's presence, it was that he somehow felt familiar. Li Wen never used cologne. Suwei did not like body scents. Diablo had no scent.

If it had not been for Li Wen, Suwei would never have told his mother about the black holes in his eyes. There had always been secrets between him and his mother. As long as he did not divulge his secrets, no one would know until one of them died. For a long time now, he and his mother had been like two magnets of the same polarity. They were identical. There had never been any possibility that they would attract one another. Although she was frighteningly intelligent, only he knew he had black holes in his eyes. They were less easy to spot than his muteness. If he just kept living with his black holes without saying a word, they would never grow bigger than his own eyes. Besides, he had calculated every inch of Diablo. Even if he went blind in both eyes, he would be able to see what was happening in the game.

People said, 'He shuts himself in his room every day and plays games.'

But they were only half-right.

He could be a master learned in the sutras, an archer, a warrior in armour, or a Necromancer who summoned the souls of the dead. He spent day after day immersed in Diablo's terror, in a world in which he could defeat the dark red behemoth time and time again. But he could never really kill Diablo. Every time he turned on the computer and the monitor, the Lord of Terror was resurrected, and then he had to keep the faith and destroy Diablo's heart once more. Suwei felt that he and Diablo had established a relationship that was much more honest and real than that between him and his mother: Diablo never appeared when you had nothing. He would wait for you in the darkness, never going back on his word, wait until you were strong and confident enough to deal him the final, fatal blow. In that instant, fear did not break apart, and he, Suwei, saved the Promised Land and shattered the abyss by his own efforts. There was no need for him to distinguish between good and bad here, he only needed to be the warrior who saved everyone. And so his life flowed faster and faster, becoming increasingly meaningless.

If he said nothing, Mum would probably not find it unusual (this was one of the many benefits of being classed as different). It was only when he went downstairs or had just eaten that he would feel a kind of intense discomfort, as if his eyes had been shrouded. Or as if a bottomless black hole had suddenly appeared in the pastel hues of the decor his mother had chosen. The difference between the light given off by each was too great, and he was overwhelmed by dizziness. He almost needed to hold on to the bannisters as he walked down the stairs, reaching out to find where the next step was, like a cat.

Six months before, he had heard his mother and Li Wen discussing him. It must have been Li Wen's first day, and they were saying that he took refuge from the real world in his games. He was confused by their use of the word 'real', but he could not be bothered to argue, although he had his defence: 'I'm not trapped in a fantasy world, I'm trapped by reality.' Once, he had recorded himself saying this on the portable recorder. It made him laugh. It sounded both innocent and phoney in the quiet of the night.

Eight in the evening was the time Mum was supposed to come home, though she was rarely punctual.

He almost turned around and went back upstairs to avoid speaking. Every time he spoke, he needed to defeat not the words themselves but the dense vapour that shrouded his speech. The droplets were so small as to be invisible, but Suwei could see them. The vapour would start to swirl upwards even before people opened their mouths, dense with suspicion, hypocrisy, hurt, love and hate, and Suwei had to conquer all this before he could open his own mouth. It was a lengthy process and, most of the time, these past few years, he lost his chance to speak, because by the time he finally calmed the droplets, people had walked away.

'Mrs Luo, the soup's in the pot. I'm off now. Message me if you need me to do anything.'

Mrs Zhao said the same thing every day. It was her way of saying that she had completed her tasks and was ready to leave. Most of the time, dinner was soup. Mum only drank soup at night, and so did he. That was the reason why mother and son never put on any weight over the years. Even though she was not at home all day, he certainly was, and yet their body shapes had not changed much. They had trained themselves not to need much food.

Mum had been back home on time recently, and Suwei guessed that she was waiting for Li Wen, just as he was. He had no idea why. He came downstairs, and a load seemed to fall from his mother's shoulders when she looked at him. Now, studying her expression, he finally figured out an answer: his mother had never worried because he stayed home all day. For a while, he even firmly believed that his mother wanted him to stay home, upstairs, in Diablo's world.

His mother's face was bloated again. He could see it reflected in the crystal ceiling, so brightly as to worry him. Every few days, his mother's face would inflate like a balloon and assume a stupefied expression. It was impossible, then, to tell how old she was.

Her face was almond-shaped with a slightly upturned chin, bright eyes that tilted upwards at the corners, and exquisite eyebrows. When swollen like this, her features and her skin were firm where there should have been wrinkles, and you could not see her breathing. Her face became as icy cold and expressionless as the white marble coffee table in their lounge. It should have been a vivid, obstinate face, but the air around it solidified every pore, immobilised every movement of the eyes, nose, eyebrows and mouth. A few days later, this horrible bloating would dissipate, and Mum's face would appear sleek and smooth, smoother even than before. The whole process made for a very strange face, wrinkle-free, flat and shiny. It was incredible.

In Diablo's world, you could tell the age of all the characters by their wrinkles. They were the real deal, and he never doubted them: the people who gave him their wisdom had shrivelled, kindly faces, those who gave him strength were tall and strong, and those who helped him with their wealth were smooth-skinned. He met certain people at a certain time and place. There was no need to guess whether they were about to spring unpleasant surprises on him.

There were rules for everything, and they made him indomitable.

For Suwei, the way his mother's face swelled up and went down was a highly accurate indicator of time and what might happen in it.

Every time the swelling disappeared and her face was as smooth as glass for a few days, they would have guests. Suwei was never sure what to call these young men. They were guests, because they always stayed for a night and then left, and never had anything to do with his life. His room was on the third floor, and his mother's room was on the second floor. For these young guests, the third floor was a forgotten corner of the house. No one ever passed his door. If they did come across each other downstairs (and that did not happen very often), they would stand on tiptoe, bend backwards and try as far as possible to make themselves invisible. It was just that these guests stayed longer than the normal sort. So Suwei would scrutinise his mother's face and make a careful note of the time, so that he could avoid bumping into the men.

He remembered that one of them had a sharply defined square jaw, just like one he had seen when he was a little boy. He scooted upstairs and shut the door of his room, leaving Square Jaw looking startled. He could tell that Square Jaw was more nervous than he was, and had only come down to get a glass of water. He also thought that half the young man's alarm came from the crystal ceiling above his head. It glittered and reflected back at his young face and his bathrobe-clad body. After that, Suwei was more cautious, because these young guests were as easily scared as the handsome deer that lived in the woods. They and Suwei also shared a secret that they did not need words to communicate: Suwei knew that these young men would always leave, and could never be part of the family. The family consisted only of himself and his mother.

Suwei could read from their eyes (although most of the time they did not make eye contact) that this was not their aim. They had no intention of becoming part of the family. But that evening, when Li Wen – unusually – stayed over, Suwei spotted the passion in Li Wen's eyes, and it struck him that he had almost never seen such strong emotion in the eyes of the other young deer. For the first time, Suwei began to think that Li Wen might stay, treading like a lion over the scattered white bones of the others.

One of Suwei's first memories was the most important thing his mother had told him: 'Dad's gone, Dad's missing again.' He remembered his father as quite strict, neither very close to him nor very harsh. But gradually, as time passed, his memory of his father faded. He was not the kind of kid to tell himself fairy tales, in which his father had gone on a long voyage, or was far away sorting out some long and complicated matter. He knew that was a lie. He had occasional flashbacks, which he could not remember clearly, that his parents used to fight, that his father had fastened the top button of his shirt very tightly.

The home they lived in was large, so large their voices were deadened by distance, as if mountain ranges and rushing rivers lay between them. One day, after his father went missing, workers in grey-blue uniforms installed soundproof panelling on the walls. They attacked their task silently and swiftly. Fortunately, he fit right in with the neighbourhood; he never set foot outside, so no one could hear him, and he couldn't hear anyone else either. He was the baby bird dangling from his mother's beak in the nursery rhyme: he opened his eyes and saw the world she wanted him to see.

Mum took him to an expert in a white dress shirt who said the boy had a 'cognitive blind spot' in his brain, an emotional barrier walling him off from the rest of the world. He still remembered the question Mum had asked:

'Is he a danger to himself?'

'No. At present, he has no tendency toward self-harm.'

'Can you guarantee that?'

'Generally speaking, we don't make guarantees. What you need to know is that the arteries of his interior mental world have hardened. There are no pathological changes, but it's impossible to say if or when the condition might improve.'

So he learned precisely what Mum's bottom line was: she needed him to lie back and slide compliantly into the world mama bird had made. He did not reply, remaining absorbed as ever in his ceaseless pursuit of Diablo. It didn't bother him to be confined, bruised and bleeding, to Diablo's dark inferno, because he knew he could revive again and again, he knew no one could hurt him. He had other names here, names drawn from ancient scriptures, implying that he was the offspring of a demon and an angel.

But at the same time, Diablo revived again and again too, because other people willed it. The Lord of Terror seemed to have no true form. Suwei was starting to believe that the secret of Diablo's world of fear lay in the spinning CD-ROM filled with code and the antiquated computer setup that controlled it – it was a truly closed-loop system that could generate countless complete stories based on endings determined in advance.

Mum had bought him several mobile phones, wrongly assuming that he was interested in every kind of invented world (or maybe she had just been trying to drop him a hint). The games on the phones frightened him – they were never-ending, all you did in them was move forward, there was no endpoint, no sense of reality whatsoever. The worst part about these games was that you had to wait for other people to join before you could start, you had to be either a follower or a leader. That meant everything depended on your own decisions and other people's subterfuge, truth interwoven with falsehood, and that frightened Suwei, so he tucked the unused phones away in a drawer, not knowing where else to inter the white cuboids.

Suwei had his own secret language.

He had a portable recorder, a gift from a young guest who had visited them years before. He loved it. He covertly stored audio tracks on the recorder. He extracted the stories from his memory, things he happened to recall and things he had forgotten, certainly not things he had any desire to do. It was as if he were being buried alive by vanishing time. No one else would hear, or so he thought at first, imagining only Diablo heard the audio tracks he recorded. In fact, there were not many audio tracks, because the recorder had limited storage capacity. What he didn't tell Diablo was that he longed for the Lord of Terror to someday swallow everything, to unleash the legendary destructive power of the Worldstone.

'This happened once before, one year when there was a violent sand storm. Something blew into my eye, and Mum took me to the doctor to have it taken out – it was a fleck of coal cinder. Everything looked blurry, and it worked its way further in every time I blinked. With each blink, it felt as if a hole were being bored in my eye.'

The recollections he retrieved seemed to grow more fragmentary by the day. It seemed as if the black holes in his eyes had begun eating into his memory, too, penetrating his brain, splitting it into two unrelated halves. It was strange: weren't the things in front of your eyes the only things your eyes could see? At first, people believed the material world was trustworthy, then it couldn't be relied on any more, and the internal spiritual world took over. The spiritual world was invisible to the naked eye, so the material world won out, but by the time your eyes were so full of material things you couldn't see, the spirit had long since evaporated, and it turned out everything had been an overly optimistic guess.

Suwei thought it over. The real reason he was eagerly awaiting Li Wen wasn't to discuss whether to tell Mum about what had happened to eyes, but because of the recorder sitting in the drawer. All Suwei had to do was leave the drawer open a crack, and Li Wen would pull it the rest of the way out while Mrs Zhao was giving Suwei his bath. The recorder was their shared secret. He knew Li Wen had heard some of the stories crammed into the black box (what wasn't certain was how much he had heard), so there was a bewitching selectivity to the tales he told to the device: he became a narrator, weaving stories from his memories, like a dejected aside behind Diablo's back, until the truth he firmly believed in no longer rubbed like grit in his eye, and he even began to suspect that authenticity involved a degree of confabulation.

In Mum's opinion, his growth was stunted.

Mrs Zhao had been tasked with bathing him since her second year with the family. He felt like a child when Mum bathed him. If only he were a child, he could have remained sexless for a while; he could have faced adults without any physiological awkwardness. When he thought of this squat, homely woman, Mrs Zhao, cooking him wholesome meals, her sex was temporarily erased, but when he actually stood stark naked in front of her, he immediately discovered he was an adult disguised within a child's flayed pelt, and he flinched, withdrew into himself, twisted with shame, got goose pimples all over.

He and Mum had agreed that he would bathe just once a week. When he got goose pimples, Mrs Zhao assumed it was because he was cold, so from then on she started preparing hot towels for him, dunking them into the bathwater and draping them over his shoulders to warm him. He wavered numbly between shame and gratitude at being seen through, and he learned to shut his eyes and imagine this was all a dream that would soon end. He couldn't see his body, but he could feel Mrs Zhao's hands. He was that white rabbit he had raised at the age of five: once submerged in the water, he quickly stopped struggling.

When Mrs Zhao towelled him off, he read a certain pity in her gestures. 'Don't worry, we're just going to dry your hair off.' Submerged in the tub, Suwei looked more childlike than ever. Mrs Zhao sometimes talked to him in the voice he had used with the rabbit. He had grown accustomed to it. The fact that even at this age he still needed a middle-aged woman to help him bathe proved that he would always be a child. Even so, although he disguised himself as a silly, clumsy child, he didn't want to touch his own body. He wanted to climb to the rocks on the beach and sun himself like a fish – didn't sunlight kill off bacteria? Maybe, if he sunned himself long enough, the things inside his body would be washed out by the sunshine.

He kept his focus fixed on these jagged fragments. He got the sense that the world was a very dangerous place, and found on occasion that people were deliberately doing things behind his back. For instance, Suwei discovered that Li Wen was sneaking in while he was in the bath and listening to his portable recorder, because he found the machine slanted two centimetres to the right one time. That day, he buried himself beneath the covers and stayed hidden for a long time, until the cloistered air gave him a jolt of inspiration: he would share the audio recordings with Li Wen, because that way, if he died one day, at least someone would have heard his true memories, memories of his aborted adulthood, his failure to develop.

He dashed down the last length of stairs, his mother's face and his eyes flashing in turn across the crystal ceiling, image upon image, flash after flash: 'Mum, there are holes in my eyes!'

4

Mʀs Zнᴀᴏ arrived about half an hour late that morning. By then, Mrs Luo was pacing around the dining room and had already passed by the big window twice. She wasn't the sort of employer to stamp peevishly the instant the appointed hour went by, but she couldn't help thinking something must have happened. Mrs Zhao was never late. In Mrs Luo's opinion, the dining room was much too large. Except for some furniture and a set of fixtures that had all turned up together one day, the emptiness was filled only by the upside-down ellipse of the shadow that spilled diagonally across the room when the sun shone in, an effect the designer had referred to as 'elegant sterility', though as far as she was concerned this pairing of words was nonsensical. The developer's sales staff had explained to her that the place was suited to small gatherings of, say, twenty people, that there was plenty of space for them to mill about with wine glasses. A number of neighbours had bought in because of exactly that. People here liked to reproduce the lifestyles they saw in trending Netflix shows, practicality be damned. The probability of this space remaining unused far exceeded the faint likelihood of it someday coming into use, she was ninety-nine percent convinced of it, but that one percent possibility made her catch her breath, and the place was set up exactly as it ought to be; it wouldn't do to make rash changes. The more expensive something was, the more wasted space it contained, and the less freedom it offered. Many years had gone by and Mrs Luo had thought everything through. She didn't mind an additional, shadowy dining room.

She thought she saw Mrs Zhao scurrying along the road towards the house. Through the window pane that walled them off from one another, she observed Mrs Zhao as if for the first time: she was a woman of few words, but she knew what to do when. After leaving home and joining them here, she had quickly acquired an unhurried manner. She didn't talk to Suwei except when necessary, a habit Mrs Luo thought of as displaying appropriate restraint. The important thing was that Mrs Zhao had arrived after the incident, she had only ever known a hermit child and his poor, headstrong mother, and so Mrs Luo didn't feel any sense of obligation toward her. Mrs Zhao was a bit younger, but her skin was much coarser, her round eyes ringed with fine, dense markings like fishing line. It was the face of a woman who had never in her life spared a thought for her looks. Though Mrs Luo wasn't exactly a do-gooder, she saved up her unused cosmetics and gave them to Mrs Zhao, mingling little bottles of shower gel and shampoo from hotels into the donations. At first she was extremely apprehensive, careful of causing offence, but later an unspoken agreement took shape between them: whatever she offered, Mrs Zhao accepted, as if these spare cosmetic items could make up for Mrs Zhao's lost youth, that gaping chasm in Mrs Luo's knowledge of her. At their age, they weren't young, but they weren't yet old. Mrs Zhao had once asked how old she was, then never mentioned it again. At some point, Mrs Luo began gathering up her unused clothing and stuffing it in bags, storing them in a transparent rectangular bin. She soon realised that, while Mrs Zhao accepted the cosmetics with no more than perfunctory politeness, she was in fact quite keen on the clothes. On each occasion, she betrayed an unmistakably authentic gratitude: 'My son collects old clothes. He'll love them.'

After arriving in Beijing, Mrs Luo became a shopaholic. To her, it was the only way to demonstrate irrefutably that she was a true Beijinger. When she first stroked an Italian cashmere overcoat at the old Saitech Plaza shopping centre, she was overcome with elation. These days, she would go to the Intime department store, furtively sweep her eyes across the shops, and realise that, other than the newest styles recommended by the sales staff, the stupefaction she sought was out of reach. She watched the old Saitech centre decay, and the day its closure was announced, she made a special trip. The French dance outfit Suwei had worn when he was little, she had bought here, on the fifth floor. Back then you couldn't find imported dance costumes anywhere but Saitech, especially for boys. It boggled her mind: in just under twenty years of playing catch-up, Beijing had become a cutting-edge world metropolis. She wasn't sure if what she felt was truly nostalgia for that twilight time, or regret that she couldn't buy boys' clothes for Suwei any more. She had once swelled with pride to see shopping centres sprouting up all across the city, happy to have the jagged-edged periphery hidden from sight, believing that her beautiful child would keep being beautiful forever, and her luxurious life would keep on being luxurious. Now, like an empty-headed idiot, she let the young sales staff steer her to the racks with this season's styles, paid and moved along as if on a conveyor belt, as trusty as the rotation of the seasons.

One day, it occurred to Mrs Luo to ask an additional question:

'Where do your son and his friends keep their collection of old clothes?'

'They pull them apart.'

'Pull them apart? You mean they don't donate them?'

'As long as the material is good, they cut apart the fabric, keep what they can use, make new clothes and send them to Africa to be sold.'

In this way, Mrs Luo learned of the existence of the scrapping business. Like everything in the world, scrappers adapted to survive. When she first arrived in the city, she wasn't yet eighteen, and back then the other ballerinas had called her Young Luo. Later on, she became Mrs Chen, and later still she transformed into Mrs Luo. She felt she had been at her most vital as Young Luo, putting her whole heart and soul into dancing the white swan's dance, emptying her mind of everything else. After joining a song and dance troupe, she used her first month's salary to buy a flashy, glimmering white swan skirt from Young Zhao, one of the other dancers. At almost thirty, Young Zhao was the old lady of the troupe, in charge of costumes and props. She knew very well what every new girl who joined the dance troupe wanted, and nimbly coaxed their money into her pockets: 'I know! I've got your size. Just give me two weeks.'

Thinking it over later, Mrs Luo realised that to Young Zhao, this was a business, and every new dancer who joined the troupe was a potential client. All their heads were filled at first with visions of white plumage, but ultimately no more than one percent would get the opportunity to wear that particular skirt onstage. For her first few years as Mrs Chen, she enshrined the ballet skirt on a special shelf in her wardrobe, like a sacred object on an altar, and waited. Then, finally, she had Suwei. She went out of her way to play all sorts of ballet music for Suwei, even when he was still too young to talk, to teach him a sense of rhythm. It took subtlety to teach someone a sense of rhythm. Once, when she was still at ballet school, determined to learn, she had stayed behind and spied on a rehearsal by Siyuan, the only one of them to actually take the stage as the white swan – Siyuan's insteps arched about one-tenth of a centimetre higher than hers, her fingers extended an additional knuckle's length, and when she spun she paused for an extra second – but in Siyuan, these slight precisions added up to a relaxed yet graceful sense of rhythm that she embodied with every breath, declaring to them all that her position at the top of the troupe was unshakable.

All art depended on innate talent. As Young Luo, Mrs Luo had been absolutely unwilling to admit it, until she realised at Suwei's first ballet class that he had a sense of rhythm like Siyuan's, after which she became a zealous adherent of the 'natural talent' theory. She daydreamed of dressing Suwei up like a prince, a pirate, Don Quixote, yearned to see him fulfil the dancer's dreams that had proved out of reach for her. She couldn't wait for Suwei to grow up. Her longing cast a shadow over him, until he gradually merged with her memories of Siyuan.

The previous day, she had wavered numerous times: should she let Mrs Zhao have the white swan skirt too? In the end, she dropped the idea, folded the skirt, slipped it into its white polypropylene bag and stuffed that into a cubbyhole at the back of the cloakroom. Looking back on it now, the skirt had been mortifyingly gaudy, with dangling sequins and feathers that screeched hollow kitsch, like a pheasant hanging its head. It was the strangest of the cloakroom's cubbyholes, filled with her skirt, Suwei's dance outfit, and two or three of Old Chen's shirts. Left to languish there, the clothes oozed the niff of tarnished memories. She knew they waited there for whatever fate might bring: transmigration or oblivion.

When the doorbell finally rang, it kept ringing for what seemed like a century.

Mrs Luo knew that about half of the homes in the compound had live-in maids, and the husbands of almost all of these families lived at home. Mrs Luo had always believed that where there were live-in maids, there were prying eyes: not only did the maids spy on the families they lived with, the husbands peeped into the basements and storage rooms while the maids were sleeping. Mrs Luo was as afraid of being spied on as ever, especially by a live-in maid in a family with no men. She didn't want spying eyes ogling her and Suwei, so she was alarmed and puzzled by the sly glimmer that flashed intermittently in Li Wen's long, narrow eyes – his prying gaze spied not only on her, but on the enormous reflection of the pale-yellow house.

She remembered the day Li Wen first arrived. She had been at the big window in the dining room looking out, just as she was doing at this moment. In the words of the designer, all the windows in the home were 'secret rendezvous-grade'. Whether it was these words that satisfied her or the actual final effect once the windows were installed, Mrs Luo was completely content. The windows had the same shape and the same sheen as any others, but mysteriously, although the view from inside looking out was as clear as could be, a sheet of black mist blocked the view from the outside in. Yes, it was just like the tinted windows of the Maybach she kept parked in the garage. The designer was the first young man to declare explicitly that he wanted something from her that wasn't business-related. She had known it from the first time he showed her the renovation plans, because the look in his eyes was the same as hers when she had eyed Old Chen all those years ago. The difference was that the designer was a southerner, whereas she came from a small, gritty city in the north, and had always mistrusted men from river towns (they loved themselves too much, and it made them soft).

In the end, she hadn't slept with the designer. Back then, Mrs Luo had believed what Mrs Who's-it and Mrs What's-her-face from the social club said: any woman under the age of forty had the right to wait for love. Some of these women had husbands who were acquainted with Old Chen, and others had joined because they were the friends or friends of friends of one of the other wives. She had whiled away a year with them. The monotony: another day, another party; tea parties, dinner parties, dim sum parties, music parties, art parties, book parties . . . She disguised herself as a cheerful marionette, lost her sense of smell and hearing, no longer the B-grade dancer eternally waiting in the wings, now gyrating crazily in place, unable to quit, never getting tired, and also, waiting for someone to come and love her.

When she passed the age of forty, she realised for the first time that she had lost much of her flexibility. She could no longer extend her legs into the splits as a true ballerina should, she wasn't as light on her feet and she had started to puff and pant. Her bed even seemed harder than it had been, and she would wake in the morning with knots in her shoulders. Not even her stomach was as supple any more; even dainty mouthfuls of food got caught in her throat, refusing to descend. To stave off the inevitable, she maintained a habit of practising ballet each day, wriggling her limbs and stomach to keep them as elastic as she could. She turned the basement into a dance studio. In that respect, she appreciated the young designer's cleverness – he was the one who had suggested putting the dance studio in there: 'You've got no need for maid's quarters, so you can do what you want with the space in the basement. No one upstairs will know. You'll have privacy and silence.'

She had merely hinted that Suwei despised anything to do with ballet, and the young man had promptly learned to avoid every possible trigger. He seemed to know that Suwei would never under any circumstances climb down the stairway to the forbidden zone, just as a clever mouse wouldn't get caught twice in a mousetrap laid by a human. Or maybe the young man was trying to imply something: for instance, one night when the timing was right, Mrs Luo could use alcohol to lure him (they would both know it was bait but it would work), and then, he would get his hands on the key to the car in the garage, and she would take him shopping and buy him fancy gifts. As a newly-graduated construction and design specialist, this shower of favours and these glimpses of upper-crust society would provide him with durable conversation fodder, and if he was lucky, Mrs Luo might become his firm's first patron.

Was all this happening now to fill in the gaps of the past? She remembered the young designer's face and voice so clearly, but she couldn't remember the first young man she had lured to spend the night with her, what he had looked like, what his name had been.

Maybe this chance occurrence had materialised to make up for her missed chance with the designer.

There were more and more young men these days. To make sure she didn't miss any more chances, Mrs Luo used some of the money Old Chen had left to start a company. Several years earlier, she had learned from the other women how to spend money – you didn't do it vengefully, because money was capital. The truth was it didn't matter much what she did, what mattered was finding a resting place for this agglutination of chance occurrences. These young men needed a pillow-soft landing pad. Most people didn't want to be provided for without doing anything, living that way made them feel they were being kept like pets, and she was a sensible person, so she built them such a platform. That way, there was no squabbling, and nobody got any silly ideas about staying.

So once she was introduced to Dr Pei by Mrs Who's-it, no matter that Mrs Who's-it generally utterly repelled her, a mysterious sense of trust welled up within her in the doctor's presence. Dr Pei stood almost six feet tall, with swarthy skin, a well-proportioned face, and a pair of full, round earlobes that were everyone's envy. Mrs Luo had learned two things from Old Chen: one, people with round earlobes are good at business, and two, people with long arms make good leaders. Dr Pei asked for her advice on a plan he had devised – a ten-slide PowerPoint presentation, concise and comprehensive, with self-seriousness to spare. There was nothing dreamy about his way of speaking. Every sentence took a hard swing at reality:

'Such a beautiful set of teeth. I'm sure you're aware of the social impact of tooth manufacturing, as well as its economic benefits.'

Mrs Luo knew that Dr Pei's expert eye had spotted her mouthful of shiny white porcelain teeth. Both were well aware that the teeth were fake, yet one complimented and the other basked in the flattery. She had always liked it when people said her teeth looked good, the same way she liked it now when people praised her wrinkle-free skin. The delusion brought about by the reversal of the flow of time felt much more vivid to her than real life. She thought Dr Pei had probably deduced that the porcelain teeth were Japanese-made, since they were still in such great shape all these years later. Ten years ago, only one dental clinic in Beijing had offered this material and this technology. People had gossiped that such-and-such celebrity or such-and-such rock star went there, and when she emerged from the clinic, self-satisfaction had lacquered over the agony of her filed-down teeth: she had gained a new lease on life. When you got 'porcelain teeth', the dentist filed your teeth down and applied a thin layer of artificial white enamel on top. Once inculcated into your mouth, this parasitic enamel harassed you callously, and for the rest of your life you recoiled from cold drinks and crunchy snacks.

She knew that what Dr Pei hadn't said was that there were new technologies that could fully restore the beauty of your teeth, there was no need to endure the lifelong agony of having them filed, you could pay a little more and get a completely new set of teeth. She had seen advertisements for these new technologies, but had no regrets. She actually preferred her tiny filed teeth and the layer of artificial enamel that concealed them. Her original teeth had been covered by a concrete-like layer of grey tetracycline pigment, a side effect of taking tetracycline for acute pneumonia as a girl. She thought of it as the mark left by her upbringing in a drab northern city – grey coke haze floating in the air all year round, greasy alleys splattered with swill. The dark brown swill sent up a sickening acrid stench, and there were deep pools in some of the alleys, so she had to cling to the shoulders where the vendor's stalls stood, hopping and skipping around the swill like a fainthearted rabbit bounding through the bushes at night. Her dance instructor had no idea that the bright-eyed Young Luo always associated this brown swill with the green paint that ran halfway up the walls in the studio: they were two sets of coordinates marking the same path.

All traces of her provincial past had been lacquered over, like her filed grey nubs. She didn't want to live life with markings on her. This was her Beijing, and she wouldn't let anyone change that. Old Chen had never given her any real physical pleasure, but he had turned her into a Beijinger, given her a sparkling white smile. It was easy to erase your place of origin – a touch of fakery worked miracles.

It was subsequently demonstrated that Dr Pei ran his clinic masterfully. You got off the Fourth Ring Road after passing the enormous billboard, and the cosmetic dentistry clinic was right there at the bottom – the beautiful girl on the enormous billboard smiled tirelessly through all seasons, baring seven teeth the same snow-white shade as the clinic building. At some point, people had started preferring monochromatic spaces over places painted in flashy colours. Maybe single colours eased their anxiety over making decisions, or maybe the front of false modernity projected by single colours tricked people, convinced them that everything within was trustworthy. Dr Pei had pragmatic, crafty ideas: he decreed that all the mouthwash and fluoride gel in the clinic would be fruit-flavoured; he demanded that every bathroom be spotlessly clean, and that hygiene posters be put up on every wall; he furnished the waiting room like a sitting room, putting in bookshelves and even an imported coffee maker. These little schemes of his were, in fact, overkill, like embroidering flowers on brocade. As far as Mrs Luo was concerned, Dr Pei's true genius lay in turning every dentist in the clinic into a kindergarten teacher. The doctors all had a particular way of speaking, soft and coddling, as if comforting a five-year-old child, replacing 'you' with 'we':

'Does it hurt?'

'Hang in there, we're almost finished.'

'What a champ! Just a little jolt of pain. It'll be over soon.'

'We're going to get a beautiful set of teeth out of this, you know.'

At first, Mrs Luo thought such cajolery worked only on women and children, but she later discovered it was in fact intended to comfort the men, the middle-aged ones as well as the young ones. Dr Pei was more than capable as a doctor and as a businessman. He had a fatal bag of tricks, which gave Mrs Luo a satisfied gleam in her eye. She opened an office next door to Dr Pei's, though, as they had agreed from the beginning, she did not take part in any specialised work. The dentistry business was completely beyond her ken. Her investment approach was as clean and economical as ballet dancing: she simply appeared at the clinic at precisely the same time each day and it didn't matter whether she shut the door and watched television or chatted with friends, her presence there was enough to intimidate the actual dentist in the office next door. And one more thing, she needed a 'mate' to work by her side. The relationship she envisioned was like that between a queen bee and her polyamorous partners: no lifelong commitments, no delusions of love, and the next day the male worker bees would go on gathering honey as if nothing had happened. Mrs Luo couldn't manage that, the best she could do was hire a string of young male secretaries, then dissolve the working relationship as soon as they got tangled up together beneath the sheets, a clumsier approach than she would have liked. When she thought of it that way, she realised she really did admire Old Chen. She couldn't duplicate the way he did things, would never be like him no matter how hard she tried.

*

Mrs Zhao burst through the door and told her there had been a terrible accident in the estate. A crowd surrounded the row of houses across the way, the ambulance had left just moments ago, and 1-1-0 was on the scene. Mrs Zhao also told her there was blood spattered on the ground. Someone had fallen, a middle school student, people were saying. Mrs Luo felt as if her heart had defenestrated itself. Since moving in, she had been dreaming continually of Suwei plummeting into an inky black abyss. He hadn't fallen from a cliff or the top of a tall building, he had simply been inhaled by a maw in the cosmos, never to emerge again. She always watched him falling and falling, and she opened her mouth to scream, but no sound came out – Suwei just kept tumbling through the ether, toward a baby who hovered in the depths of the abyss. Eventually she would wake and stare straight through the ceiling at the uppermost roof beam. Thankfully, among the options offered by the developer, she had opted for 'topping out'.

Mrs Luo glanced at the floor above, where Suwei must still be sleeping, or perhaps he was awake and just pretending. She had long since acquiesced to a tacit agreement with Suwei, an agreement to pick up the pieces and make the best of a mess – Dr Zhong said Suwei shouldn't be forced to speak, especially not by the people closest to him. It would backfire, there was no law that said people had to bare their hearts to each other. She calculated that once she left, it would be essential to call the property manager and find out what had happened. In truth, when Dr Zhong first told her Suwei could be treated at home, she had the clear sensation of a stone being rolled from her heart, and her first reaction had been, *Thank goodness, we're safe.* From the very first day Suwei began growing inside her belly, she was assailed by fear and panic – she feared he would disappear without warning; she feared he would turn out to be physically weak, with a deformed appearance; she feared his teachers and classmates would gang up on him; she feared he would get injured in ballet class . . . She could spend the rest of eternity reciting an inner litany of all the catastrophes that might crash down on Suwei, as if the world itself were a nebulous array of fierce floods and ferocious beasts, and her little Suwei would only be safe in her embrace.

Dr Pei had gone to Dr Zhong, China's top autism expert according to Dr Pei, and if Dr Pei trusted him, so did she. Before Dr Zhong got involved, Mrs Luo had assumed that Suwei was tired, he just needed a few days of bed rest. After all, that was just what she and Suwei had settled upon: silence and seclusion. Maybe Dr Zhong's expert conclusion would coincide with hers, which was that Suwei was just tired and needed to seclude himself, wrap himself like a silkworm in a cocoon and get a good sleep, stop growing so quickly. All growth had ever done was get them into trouble.

In the car, Mrs Luo called the property manager. When Li Wen and the others weren't around, Mrs Luo never drove on her own. She was deathly afraid of random occurrences. Traffic accidents, for instance. Paying no heed to the driver's gaze, she slid the phone back into her bag. She was sure she had seen that cat, the ghostly blue one, somewhere before. The manager said the boy had somehow managed to climb from a flower rack up onto the roof, chasing a pet cat, but the quick-footed cat had hidden on the opposite corner of the roof, and the boy had somehow slipped and fallen. It was an absurd story, that was for certain, absurd enough to keep secret, even though everyone knew it. Anyway, it had nothing to do with her or her family, so what was she doing rummaging through other people's secrets? She could have sworn she had seen that blue cat perched on the edge of the roof looking down wordlessly on the boy, golden pupils flashing.

5

A real man does what his mother says, Li Wen told himself.

*

But life was a path that led forward – that's what his grandfather, his mother's father, had said when he was alive. As a little boy, he had believed in what he saw with his eyes, only a family pet waiting to be fed would do such a thing: he depicted every relationship by drawing straight lines between things. For instance, his grandfather's line was linked with a delicious hongshao braised fish on a greasy wooden table; his mother's line was linked with his final burst of breath on the brink of collapsing in the final hundred metres of a long race; his father, meanwhile, was linked only to blank space and gaping lack. He had no memories of his father, his recollections and sensations were like a bunch of empty boxes with no check marks. The day finally came when his mother hung the house key on a grass-green cord and fastened it around his neck. He remembered kicking a stone down the road as he headed home, and he remembered that the food beneath the plastic cover on the stove burner had been eternally cold. He was seven when it happened. To him, the phrase 'passed away' was a description of a state of being, like 'at home'. He remembered that he had disliked the odour of the hospital, lethargic decay overlaid with disinfectant. His mother had sat by the white sickbed in the far corner, silent until the end, her hands balled up into pentagonal fists, ashen and ice-cold.

It wasn't necessary to plunge too deeply into memories. Time was shaped like a soft rubber bouncy ball, shifting between colours and spaces, bouncing ceaselessly between multiple temporal strata. The only person to be found anywhere among these thin, overlapping layers of time was a baby-faced boy with tiny eyes, a tiny nose, a tiny mouth, and a tiny chin; you could imagine him growing into a tall, strong adult with an incongruous baby face. Fourth period was almost over. At noon, Li Wen would cut through the scorched rubber stench of the sun-baked running track to the middle school teachers' building. His mother's office was on the second floor.

'He's gone to see mummy again.'

He could hear his classmates talking in whispers, murmuring derisively. It had never been a secret: each day at noon, the same stainless-steel lunchbox awaited, always in the same clean flower-printed cloth case, and then there was the woman sitting across from him. When he was little, he had loved to pull her glasses off, then put them back on, but at some point he had quit. At some point, out of the blue, it had suddenly begun to feel too intimate, too childlike. They sat across from one another, picking food from their boxes, like taking communion over and over on loop, a cycle that had to be completed to ward off disorder. When they ate together, they were the only two people in his mother's office. Her co-workers were all out. Only later he heard the voices of those people whose faces had long since misted over, emanating out of nothing: 'That poor mother and son, clinging to one another for dear life.'

He had never felt there was anything pitiful about him, but he was used to it. He was every bit as entrenched in a ditch of convention as a worker on an assembly line. It took just ten minutes to get to school on foot from the building that housed the families of the middle school teachers, no need to go by bike. He was jealous of the students who rode their bikes to school, jealous of their pretty keychains of every colour strung with bike keys. He was also jealous of the cliques of kids who went foraging at lunchtime, forming small groups, sharing their lunch expenses, sitting around chatting and laughing. He had no friends. The whole school left him and his mother to rule over their landlocked kingdom. Nobody talked to them, nobody cared what they did, nobody sought them out. Many years ago, his mother had declared to the world, 'My son has a bright future. He isn't going to languish. He's going to get into a good school and get out of this godforsaken place.'

'Every moment is precious.'

His mother's protective attitude toward time reminded him of the way she would hand him a bowl of rice when he was little and instruct him not to spill a single grain. She didn't like it when his aunt and her family visited, looking down on them as lowly peddlers, the owners of a small supermarket, so he never told his mother that the cartons of milk and the colourful cornucopia of snacks they brought whenever they visited were actually quite delicious. Later, he realised that his mother didn't like it when other people brought them gifts. Her shoulders would hunch slightly, like a wildcat on guard against an unexpected guest: 'Thanks, but we're in no need of anything. Next time, leave it at home.'

The city they lived in was just the right size, not too big or too small. Apparently, there were many Tang dynasty buildings and monuments there, but he had never been to see them. His world was very small and tightly sealed against leaks. Sometimes, his mother took him on the number 2 bus to see his grandfather on the western outskirts of the city. On several occasions they had arrived in the first half of the afternoon, in time to see the half-sunken sun smear an unnatural orange pigment over a swath of the sky. There was a reservoir by his grandfather's house, and when he was younger, he had sneaked off to see it a few times, the other kids in his grandfather's courtyard compound had shown him the way. In fact, he hadn't known those kids at all. A few days would go by and they would forget each other's names. Kids didn't need to be introduced by anyone, they acted out of primitive instinct, eagerly sharing places and things, keeping the adults in the dark. He liked the reservoir. The water was cold, and when you looked out across it, it seemed to be infinite, no shoreline in sight. Amid billowing steam redolent of hongshao fish, his mother grabbed the waistband of his dripping wet pants, made him hold his hand out and slapped it viciously: 'You could have drowned!'

He saw that his mother's hands were once again balled up into pentagons, and he felt true fear, became aware for the first time of the second thing his mother was afraid of other than him shirking his studies and pissing away time, and it was also the first time he realised the frightening accuracy of his mother's predictions – the next time they visited his grandfather, none of the kids came to play. There had in fact been a terrible accident at the reservoir: a boy had drowned. For many nights on end, he dreamed he was the drowned boy – he bobbed on the surface, his body light as a feather, but bloated like a balloon. The kids who'd shown him the way wanted to go home and get help, but they couldn't remember his name or which building his grandfather lived in. They crossed paths with his mother, who was shouting his name in the courtyard, but no one else could make out the words. He saw his waterlogged face contorted by a smile, the vile grin of a child playing hide and seek under cover of darkness, watching while the other kids searched in vain. This time, the word 'death' felt still closer than it had when Dad passed away.

Each time he heard someone else had died, Li Wen realised he was approaching adulthood, and that was a word his mother couldn't dispel. The nights grew longer, and on many occasions he constantly tossed and turned, got up and sat on the edge of the bed, then lay back down. He thought of the scent of shampoo that would suddenly slap him in the face sometimes at school, he knew it had come from someone's luxuriant black hair, but he couldn't recall whose. He tried hard to silence himself promptly, wished it were as easy as hitting the off button on an alarm clock, because if he made any noise, his mother would worry about why he wasn't sleeping. His worries frightened him, he needed to demonstrate to her every second of every day that he was normal, that he was pressing unswervingly forward, and there had been no mishaps. He had less and less to say when they were together, and he found himself cramming more and more words down into his abdomen. He still had that childhood impulse to stroke her hair, to curl up like a snail and conceal himself in her embrace, but he had sworn a solemn oath to be a man, and now when his mother tried to grab his hand, he deliberately shrank back. He supplanted every instance of 'boy and mummy' with 'man and mum'; the ghastly intimacy sent shivers down his spine.

The nights grew longer, and the days diminished. Around the three-kilometre mark, everything around him, including the air, was sucked into a vacuum bag, and his head spun in jet-black nullity. He had to constantly contort his lips into a goldfish shape so that he could exhale without cease, forgetting the limits of his hyperaemic limbs. Each day he set aside this time for himself alone. The finish line of the five-kilometre race was soundless and clear, the stopwatch right on the nose. For a moment he forgot about his mother, about the stainless-steel lunchbox and the shapeless unseen goal. His mother ultimately came to terms with him joining the track team, because he said to her, 'If you play sports you live longer, and it's easier to get into college.'

He knew that if he trotted out this argument, his mother would more than likely step out of the way. If he could just get into a good college and get out of this place, he knew his mother would exhaust absolutely every means at her disposal for his sake.

Maybe he had simply spent too much time trying to cram everything into his brain, until in a strange sort of way the words grew to be a part of him. As he and his mother recited from Obama, her voice swelled, incandescent: 'Let it be told to the future world, that in the depth of winter, when nothing but hope and virtue could survive . . .'

And then there were other famous English language speeches, compiled by a publishing house into an oratory anthology for advanced pupils of English.

'Virtue', 'hope', and 'light' made countless appearances in the sentences he had memorised. He read these sentences aloud along with the CD, imitating the affectedly perspicacious pronunciation, imagining that he too wore a dark suit and stood beneath the stars and stripes, facing a populace unconditionally under his thrall. 'Words of wisdom! Long live democracy!' These stirring utterances had infected his mother, and she wanted to infect him, too. As he recited and recited, the urge would strike to run into the street and cry at the top of his lungs, 'We should ask what we can do for our country, too!'

In a flash, he understood his mother's disdain for his aunt – only a self-centred plebeian would go into business as a shiftless peddler, but her ambitions for him were so much bigger. He belonged before a podium, the eyes of the people fixed on him, delivering a righteous performance to preserve the world's virtue.

As time went on, he wasn't sure any more whether he was doing these long-distance drills to get into a good college (and save the world by a roundabout route), to torch his muscles and taste sweet leisure, or to break free from the smouldering echoes that flared in his brain: 'virtue', 'hope', and 'light'. The only other student in his grade who did long-distance running was Wu Shuisheng, a swarthy runt who stood half a head shorter than him. The ramparts of an orthodontic correctional apparatus fortified his mouth, and his tongue sometimes skidded over words. Though Shuisheng was not in the middle school's so-called 'experimental class', he had joined the track team half a year ahead of Li Wen. At first, they didn't talk much. Everyone on the track team treated running as a confrontation with their own belaboured breathing, and had no time or inclination to chat. Something about Shuisheng powerfully attracted him. When he ran, his entire body was relaxed, and Li Wen envied that ease. Though he thought he was relaxed when he ran, even at the pinnacle of his relaxation he was wound much tighter than Shuisheng.

'No need to take running so seriously. It isn't a race.'

No matter how much time went by, Li Wen clearly remembered the first words Shuisheng had said to him. Shuisheng had detected at a glance that he was constantly on guard against something. Not even Li Wen knew what that something was. Since realising that his mother's expectant gaze and the ever-present sense of uncomfortable intimacy had seeped into every pore of his existence, he had been constantly at the ready. The atmosphere of the experimental class raised his hackles, too. In spite of his best efforts, his class ranking remained lodged in the thirties, and he knew that was as far as all his natural talents could take him. But the instant he turned his head, his mother's expectations and unspoken entreaties once again wove into a fluorescent green binary system and flung themselves at his face. He rapidly and instinctively decoded the signals, and like a small boat battling the current, clung to the periphery of the experimental class and somehow managed to avoid being swept away. If, after joining, his departure was overly prompt, his mother would lose face. For her, everywhere except the experimental class was a limbo from which her son might never emerge into a brilliant future. There was no time to do anything or see anyone on the side.

Daily track practice was the only time he and Shuisheng ever saw each other. His mother would certainly be unhappy to discover that he was associating with someone from outside the experimental class. His mother strongly believed in the educational system's compartmentalised categories. As far as she was concerned, no one outside the experimental class would be getting into a good school. Li Wen never asked Shuisheng which university he wanted to go to, and he didn't share his goals with Shuisheng either. As far as he was concerned, sharing and asking were the same thing, and he would rather not go there. They were more like battle-weary soldiers leaning on each other as they marched along than middle school students with indeterminate prospects. He felt the urge to consciously defend Shuisheng, and he didn't want his mother's prying eyes to see them together.

*

At six-thirty in the evening, Li Wen should be on his last free study period, Mrs Li calculated, glancing at the watch on her wrist as she walked into the Chengnan food market. There were scratches on the stainless-steel watch bracelet, and the mottled marks glinted in the rays of the setting sun. It was an Yibo watch, a gift Li Wen's father had brought back when he went to Shenzhen on business. At the time, Yibo had been a big brand name. There was a quality guarantee certificate attached to the box pledging lifetime maintenance, all written down in black and white.

'Now's the time,' Mrs Li murmured to herself. Younger teachers had long ago stopped wearing watches to check the time, preferring their mobiles instead, but Mrs Li still wore her watch. It gave her a sense of security to hold it to her ear and listen to the ticking of the second hand. It was soon afterwards that Li Wen's dad had been diagnosed with kidney failure, and Mrs Li had relied on this watch to apportion her time. Suddenly, everyone needed her: her husband in hospital, her pupils who had just started junior middle school, and her son, Li Wen. She looked at the family members of the patients in the hospital ward – all either weeping and wailing or breathing sighs of relief at their recovery – and made a resolution: she had to ensure that Li Wen would grow up to have a decent life.

After her husband's death, the school authorities made several attempts to find her another husband, but she fobbed them off. So they let the matter drop. As time went on, everyone accepted that she and Li Wen were a family unit, and it would have been wrong to add a stranger to their set-up. Mrs Li had also thought about remarrying, but then put it out of her mind. The very thought made her so anxious that her palms would sweat. She was afraid that a new husband would treat her son badly, or that Li Wen would not like it. She was also afraid for another reason, of which only she was aware: a new husband would never measure up to Li Wen's father. Bringing up Li Wen on her own made her feel as if she was holding fast to the last shred of dignity of her former life. She did not believe that losing her husband made her an unfortunate woman. She still had Li Wen, and her life and her dreams would be focused on him from now on. When others were trying to matchmake for her, she used to joke that when you had a son, no matter what surname he had, he became the ultimate metaphor. In every sense, he was always her son.

Mrs Li firmly believed that there was nothing at all noteworthy about any part of their lives back then. It was just a stage her son was going through, from the microscopic egg from which he would incubate, to the gigantic roc-like bird that he would grow into before flying away. Her colleagues, their families, the middle school – they were all pitifully small. She had missed out on life, but Li Wen was not going to. She had managed to wriggle like an earthworm into this dirty old town, ultimately succeeding only at making her way from the west to the south. When she was studying in the English department of the local teacher training college, her professors, some of whom had lived through the last years of the Republic, had introduced her to Browning and Shakespeare, but in the end, the only outlet for her English skills had been the primary school classroom attached to their college, where she taught the same basic texts over and over again. When she first graduated as a teacher, she was still hopeful of finding even one promising pupil to whom she could hint at the paradise that lay waiting in English literature, but as the years passed, she gave up and stopped looking.

She still treasured the foreign novels with their mustard-yellow covers that she had loved back then. A while ago, it occurred to her to show them to Li Wen. She got one book out and leafed through the dog-eared pages. It reminded her that she had once wanted to be Madame Bovary and had dreamed of having fashionable young lovers who lived somewhere in the countryside. She had stuck a picture of Madame Bovary on the wall next to her single dormitory bed, imagining that one day, she too would have beautiful wavy hair and drink coffee in a city in the West. She thought that coffee must be a creamy beverage, just as she had read in foreign literature, a strange and wonderful elixir that could heal all her troubles. Until one day, Li Wen's dad brought her back a sachet of Nescafe. It was scalding hot and very bitter, but still she told herself that if she had the opportunity to drink this stuff every day, she could get used to it.

It was all her chemistry teacher's fault. When she was just a young woman in a simple seersucker dress, the teacher had been quite keen to introduce her to a 'very fine young man'. She had been thinking about applying for a place on a postgraduate course so that she could get out of this stagnant town and study in a big city, or maybe even in America, but she had not dared share her thoughts with anyone around her. Who would listen? Not her parents or her friends in their small community, or their parents either. It was a fantasy. Time passed, she married a colleague of her chemistry teacher, and the two of them made the daily trip to work and back home together. Time fled as if someone had stolen it. Then there was Li Wen. As she lay in bed at night, she realised that her son made her happy and she quietly locked all the materials for the postgraduate examination away in her bedside table. When the time came to move house, she couldn't find the picture of Madame Bovary. Maybe it had stayed on her wall, been torn down by the young woman who took her bed and thrown away. For the first two years after Li Wen was born, she remembered running around chasing her tail. Life was chaotic but exciting. She felt that she was always chasing after time, of which there was never a sufficient supply. She did not mind living like this. After all, there was no guarantee that if she had pursued her studies and left this small town, life would have been any better.

Her husband had died very suddenly. For a while afterwards, she could only sleep if she had Li Wen in her arms. She told Li Wen that she was afraid that he would miss his father. In fact, she was concerned about herself. She felt extremely lonely at first. She slowly stopped thinking of herself as a woman, only as a mother. As before, she went to school and came back home along the same road as she had always done, teaching the same English classes with the curriculum that repeated every three years, asking her class the same questions that the pupils were never able to answer. She cooked the same amount of food, too. Li Wen was growing and getting bigger, he could just eat his father's share. The school remembered that the couple had both had jobs and topped up her wages with a subsidy every month. She no longer spent any extra money on herself; she saved up the extra payments, and when Li Wen went to college at the age of eighteen, she opened an account for him, with a bright red passbook. When his father was alive, she had never had this urge to see Li Wen grow up quickly. But now, she heard a forgotten valve in her heart loosen a little: she was convinced that some of the beautiful urge to escape that she had had before she married Li Wen's father had returned. The foreign names she had known through translation came alive again, convincing her that some strange power had once more endowed her with spiritual wealth and nobility. Li Wen was her son, and he was destined to take that nobility with him as he strode away.

Until now, she had been moving from square to square on a horizontal board: from the community where she lived to the school, from daughter to wife to mother. 'Growing up' had nothing to do with her. Her life had been sucked dry. She had become one of countless middle-aged women who hurried down the street without being noticed. She knew that quite well. All her hormones had also dried up, and her face was growing more desiccated by the day. Every morning, she became aware of the inexorable increase of fine lines on her face. Washing herself became a matter of mere routine, meant only to keep her clean. Her body had long ago lost all its elasticity, and all its desire. She knew that her pupils were afraid of her. They nicknamed her 'Liangfen', after the bean noodles, because she looked so stiff. When she walked into the classroom, they hurriedly hid all their snacks, mobile phones and comic books in their desk drawers. She was not angry. She could only have been angry if she cared about them. And she did not care. Every day she endured the same routine in order to scrimp and save so that her son could fly away. Her goal increasingly filled her with passion, until she was almost boiling over.

She was careful to keep out of sight behind the windows of the corridor connecting the junior and senior middle schools, as she scanned the open space in front of the senior middle school building and the playground. When Li Wen was eating his lunch in the office the day before yesterday, a newly-qualified teacher on her practice year smiled at him. She saw Li Wen blush. Young teachers nowadays had no shame. They wore makeup and tight clothes to school, and didn't give a damn for their reputations. Mrs Li had always disliked them. But Li Wen's blush made her wake up. He was not a kid any more.

She was struck by terror. Then she put the thought out of her mind. She wanted Li Wen to grow up and fly away from this no-hope town, but he was developing slowly and needed to experience these things. She began to make a habit of skulking behind the corridor window outside Li Wen's closed door, listening to every breath he took, identifying every movement she heard. Everything had to be her son's and his alone, and must not be contaminated by desires for the opposite sex. In the dimness, she imagined an invisible enemy, a local girl who had to be prevented from sinking her claws into him. His future and his happiness lay far, far away. He must not be held back by juvenile physical impulses. She actually feared that one day Li Wen might stop growing up. In that case, her life would end here.

There were so many forbidden topics between mother and son that their conversations were often limited to:

'How was your day?'

'Ten students are going to be leaving after the end-of-term exams.'

'I heard that Ms Zheng has set up a tutor group. Shall we sign you up?'

'Don't bother, I'll just revise more, then you can save the money. She's only repeating lessons we've already done.'

'It'll do you good to repeat the lessons. I can afford it.'

'I'd be better off spending the time revising my English. That's the way to raise my marks.'

But sometimes, Mrs Li felt small and defeated, completely bereft of the noble spirit she imagined would power her through. When Li Wen was young, she saw her son speaking beautiful, fluent English, playing the piano, mastering chess, doing calligraphy and painting. As these ambitions edged closer to their projected deadlines, she realised that she had never heard him speak the eloquent English of her daydreams. And the school took only a perfunctory interest in extracurricular classes, whether it was the national youth Go championships or calligraphy. Not even Li Wen's teachers had any aspirations, and they were the best in the school. It did not matter how much money she saved or how hard she tried, there would always be a ceiling above her that she could see without looking up. She and her son were well known in the area where they lived. The neighbours regarded the junior middle school English teacher as an 'intellectual', but that was as far as it went; they were all small people. At parents' evening one year, she picked out the top two names in Li Wen's experimental class, a girl with a big head and a short body and a tall boy with a small head. Their home background seemed quite humble. How come they were so determined to get into Peking University?

Finally, in his third year of senior middle school, Li Wen came to her one day to talk about which college to apply to.

'I thought about it, and it's unrealistic for me to try for Peking University. I'd rather go to one with a better English department. I'll study hard at university, and then I'll pass the postgraduate examination.'

Mrs Li thought how grown up he had become, how he was a better planner than she was. University must surely be his opportunity to really take off. The key thing was for him to get away, then they could think about his future.

6

LI WEN still thought of fatty pork every time he touched his stomach. Their track coach was an old man with a flat head called Wang. He always wore a blue tracksuit, supplemented in winter by a dark green army greatcoat. He had a whistle around his neck, hanging from a long cord. It reached as far as his beer belly, which bulged so much it looked like a grotesque growth on his body. That whistle was the source of all Coach Wang's power. According to Li Wen's mother, Coach Wang had been the best-looking teacher in the school when he was young. He was ex-army, and all the girls fancied him. In time, he married a teacher who taught guzheng in the music department of the teacher training college. She had run off with a tradesman, leaving him pottering along on his own. He never remarried, and they had no children. Nowadays Coach Wang was no longer the big man he had once been. He seemed to have faded, gone rusty. In summer, you could still see the muscles in his legs, but his bulging stomach gave him a comical look. Coach Wang was a strict instructor, but he never got angry with the students. When their daily training was over and they headed back to the classroom covered in sweat, they occasionally looked back and saw Coach Wang still standing there. He looked lonely. When this word popped into Li Wen's mind, he was surprised at himself. He never told his classmates Coach Wang's story. In fact, he felt guilty that he knew it himself. Whenever he looked at Coach Wang, he could see that he had nothing but his emotional wounds. The story he had heard seemed to envelop the old man in an impenetrable black cloak.

Coach Wang sometimes put his arms around the team members' shoulders, like they were mates. But he never did this to Li Wen or Shuisheng. Instead, he nodded to them. At first, Li Wen thought this was because he had joined late, and had to work harder to get into the boss's good books. He had a good physique and his muscles were firm, but when he started real fitness training, the press-ups made him feel sick. Exercise was exactly the same as studying, involving constant repetition of mechanical movements. The difference was that pushing his body to its limits gave him freedom, while studying was a Sisyphean task, there was never any end in sight. Coach Wang always told him that if he didn't do his press-ups, his muscles would go soft and flabby. They were like fatty pork on the chopping board – a few chops and they went mushy. Training was needed to strengthen those tendons and muscles. Coach Wang's words, spoken in his almost unintelligible accent, were engraved in Li Wen's memory. Sometimes in his dreams, his whole body was sticky and greasy like streaky pork. In the evenings, he used to pull up his shirt and carefully poke his belly. He was afraid the tendons he had trained up might disappear overnight.

Of all the teachers in the school, it was Coach Wang whom he remembered most clearly. The man had a kind of submerged tenacity. Other people did not dare to transgress the rules in the way they lived, but Coach Wang seemed to punch back at life's inertia by means of failure. His mother felt that Coach Wang was not pushy enough, but Li Wen saw him as a bad-boy hero. On the track and field team, he and Shuisheng were the only boys who took sports as an extra module, while everyone else was going straight to the sports academy. Wang taught them all in the same way, but it seemed like there was an invisible barrier between him and these two students, Li Wen and Shuisheng. Once they had completed their exercises and could not take another step, Coach Wang had nothing more to do with them. Li Wen realised after a while that Coach Wang never regarded the pair as real athletes, and this created an unbridgeable divide between them. Perhaps Coach Wang despised them in his heart of hearts. He was once heard to mutter, 'Too ambitious.' Li Wen felt Coach Wang was talking about him. Coach Wang always used to say that sport was the fairest kind of competition, but Li Wen paid no attention. Even the concept of sport in general meant little to him. He ran because it was one of the few things he did that were completely under his control. He practised it as a personal skill.

Li Wen lived life on two levels: the first was a closed circle, in which he was constrained to loop constantly between point A and point B. He ran round and round the targets marked for him by his mother, getting dizzy, but also feeling at ease with himself. The other level of his life was open, and just outside the first level, without any markers or fixed points. Sometimes he tried to measure the distance between the two levels from the inside outward, but was unable to make any measurement, or indeed see anything.

In June and July, the heat in the north was relentless. There was no getting away from the sun pounding down onto the rubberized track. Li Wen felt his hands burning where they touched the ground. Beads of sweat dripped from his forehead, spread out on the dark green track and then instantly evaporated. He loathed the hot weather; the inexorably rising temperature upset him. He was lucky that the sports tests were scheduled for the cooler months. Just like Coach Wang said, he treated the competitions and assessments as personal tests to see how fast he could run. Once he was running, no one looked at him, no one urged him on, no one had any expectations of him. Everything, including the air, seemed to move backwards. He left the whole world behind him. He was reduced to his feet and hands, fighting against the resistance in the air currents. He was in command, a hero. He ran well.

Li Wen was an anxious boy. His classmates thought he was taciturn by nature. In fact, most of the time he chose not to speak because he didn't want to embarrass himself. He knew that he could not break any of the rules within these walls. Sometimes, he secretly hoped that his classmates would deliberately provoke him, to give him a reason to break out of his shell and have a good punch-up. He couldn't do it on his own. There was always a teacher nearby, ready to tell his mother and reprimand him for immature behaviour. But none of his classmates ever picked a fight with him – they found him too boringly hardworking. He had clearly made a vow to grow into a real man. His mother's frown and her clenched fists made him feel guilty. Her increasing frailty seemed to him to be a sign of a woman who had almost faded out of existence. He blamed himself for being a burden to her, just as the years themselves were a burden. Although it had been a long time since he had taken his mother's hand, in his memory, those hands were soft and warm.

Now that he had made running into a bargaining chip, there was only one hurdle left until his mother got her wishes. In the past few days, he had started taking out the stopwatch he used for running, pressing start and then stop again, sometimes for a few seconds and sometimes for a few minutes. He did not know what time he was calculating, but the nearer the time came, the more hopeless he felt.

Shuisheng's revelation came one day in the rubber-smelling heat. They were running together, into the sun. The beads of sweat they left on the track made a string of tiny beads. As the temperature climbed, these beads would disappear without leaving a trace. Li Wen remembered their first day of training, when Shuisheng had stayed behind to time him and asked, 'Do you know the difference between long-distance running and sprinting?'

It had never entered his mind. Nor had he questioned why having his run properly timed somehow made his feet feel leaden. He shook his head. He badly wanted to know the answer.

'Only animals with sweat glands can run long distances because they can expel heat,' said Shuisheng. 'Some fleet-footed animals only sprint because they don't have sweat glands to help with long-distance running. We humans don't run fast, but we're better adapted to long-distance running.'

Li Wen looked at the sweat traces he had left on the ground. The fast-vanishing liquid was the condensed energy discharged by all those powerful sweat gland systems that only humans have. Was sweating a waste of energy? He did not know. He looked up and took a deep breath. Compared to the rest of the track team, neither he nor Shuisheng were particularly tall or strong. As Coach Wang put it, they had short Achilles tendons. So every time someone else was running, he and Shuisheng sat down face to face with their feet pressed against each other, to stretch their Achilles tendons. At first, he could only reach Shuisheng's wrists, but after a bit of practice, they could hold each other's waists. Coach Wang told them to keep trying; with a bit more stretching, they might catch up with the others. But he had done enough. These stretching sessions were like private conversations between Li Wen and Shuisheng. Sometimes, when Coach Wang was next to them, they just made eye contact. At other times, Shuisheng used to ask him to meet after school at the gate. Then they would go back to the playground and listen to music on Shuisheng's portable CD player. Their sweat steamed off them, smelling of grass, the way teenagers' sweat did, leaving them just moist enough.

After the tests were over, the two of them, the non-athletes, bent over clutching their knees, panting.

'Ten more days. Have you done your preparation?'

'I . . . I'm not taking the college entrance exam.'

Li Wen caught his breath, scarlet in the face. 'You're not taking the gaokao?'

Shuisheng grunted but did not look at him. His voice was quiet, as if he had done something wrong, and he muttered something Li Wen could not catch.

'You're not going to college?' Li Wen repeated, staring at the pimply boy beside him. He only knew that Shuisheng was not in the experimental class, but even so, he should have been able at least to get into a second-tier university as a level two athlete. He suddenly had a premonition, just like when he used to eat jiaozi dumplings at his grandparents' house when he was a child and got one with a coin inside. It had occurred to him just at the moment when he bit down that if he was not careful, it was going to hurt his teeth.

'I'm not going to university here.'

Shuisheng's voice was getting even quieter, as if he was trying to muffle the truth, but the words rang out anyway, 'I'm going to college in the United States.'

Li Wen stiffened, trying to stop shaking, although the trembling was only a sign of his desperate envy. He had so much he wanted to say, but nothing came out. Scarlet in the face, he finally said, 'Why didn't you tell me earlier?'

In fact, what he remembered was that he had told Shuisheng that his ambition was to get into the English department and then go to the United States. He thought he was treading carefully around Shuisheng, but now he realised that it was Shuisheng who was treading carefully around him.

'My dad arranged it, he's gone there to work,' Shuisheng said, trying to make it sound like this was not his doing, that it was his family who had fixed it.

'Why didn't you tell me earlier?' Li Wen kept repeating. Years later, when he thought back to the rubberized running track, he saw how pathetic he had been. A boy who ran so that he could carry his mother far away, and when he got to the end, found his silent partner had left this little track long before. His mother's hopes were hard-wired into him. He always thought that he could become a man by walking forward one step at a time, but when he looked up, he realised that other kids' parents had given their children wings. 'Poor mother, poor son.' And now, for the first time, he did not want to be 'poor'.

He imagined himself carrying his mother on his back through a city encased in a translucent eggshell. He ran and ran, but could not figure out how to break through to the outside world. His mother was getting heavier, and her arms and legs kept slipping, so he had to slow down and hoist her up again. By the time he finally saw a crack in the eggshell, his mother had become so heavy that he had to let her go and almost drag her towards it. When the gap was almost within reach, it began to narrow. By now, his mother was heavier than he was, and despair was sucking him into a quagmire.

The world had suddenly gone quiet. He did not say a word, just stared at Shuisheng, as if he could transfer his soul into that pimple-faced body.

*

Ten days later, Li Wen was unsurprised when he suffered a crushing defeat. His brain had been spinning at top speed the whole time. He seemed to have grown into an adult overnight. 'Everything's Gone Quiet' repeated itself madly over and over again in his head – this was a number by a Beijing band that Shuisheng had introduced to him. Apparently the singers were the same age as they were, and had lovely Beijing accents which made them sound completely carefree. As soon as the door to adulthood opened, Li Wen was like a warrior who had secretly used a modding app and swallowed hundreds of thousands of experience points in an instant, after which he had to stand and wait for his appearance to transform. Somewhat confused, he wondered if he was going to become more powerful or more hopeless. Yet at the same time, he was crystal clear about one thing: as his memory hurled itself at the exam questions, he did not need to look up from the paper to know that his mother was standing just outside the sealed-off exam room, waiting for him, probably still wearing that metallic blue, short-sleeved polyester blouse. If he used his limited running skills to rebel against his mother's ambitions for him, would his future be his to control? If he managed to squeeze through the crack, would life outside the eggshell be the place of hope that his mother had promised?

That summer, they barely exchanged a word. As soon as the college entrance examination was over, his mother took him to McDonald's in the centre of Jianjun Plaza. He ordered a set meal that cost more than a hundred yuan, and a large glass of Coca-Cola to wash it down. His mother ordered a Filet-O-Fish which came in a paper wrapper, but she only took a bite of it.

'How's this supposed to be good to eat?' she grumbled. 'It has no texture or flavour. We'd be better off at home making jiaozi dumplings.'

Li Wen's was a sad generation. Their parents had fought a war, but all they had bequeathed to their offspring was junk food. Li Wen stuffed the burgers into his mouth one after another. Eight or nine years ago, when McDonald's first came to their town, the square had been full of children of about his size, hand in hand with their parents, bubbling with excitement. Nothing else had existed for them apart from the fragrance of hamburgers. His memories of his father that day were the sharpest he had. Dad had stood in the queue wearing a navy-blue tee-shirt, squinting and holding a newspaper over his head to keep the sun out of his face. His mother had asked for a Filet-O-Fish, and said it was delicious.

He knew in his heart of hearts that he might well end up obediently accepting a job at the teacher training college his mother had attended. A few years down the line, he would probably take over her position and read the same English texts on the same three-year cycle to the pupils. He would marry a colleague and settle down here. It would be the ultimate revenge against his mother and her ambitions for him.

When the exam marks were published, his mother did not yell at him or beat him. She sat bolt upright on the kitchen chair, as if she had turned into a tree accumulating yearly rings in her trunk. She seemed unable to grapple with the void which confronted her – it had never occurred to her that he might get results like this. Or if she had, she dismissed it instantly. Li Wen stood with his hands behind his back gripping the metal door frame separating the kitchen and living room area so tightly that red welts appeared on his hands, although he did not feel any pain. He was adapting: what he feared was no longer his mother punishing him, it was what awaited him afterwards, her anxious fears, which he had to appease over and over by reawakening her expectations. They had a standing fluorescent lamp which stood tall and straight, just as his mother curled into a ball, while he loomed over her like a huge carnivorous plant. Li Wen felt a strange pleasurable sensation surging from the soles of his feet into his peripheral nerves, and a little voice whispered in his ear, 'You're going to stay here, you have nothing, this is the end of her, and you.' This was followed by a wave of terror, and his mother, still motionless, seemed to evaporate, to become invisible and intangible. Where her body had been, there was only a boundless emptiness. In his mind's eye, Li Wen saw himself as a child, curled up in the darkness when there was a blackout. Then his mother had come, put her arms around him gently and lit a candle. The light from the candle had been just enough for the two of them. Now it was his turn to comfort her. He told her that he would put down 'willing to be flexible' on his application, he had no objection to being open with his college choices. He also had a level two athlete's certificate, which would definitely help.

'Yes, the athlete's certificate . . . It'll definitely help . . . We'll find a way . . .'

His mother suddenly looked up. Li Wen was taken aback. He had seen a glimmer in his mother's eyes, like the glimmer of an oar reaching out to save someone who had fallen into the water in the dark.

'Let me find out what "willing to be flexible" actually means. There must be a way.'

Li Wen had no memories of a director called Dr Yao when he was growing up, nor did he even remember the name. His mother must be planning something big – she seemed fired up with excitement and a desire for justice in a way that he had never seen before. He watched as she filled a stainless-steel lunch box with baozi dumplings stuffed with steamed shredded cabbage, folded their clothes and packed a black canvas suitcase they had not used for many years. She tucked a leather document folder between the bottom layers of clothes and zipped the suitcase shut – then opened and closed it again indecisively. Finally, she took the folder out and put it into the black leather shoulder bag she carried with her. That night, they got on the train to M City. In their hard sleeper compartment, he slept on the lower bunk, and his mother slept with her shoulder bag in her arms in the middle bunk. The compartment stank of sweat and instant noodles. He did not want to eat his mother's baozi. Instead, he peeled an orange, and they ate half each. This was his attempt to mask the stench in the compartment. His mother, however, kept trying to force the baozi in the stainless-steel box on him, even though he kept repeating, 'No thanks, I'm not hungry'.

He felt everyone's eyes on him. He did not want to reject her, nor did he want to look like a baby bird being fed by its mother. After repeated refusals, he suddenly found himself knocking the lid of the lunch box and the buns onto the floor.

'Leave them, they're dirty,' she said. She picked everything up, blew on buns, put them on the pull-out table, thought for a moment, then got a roll of toilet paper out of her bag. She covered the buns with a few squares of toilet paper and handed the roll to Li Wen.

'Take it when you go,' she said.

Li Wen put the paper on the dining table, next to the condemned buns. His mother had told him that they were going to see Dr Yao, a director at M City University, and it was an overnight trip. 'Sleep well,' she told him, 'tomorrow is the big day.' But he didn't sleep. He kept looking at a girl in the opposite bunk. Her face appeared and disappeared, starkly illuminated like clean white bone. She was wearing black earphones. He had no idea what she was listening to but he imagined the music filling her entire world. His own ears were filled with the sound of the train moving along. All he could remember at this particular moment were some presidential inauguration speeches he had memorised. *When we imitate those triumphalist tones*, he thought, *we're completely detached, as if the whole world has nothing to do with us.*

They returned on a night train too, and the upper bunk across from him was empty this time. He and his mother had been to see Dr Yao. His memories of this were like slides being projected into the air with the sound muted, telling him that he could never look back now: his mother and Yao had reached some kind of agreement, and at the appropriate moment, he saw his mother transfer the leather folder to Yao. He was unable to estimate from its thickness how much money it might contain. He had no idea why or how Yao had fallen from the sky. Was it to solve his problems, or to lock him up in an unsolvable formula? He sat feeling useless in the side room of M City Restaurant where they had reserved a table. He was redundant. It was as if he was watching a film that was oblivious to his presence. He was being displayed just like the dishes on the table. Dr Yao seemed to be someone he could trust. At least he did not grumble continuously, 'You young whipper-snappers!' and 'You punk kids!' Yao's calm attitude toward him made him feel differently about himself. He felt like he was on the way to adulthood, and the rite of passage was imminent. He suddenly thought of Shuisheng. By this time, he should be in the United States.

Back at the express hotel that night, their room had a damp, sour odour. Leaving most of his clothes on, he hurriedly slipped under the covers which still carried a whiff of the previous occupant's hair. He lay facing the wall in order to avoid looking at his mother in the bed next to him. The sight of her underwear folded on the bedside table confused him, and his whole body went rigid. Without a door and wall between them, he felt like he was itching all over. He could no longer stomach sharing a room with his mother. He could not suppress hateful masculine thoughts when he looked at her peony-coloured bra, and he loathed himself for that. He also hated the silence that the inseparability of their relationship imposed on them. His puberty had been depressingly short. It started from ignorance one morning and ended with an ejaculation that soaked the quilt. The whole process took less than five minutes. He did not even know whose image he was imagining. He only knew that from that day on, his mother lay awake next door like a female panther lurking in the dark on the grassland, straining her ears for any noise that her prey might make. Once, while his mother was away, he sneaked into her bedroom and opened her bedside cabinet, as if it was the door to a brave new world. He felt his heart pounding in terror that his mother might suddenly appear behind him. There were two red passbooks at the bottom of the drawer, and a black Bible lay on top of them, he did not know why. Nor did he care how much money the passbooks contained. Then his attention fell on a small foil packet, which seemed to get hot in his hand, until it threatened to catch alight and burn the place down. It was not until a few years later when he lost his virginity to Zheng Xiaowei and she tore open the little packet that he figured out it was never going to set the world alight.

His memories of his mother's words faded with time, some of them slipping away before he even understood them. That autumn, he was to register at M City University as a sports student. His mother said that Dr Yao had promised to find a way to transfer him to the English department for his second and third years.

He became extremely compliant; outside the translucent eggshell was another one just like it. He obediently ate the three meals a day his mother cooked, obediently went out for walks with her, obediently stood beside her and listened as she told her friends that he had a place in the English Department of M City University. The pair of them never mentioned Dr Yao or the passing over and disappearance of the leather folder. For the first time in their lives, he and his mother tacitly understood each other. His acquiescence confused him: Was he hoping his mother would find a way out of his current situation for him? Or was he passively admitting that there would never be a way out, and he was stuck?

7

'IT's a spaceship.'

Mrs Li was surprised to hear herself say the word aloud. Nowadays, she had to wear a scarf around her neck all year round. She hated the cold, and from her forties onwards, she had had increasing trouble with her cervical vertebrae – first, curvature of the spine, and later, compression of the nerves. She was reluctant to go to hospital, regarding it as a place where judgements rather than cures were doled out. She had seen the white rooms where people's bodies grew saggy and cold and their eyes closed forever. Although she knew that eventually she, like everyone else, would end up going that way, there was a moment in which she suddenly saw herself no longer moving forward – in fact, retreating at least one year every year. Even if she did go forwards, it was a kind of going backwards so that when the last day came, she would have become a baby again. She looked in the rectangular windows of the school building and the sun looked very small, even smaller than the sun she saw by the reservoir when she was a kid. The rubberized running track had welcomed a new set of students, accompanied by Coach Wang, still wearing his blue, threadbare tracksuit. She touched the scarf around her neck, and its slippery feel filled her with pride: real silk kept its texture, especially Hangzhou silk from ten years ago.

She was well aware that her students nowadays talked behind her back, commenting on how her clothes were old-fashioned. They also blatantly passed notes to each other under their desks and gossiped shamelessly on their WeChat groups during class. As time went by, she found that she understood these children of thirteen or fourteen less and less. The same went for the new young teachers. They had new clothes every day, all bought online, but the garments might as well have been made of paper, they wore out so quickly. As for the students, once they graduated, they never came back again. When Li Wen had been at the school, she had only taught the junior middle school classes. She thought now she might have a go at teaching the seniors. Maybe that way she would not feel time was going so slowly. She had not noticed before that the two ends of the school building were connected by a long corridor, and it cast a shadow shaped like a spaceship on the sports field.

When Li Wen was around, there had been many things she had failed to pick up on. But after he went off to M City, her head seethed with a mixture of memories and imagination. In her mind's eye, she often saw Li Wen as a baby, and occasionally at thirty years old. For her, Li Wen was Li Wen. She did not see him as progressing through life the way her pupils did – through school to graduation, through adolescence to adulthood, from a spaceship-shaped campus to a whole new world where she could no longer keep a grip on him. She cleaned Li Wen's room with an ocean-scented disinfectant. She had forgotten what the ocean really smelled like, but the concentrated fragrance made her head spin. She was getting old. She yearned for a secret radar, for a nameless cavern tucked away under Li Wen's pillow, in a corner of his desk, or in a crack in his bookshelves, in which to hide. She had seen how her pupils did it: the books they hid, the flip phones hurriedly snapped shut, the girlish blushes, the scraps of paper stuffed into their desks. She found almost nothing, apart from a few *Slam Dunk* manga and some CDs of singers, girls with brown curly hair on the sleeves. Li Wen was not that kind of kid. Anyway, he was gone. The boy was well on the way to becoming an adult. Mrs Li sat for an afternoon, her head swimming from the ocean fragrance, trying to get some balance back in her life. Then she went to the kitchen to boil an egg and, once the water was at a rolling boil, took out her phone and messaged Li Wen.

'How are you doing today?'

After pressing send, she realised that what she really wanted to know was how Li Wen was managing, living alone. On the one hand, she had managed to dig out Dr Yao's details, an instinctive human response when all her attention was focused on how to grasp a fleeting glimpse of the future. Intuition, you could call it. It had been a miracle. She had called Yao fully expecting that no one would answer; she had kept his phone number when he visited Li Wen's father in his last days in hospital, never imagining she would need it for just such an occasion: to ensure that Li Wen could get into the English department at M City University and be different from the others. On the other hand, when she took Li Wen to meet Yao, she had been utterly calm. She would carry that black case for her son, come what may. It was her natural instinct as a mother, even though Li Wen was now a head taller than her. As the train started its journey, it felt like she had set a chain of events in motion. She stood alone on the empty platform for a long time. She had given Li Wen the red passbooks, a third of her life. The fifty thousand yuan was her last scrap of strength, which she hoped would catapult Li Wen into a new and better life. She was sorry that she no longer had the power to save up for Li Wen to go to the United States, but perhaps that was altogether too ambitious a goal for them both. If they needed more, she could always sell the house. She was like a bee drowning in a psychedelic aroma, carrying her son on her back to some nameless, paradisiacal blossom in search of his salvation. She marched with resolute determination out of the train station. She could see that this dirty old town was full of people bereft of ideals and yearnings, all with the same grey faces and glazed looks in their eyes. Her heart thumped with excitement. Li Wen had finally escaped from this suffocating hole in the sand.

It was the second time that Li Wen had vomited in the communal toilet on the twelfth floor. The walls of the school's toilets were inlaid with innumerable tiny flesh-pink tiles. He finished each practice with a spinning head and a frenetic heart. Before long, like the bona fide physical education students around him, he learned to quickly gauge his pulse by palpating his face. No matter how fast his heartbeat, the voices told him to press on, give it his all, go even faster next time. He agreed with Coach Wang: he didn't understand sports training and lacked a grasp of the essence of exercise. In the past, he had protested, and Coach Wang's aloofness had led him to conclude it was a wise move to use sports training as a bargaining chip. But he feared others would think of him as overly clever, overly ambitious; his mother always stood in his way, so he had to step aside and yield to her forward drive. That day on the train, he swore a luminous oath to never again let his mother carry heavy objects for him, yet in reality he had no choice but to surrender his power and leave the suitcase in her hands. One day, this powerlessness will be the death of me! The thought adhered to the lobes of his brain, like the motherly kindness that slimed his skin. It was a paralysing, immobilising kindness: no, he would be tormented by guilt; yes, he would be suffocated and submerged.

It was nothing like the rubberized running track at the middle school. Each long run in M City was a risky bet, a tightrope undulating with dopamine. The other competitors took themselves to be genuine athletes, and in fact they were. There were just ten or so girls and twenty boys. They had the distinctive stance and stride of professional athletes: backs subtly arched, betraying readiness to attack; hands in their pockets, springs in their feet; cold and uncaring, putting on an act, utterly without fear. He only realised later that the greatest delusion physical strength and arousal could bring was the belief that the world could be conquered. Beginning on the first day, he came in last in the class every single time, his timepiece numerals adjacent to the girls'. He had to learn to live in exile in the alien world of track and field. He had never longed so fervidly for the second- or third-year 'turnaround' of which his mother spoke. Being a poor fit for the world of sports training, the twice-weekly public English language class became his gospel. For the first time, he tasted the almost hallucinatory beauty and redemptive power of English.

The class was taught by a bespectacled teacher rumoured to be a newly minted PhD, a young man with an air of tactful reserve. These days, teachers didn't dare pit themselves against students. The relationship between the two parties had undergone an earth-shattering transformation: university was no longer the final confession booth of adulthood, and students relied upon the synergy of youthful vigour to gain the upper hand in the chess game of student-teacher relations. Li Wen's sole golden moment had already started to fragment: a month into the semester, the classroom was consumed by intolerable cacophony, half the seats were empty, and cheat sheets circulated brazenly beneath the desks. Li Wen always arrived ten minutes ahead of time, when the classroom was invariably deserted. He was the only one who rushed to secure a front-row seat and fix his eyes on the blackboard in the empty room. One day, he had arrived early and was sitting in the front row as usual when the young male teacher walked in, shot Li Wen a glance and asked as he powered up the projector on the podium, 'So you like English?'

'Mm-hmm.'

'Following along okay in class?'

'Every word.'

'This class is full of losers. Do me a favour, try and scrape by with a D–.'

Li Wen turned to look to the left and watched as a few athletes filed into the room, speaking a southern dialect too coarse for him to make out. When the athletes passed, a certain peculiar odour stirred in the air, a rust emanation covering over the lilt of green grass. The teacher thinks of me as one of them, judges me by sports students' standards, he thought. Sports students were expected to only barely pass English. This language was of absolutely no benefit to their training, did nothing to increase their competitive capacity or channel their raging hormones. Suddenly, Li Wen's back straightened with a sort of secret complicity: salvation was just a year or two away. That day, after class, he made a point of staying behind, shuffled over to the young teacher and said:

'I really want to learn English, Sir.'

Without lifting his head, the teacher slid his mobile phone into a canvas bag: 'It's a matter of practice. Read and read and read some more.'

A self-evident elaboration – a certain turbid emotion instantly stopped up his neural pathways. He wasn't sure if it was hatred, but he knew he had hit on an appropriate attitude with which to confront the sports students – it was because of them that the standards of the English class had slowly slipped. Individual students learning at faster and slower speeds went unnoticed in their midst like small, flat stones which left ripples on the water but were never seen skipping. At that instant, Li Wen was struck by the urge to sit in on some English department classes, and he understood why the young teacher always seemed to be delivering longwinded monologues. What did it matter if half the class skived off and the other half slept at their desks? Sports students' English marks didn't matter – the school simply had to assign staff capable of ushering them across the finish line. Freshman year was nearly over, summer was fast approaching and the inexorable dry heat was harassing his senses. He had had enough of the daily drills, he had had enough of the stifling rust odour, he had had enough of the dorm with its two sets of bunk beds. This was in spite of the fact that he always convinced himself that the dorm was just a place to sleep, and as soon as he climbed onto the top bunk and shut his eyes he had no obligation to converse with the other occupants. He went online and bought a blindfold and earplugs, but still, each time he returned from the library, he sensed the awkward transitory stiffness of the other three, followed shortly by the din of a further explosion. His brain was stuck in cramming mode: he roamed the library and the cafeteria, striving to maintain the state he was in when he returned to the dormitory half an hour before lights out, to preserve the cloistered reticence of a lone traveller. His sphere of activity hardly ever overlapped with that of the sports students in the class. He was as busy and orderly as a shadow, bound to routine, his thoughts and actions utterly opaque to everyone.

His train arrived early on the day he moved into the dorm. He hadn't discussed attending M City University with his mother on their previous visit, couldn't remember where in M City their express hotel had been. The university campus was big, bigger than the middle school and the teachers' housing compound combined. Spread taut across the centre of the path, welcoming new students, an enormous red banner hung from the school gates: 'Toward a brilliant future.'

Li Wen had no particular imaginings of what university life might be like, which he blamed on an insufficiency of imaginational resources stockpiled in his grey matter. He essentially lacked motivation to actively seek out novelty or excavate the unknown. He had started going senile at the age of seven, his need to grow staunched by his mother's black magic.

He found the bunk with his name on it in the inner cavity of the dorm, a flat shaft of sunlight tumbling onto the white desk at the base of the bed, its texture cold and icy like stainless steel. In a clumsy attempt to square the corners of the sheets, he ended up twisting the sheets and the quilt together, and an image of his mother forcefully overtook his thoughts. He longed for her to show up and straighten everything out. He missed her.

Chen was the first of Li Wen's roommates to speak to him. A practised eye could have discerned that Chen was older, around the age of twenty, but when Li Wen laid eyes on him, he discerned only that this boy was a bit different than the others: he stood about half a head taller than Li Wen, was extremely stocky and exuded an aura of dry heat, but there was darkness in his eyes, a nihilistic gloom indicating an absolute unconcern for existence. A back-alley Beijing accent coloured his speech, recalling in Li Wen's mind the band from Beijing that sang 'Everything's Gone Quiet'. The accent intensified the sense he cared about nothing at all: 'I'm older than any of the rest of you. You can call me Big Brother Chen.'

When Chen spoke, the odour of tobacco wafted from his mouth, and the faint yellow hue of his fingertips recalled a piece of paper left too long in the sun.

'My name's Li Wen. It's my first year here.'

Li Wen later learned that Chen had trained as a kickboxer, come third in a few tournaments and ended up starting university several years behind schedule. Every pore on Chen's body was open; he knew something of the world. Actually, all the sports students had that air about them. They came from every corner of the country. It was that whiff of raw power that caught Li Wen off guard; he had never possessed it. He couldn't be sure at the time whether he had been enchanted by Big Brother Chen's accent, or if it was the envigored aura of the sports students that gripped him and wouldn't let go. Anyway, in the beginning, he tagged along with them – Chen took him and their other two roommates to the hotpot place behind campus. They said the hotpot place had stayed in business so long by relying on university students for sustenance. There it had been for years, a stalwart presence hunched at the end of an alley thick with parasol trees. Chen said hotpot was only good when you tossed opium poppy pods into it, otherwise it lacked the zest of a death wish. Li Wen sniffed with interest. He wasn't sure what poppy pods smelled like, but he did catch a twinge of tingling sweetness within the choking smoke.

Was memory a flowing river, or a heap of fragments? Li Wen wasn't sure. All he could recall were discreet shards, and the odour of deceit. For instance, he had forgotten the names of his other two roommates, but they are not important to this story. He remembered only that Big Brother Chen had opened up his pores and tossed poppy pods into the beef tallow hotpot, and it had tasted really goddamn amazing. In the very beginning, when he watched Chen and the other two playing the drinking game huaquan, the three of them all shouting over one another in different accents, he was struck by a sense of novelty. He sensed he was positioned at the very centriole of the large balloon called the world – he had caught the scent of adulthood. He remembered the time when Chen had turned to look at him through slitted eyes and asked if he was experienced in love. His face had reddened. The answer was no: other than a few flustered, transitory wet dreams, he couldn't even spoor the outlines of love through tracing paper, just as he could never make out the face of the girl in the dream. He only ever thought of the hot viscous liquid that filled his body. No matter what happened in his fantasies or how much time went by, the sheets and quilts he had slept on and under were always carefully inspected and cleaned by his mother, and he began to suspect there was filth in him, a foulness faintly enmeshed in his growth, an alluring whiff of the taboo. But now he remembered, Big Brother Chen claimed to have done it with an athlete, and a dance school student. He said sex was like the moment when a hungry lion leapt on its prey, a burst of pleasure following the fatigue of heated pursuit.

Li Wen felt his life had always lacked the intense penetrating quality of supercharged male hormones, and his sense of smell was no longer suited to his surroundings: his immune system hoisted one red flag after another. The other two quickly learned to smoke with Big Brother Chen. When they lit each other's cigarettes, they coalesced into a sealed circle, flames flashing within the ring, whilst Li Wen remained an exiled speck.

His true indisposition originated from the final row of the English classroom. For him, getting to school had always been a walk in the park: it was just a ten-minute trip from the teachers' housing compound to the university-affiliated middle school educational facility, no need to chaperone or be chaperoned by anybody. The first time he walked the cement grey paths of M City University with Big Brother Chen and the others, the jangling of fragments blew up like gusts of wind – the sound issued from the campus' PA. The announcement said, 'This is Mei Xi'an's "End Times Quartet".' Mei Xi'an? Li Wen had never before heard that name. It reminded him of the name of the soccer player Mei Xi, but the sound was truly fantastical, the smithereens multiplying endlessly.

Big Brother Chen nudged him in the elbow and said, 'Hey, what's-yer-face, let's sneak out in the first half of the period. Heard he's gonna do the roll call before class.'

Chen's English was a shambles. He was much better at speaking with his body. The ragged jingle-jangle flared and faded, and as he listened Li Wen forgot the answer he had prepared beforehand. End times was a nice name, it made people stop in their tracks for no reason at all. If there was no reason to care about other people's lives, there was no reason to care about your own life either. He asked Chen why he liked English-language hip-hop so much, and Chen cranked the sodcast to a thunderous volume and roared that he didn't care to understand the words, and then he rammed his back into the chair, which wobbled precariously, and Li Wen wondered how many days that chair had left on earth. Their other two roommates were also earnest, eager sports students, in some sense Chen's equals and abetters, and when Li Wen ingratiated himself into their enclave in the back row, he sensed there was no oxygen for him to breathe, they were creatures requiring different types of nourishment.

Li Wen acknowledged that Big Brother Chen's swaying and his tobacco tang, juxtaposed with the stereotypical rapping, indeed made him think of himself as special. It took just ten seconds, and at the count of ten, he came back to Li Wen: Li Wen, the one sports student among them who wasn't at all earnest or eager. What Coach Wang had said was wrong, physical education wasn't about spirited struggle, it was clearly a mere matter of sweat glands excreting excess perspiration, an accretion of gluey gunge. He could hear nearly nothing of what the young teacher said, saw only his mouth gaping open and snapping shut, with no expression, no sense of rhythm, flat as a beached fish gasping for air. Following along in the English textbook, he read virtue and hope into the teacher's lip movements. It was that distinct phantasmic aura of a foreign language, the same one exuded by the texts he had recited with his mother. He longed for a tempest to stir, for a lightning bolt to strike with a bang and fracture his cowardly disguise.

The first time he received the highest score on an English exam, Li Wen didn't see it as anything in particular to be proud of. Still, he sent his mother a text, meant to communicate that the two of them were still striving toward the same goal with one heart and mind. It was strange, though. Since he had arrived at M City University, his mother's face had been clouding over in his mind, and then the cloud would disperse; she would look first old, then young. That evening, Chen failed to appear at the training ground. He stayed in the dorm smoking one cigarette after another: 'You bluenose prig, why wouldn't you let me copy all the answers?'

The following inviolable principle had been emblazoned on Li Wen's brain since middle school: he wasn't to copy off anyone else, nor was he to let anyone copy off him. He had finally reached an acceptable solution, which was to let others copy half his answers. It wasn't that he fancied himself the high-minded, squeaky-clean sort. It wasn't that he was hell-bent on taking a moral stand. But his mother had told him that what a teacher hated more than anything was to find that two exams had the same answers, because it was often impossible to determine who had been copied and who had done the copying. It was as delicate as the distinction between perpetrator and victim, and it was better to accept ambiguity than to invite trouble by splitting hairs. This despite the fact that, from a young age, he had cautiously avoided his teachers' forbidden zones, and had never truly been on intimate terms with any teacher except his mother. He knew that when freshman year was over, some of his middle school classmates would return home to visit their former class teacher, a squat, stout woman. In their minds, university life was something to boast about. He had never been back home and wasn't planning on going. If you asked him, their behaviour was nothing other than self-centred conceit.

'I was afraid some of the answers might be wrong.'

'I just don't get this bloody seriousness of yours.' Big Brother Chen stubbed out the flaring fag end with a finger. A sickening miasma of smoke hovered all around. 'Drop the goody two-shoes act.'

'It isn't that I'm so serious. I just want to learn, that's all. I don't mean to make trouble.'

What Li Wen hadn't told the other occupants of the dorm was that he was leaving them behind, changing courses to English. And he had thought over how to handle them if things in the dorm hadn't changed by then. He had made up his mind to be a traitor to the other sports students, and a traitor to his own physical limitations, to set off sprinting toward a more selfish goal. At the start of the school year, the head of the physical education department had declared that physical education was an exalted human endeavour, that the competitive spirit of sport embodied equality, that as an athlete, one's sole opponent was oneself. Li Wen understood this perhaps better than anyone else present, but he knew that there was nothing exalted about his athletic skills – the boundless fervour that wafted from the other sports students, and the sense of being an observer, cut the bottom out of his heart. The others around him were like mountain climbers, taking no part in production or competitive society, rewarded only by oxygen on reaching the mountain peak. 'I don't mean to make trouble' was his heartfelt response to Big Brother Chen.

'So you're quitting sports? What do you want to be anyway, a fitness coach or a school gym teacher?' Chen had made it through several sentences without uttering a single curse word. He recognised this rare occurrence as a sign that Chen had his guard up.

'I haven't thought it through.'

Ultimately, he failed to run the rest of the race with them. In the evening, the entire dormitory went out for hotpot, like usual. In this regard, he did still retain some admiration for Big Brother Chen, or maybe it was a mere self-protective measure on Chen's part; only by opening your pores could you spot your opponent's weak point, it was just like playing huaquan. He even feared that amid the dizzying steam of the opium poppy hotpot, he might blurt out that as a sports student, he was a phoney.

On the way back to class, a crowd had gathered beneath the sole light source on either side of the street. There at the roadside clothing stand stood the old man they called Peddler Wang. Chen was the one who had introduced Li Wen to Peddler Wang, who appeared and disappeared at irregular hours, but always in the evening, when the likelihood of being spotted by the chengguan, the Urban Administrative and Law Enforcement Bureau, was lower. Wang was rail-thin and always wore billowing, baggy training uniforms, making him look even more like a giraffe. All Wang's wares were knockoffs: sportswear, socks, sometimes shoes. You might say that rather than relying on students for sustenance as the hotpot place did, it was the students who gained sustenance from Wang's counterfeit goods. Sports students from M City University made up the bulk of the clientele, and Wang knew his customers well, knew he had developed a durable business concept – each year, old students left and new ones came, and Wang couldn't remember clearly who had bought from him before, knew only that these kids didn't care that counterfeit tee-shirts failed to absorb sweat, they just wanted the latest styles, cheaply and now.

A hubbub burbled beneath Peddler Wang's cart lamp. Drawing closer, Li Wen saw two officers in blue uniforms preparing to cart away the entirety of his wares. The old man seemed to be talking back, demanding to know why his things were being confiscated, rallying the crowd to his defence between retorts. The crowd around him gradually grew, coming to resemble a posse of bouncers. Li Wen saw only two chengguan surrounded by Peddler Wang and his student supporters, like white Go pieces on the brink of being devoured by a swarm of black.

'Oh, shit! Peddler Wang's in trouble!'

Li Wen was so tipsy on liquor fumes that he almost failed to react, but Big Brother Chen rushed in, elbowing through the outer ring of students to the centre. Sound had vanished from the screen before Li Wen's eyes, all that remained was Chen's wall-like body lit by the cart lamp, fists pounding at the officers, mystically deriving the precise amount of necessary force, stopping just short of causing severe injury but hitting hard enough to counter any resistance. Their other two roommates clapped and shouted with the crowd, driven to exuberant agitation by righteous herd mentality. Big Brother Chen was their new hero.

Head held low, Li Wen pressed forward without a moment's pause. The bowl of iced transparent jelly he had gulped down had burst into flames in his belly. He quivered with youthful vigour.

8

'On 3 October 1849, a compositor for the *Baltimore Sun* named Joseph W. Walker found a barely coherent Poe on the street. According to Walker, Poe was in extreme distress and urgently needed help. Poe was taken to the University of Washington Hospital where he died at five o'clock on Sunday morning on 7 October. Poe was unable to explain how he had fallen into such dire straits.'

*

When he sneaked into the English department for the first time, Li Wen made sure to wear a white shirt, the kind he wore for flag-raising on National Day. It all went smoothly: he got hold of the class timetable without much effort, and it was not as difficult as he thought to get into the department. Among the crowd of students, he was almost invisible. After he had taken a good look around, it even occurred to him that there were half a dozen other unauthorised students sitting in too. He made sure to sit in the back row on every visit, keeping as quiet as possible to not attract attention. The strange thing was that even in the back row, the teacher's voice carried as clear as a bell, as if she was right in front of him. He belonged here, Li Wen felt. He had only glimpsed the faces of the students in front of him, those who next year, if not the year after, would be his classmates. From what he could see from the backs of their heads, they looked just like him. Both he and they were quite unlike the sports students. He also noticed that several of the boys in the class had on white shirts like his. (The sports students would have laughed at them.) He breathed in deeply, at the risk of attracting the attention of those in front of him, and felt quite sure that the smell of grass was back again.

The teacher on the podium was middle-aged and wore her hair in a bun, but a strand always escaped and hung down her cheek. She was supposed to be a well-known and prolific translator of American literature. She spoke softly, with the result that the class was always very quiet. It was as if even a book falling to the floor could startle her. The first time he went to her class on American literature, Li Wen took nothing but a blank notebook, and simply listened. Her voice was hypnotic. Once or twice, he almost caught her eye and hurriedly looked down. He wanted to remain invisible, to leave no evidence of his presence. *She knows I shouldn't be here,* he thought, *but she must be expecting me to introduce myself.* As time passed, he made a point of observing the students in the row in front of him. There was usually a skinny girl with a ponytail as thin as a frayed window sash cord. Until she turned around, he always had the impression that she was not paying attention to the lecture; the back of her head, her narrow shoulders and the rumpled jacket, which looked as frayed as her ponytail, seemed to float in the air below him.

Li Wen borrowed *Selected Stories by Edgar Allan Poe* from the library, one volume in Chinese and one in English. They were both well-thumbed, the pages dog-eared and curled at the edges. This was the first time he had come across Poe. He slipped them into his bag, glanced around, then scoffed at himself. *What are you afraid of? Sports students never come to the library.* Ever since he started attending classes in the English department, Li Wen had felt that his fellow sports students were pointing at him, watching him to see what he was up to. He knew that he felt like this because he had deserted them, but where was the harm in taking the long way round to get to where he wanted to go? By now, he was extremely grateful to his mother for that leather document folder. In fact, now that there was a distance between them and he no longer saw her, his former repressed irritability towards her had faded and he could think of her with equanimity.

He was not sensitive to words, and memorising word lists had been a source of anxiety since he was a child. His head teemed with jumbled letters, full of potential but, at the same time, objects of suspicion. When he was little, his mother had made stacks of word cards for him. She called them cards, but she actually cut them out of old cardboard boxes. He liked to play guessing games with himself, turning them over to see which came from a milk carton and which from a box of biscuits. Back then, he enjoyed the memory games. When he got five answers right in a row, it made his mother very happy. But by the age of twelve, pleasing his mother no longer seemed like fun, and he rebelled. Just as he was about to give the correct answer to the flashcard, a wrecking urge came over him and the familiar voice whispered in his ear, *Don't let her get her wish.*

The fact was that he had never seen a lot of the words in the English volume. It never occurred to him that meaningful words could be formed by putting these letters together, or that what this Edgar Allan Poe wrote was at all significant. His mother had phoned a few days before, and he had told her that he was auditing lectures in the English department. She seemed delighted, happy that he had joined the ranks of the English students, but he had not told her how interesting he was finding the course on American literature. He could not make up his mind whether these strange roaming phrases would be of any help to him in the future. Somehow, through this peculiar language, he finally grasped what his mother meant: studying in the United States symbolised for her a reshuffling of the cards. But why didn't Poe's writings offer him even a glimmer of hope? Perhaps because they were so different from the world his mother described as 'foreign'.

He remembered the message Shuisheng had sent him on MSN Messenger two days before.

'How's things? I'm in LA.'

Li Wen did not know what to say. 'I'm in M City studying physical education'? Or 'I'll be in the US too in a couple of years'? They had not seen each other since finishing their run that day. When the graduation photo was taken, he had seen Shuisheng in the distance. He was smiling brilliantly in the sunshine, and it looked like he no longer had braces. A little of their camaraderie was stripped away. He saw the rubber surface of the running track melting in the sun, and felt that the only thing he had a right to in that moment was silence.

He could not imagine what kind of place Shuisheng was living in now. This was beyond his ken, and far outside his mother's concept of 'foreign'. Was the Shuisheng without braces the same as or different from the boy he had known before? He had no idea. Shuisheng was a demon, a demon who had brought him face to face with the real world for the first time. Before that, reality had never been so close, but Shuisheng's big opportunity had made him insignificant and fragmented the world into countless spaces through which he could not see. Only passing through stages of growing up, one level after another, could unlock new checkpoints for him. Prior to this, Li Wen had almost no memory of his age, although his mother used to buy him a cake adorned with brightly-coloured spiral candles every birthday. The candles burned down and puddled brightly on the surface of the white icing. She made him long-life noodles too, long and chewy, which he ate without vinegar; she only remembered to add vinegar to hers when she was halfway through them.

Since starting at M City University, he increasingly felt like he was turning into a character in *The Sims*. Big Brother Chen introduced him to the video game – the first he had ever played. When he was in middle school, his mother had forbidden him a games console, and it would have been too big to hide. She hated anything fun: she never played cards, danced, or sang. He sometimes watched her making pulled noodles through the glass door of the kitchen. She made it seem like a strange ritual: the flesh on her upper arms jiggled along with the noodles as she shook them out. It was the only sign she had ever been young. His mother was beginning to seem ageless to him. No matter how much he probed, all he could find in the deepest part of the cave was a wizened old body, from whose dark flabby womb some stranger had extracted him.

Big Brother Chen had a PS2 emulator connected to his computer monitor. Before Li Wen went off to his English classes, Big Brother Chen sometimes let him learn games on it. Big Brother Chen and another boy in their dormitory were often to be found in front of the monitor, playing *Diablo*, they told him. To start with, Chen told Li Wen that *Diablo* was too difficult for him, he needed to work up to it with simpler games. Li Wen had to admit that even *The Sims* amazed him. In this simulated world, he could be anyone he wanted. The black controller in his hand was the hub of all action, and the virtual reality dazzled him. The human form created by the game had grown up in a dirty old town just like him, before arriving in this global metropolis, where growth spurts were marked by bigger houses, more cars and sexier girlfriends. Every year as he grew up through the game, he got something new. When his virtual self was thirty years old, he had enough money to buy a flat on the sixtieth floor of a city centre block. The moment he clicked the circle button on the controller to confirm his purchase, his memory went blank for a moment and he completely forgot where he really was. He watched the avatar he had created living in a sixty-storey skyscraper, a stupefied expression on its face. This version of him sat on the blue sofa in the screen and opened a bottle of champagne, and he was convinced that this was his true form.

But Li Wen was still forced to endure linear time. The toilets of the boys' dormitory always reeked of a mixture of sweat and urine. Almost all the boys on this floor were sports students in different years. *They're as bad as primary school kids, they can't even wipe their own arses*, thought Li Wen, fingering the fluff that had started to grow on his chin. He was sensitive to the body odour of men because he had grown up in an environment without it. When he went into the toilets on the first day, he had been suspicious enough to check over the urinal in the cubicle, although in fact, it was no different from the urinal in his middle school. Grimy white ceramic. He remembered how his Adam's apple had grown a few years ago, and his voice suddenly went gruff. The Adam's apple seemed to appear at the same time as the bum fluff on his upper lip. He guessed that his mother must have heard the change in his voice before she noticed the pointy thing bulging at the front of his throat. She said nothing, but he knew that from then on, she would eavesdrop on him at night and go through the drawer of his bedside table. It meant the end of his childhood, the end of any lingering memories of his father. It all happened too quickly, practically overnight, and there was no time for his mother or him to find a way to deal with the changes in each other. Growing up and sex, like having fun, were taboo subjects for his mother.

*

After he got beaten up by the chengguan, Li Wen became known as a wimp. Whenever he went into the English department, he felt Big Brother Chen's eyes peering out at him from some invisible corner. Chen could see through him, Li Wen was convinced of it. He was also convinced that when he went into the dormitory with Poe or other books under his arm, Chen glared at him behind his back. The looks gave him goosebumps, while the hostility was that of a creature who had been left behind in the abyss while his fellow traveller had managed to crawl into the light. Their comradeship was an illusion, and in its place was an antagonism that chilled him.

Mentally, Li Wen called the incident the 'chengguan revolution'. He did not tell his mother about it. In his opinion, this was not only Big Brother Chen marking out his territory, it was a popular revolt against rules and regulations, like the capture of the Bastille they had read about in history class. Even the adjectives he used to describe it came from the textbook. There was no revolution in *The Sims*, where virtual life moved forward steadily as if protected inside an eggshell. Big Brother Chen said that he was not up to their kind of war game, and he had to agree. He came back to the dormitory after his beating alone and climbed into bed without washing or cleaning his teeth. Chen and the others were back about half an hour later, filling the dorm with their elation and alcohol fumes.

'What a great day!' Chen shouted. 'They better not mess with Peddler Wang again. We can't let those uniforms oppress us!'

Li Wen didn't dare to turn over or cover his ears. He could hear Chen's voice and smell all of them, but had no idea why they were so fired up. After that evening, Chen and the others in the dormitory began to play games at night. They turned the volume up full blast, right up until the lights went out.

From then on, Li Wen's connection with the world of *The Sims* was broken. He had been pursuing a girl named W in this virtual world. She was gorgeous, with luscious breasts and a slender waist. They had two dinners together. W had even kissed him after dinner. The virtual Li Wen was very grown up. He kept his cool and did not blush, while Li Wen in real life was hazy about whether a kiss was anything more than an exchange of saliva. It occurred to him to wonder whether his virtual persona could simulate a woman for himself again. What name should he give her? Perhaps just W for the time being.

Anyway, the real Li Wen was now condemned as a wimp. Big

Brother Chen had frozen him out of the gang. By mutual agreement, apart from sleeping in the same room, they had nothing more to do with each other. Without any questions or negotiations, Li Wen had been banished. He spent his time roaming around, in the library, the canteen, the sportsground, in a thicket where the sun never shone, even down the alley beside the hotpot restaurant where the recycling was piled up. Amongst the sports students, he was the odd man out, antisocial, a furtive shadowy figure who never had anything sensible to say.

Occasionally he missed the opium poppy hotpot and sticky rice cakes that he used to enjoy, but he was afraid of bumping into Chen and his mates there. It took two weeks of tracking them, real cloak-and-dagger stuff, to find out where and when they hung out. The skulking around filled him with an odd sense of excitement. He was disgusted at his behaviour – all this hiding in dark corners to spy out other people's lives – and yet he felt a surge of blood pumping through his veins, almost making them inflate. He had never felt like this before, and he wondered if it was a real physical effect, or just psychological. A very quiet demon seemed to have taken up residence in his heart. He discovered that the gang never went to the hotpot place on Wednesday nights, because that was the day of Big Brother Chen's weekly boxing match. It was not exactly a meeting of equals, more a chance to beat up his opponents. Every Wednesday, Chen was the king. He frequently beat three other boxers, one after another, in one night. After that, he would go and sprint around the sportsground on his own. When he had run himself into exhaustion, he would grab a towel to cover his head and throw himself flat out on the ground, panting heavily. Finally, he would save up his elation until Friday night, when he would binge on food and drink.

Li Wen wondered if he was going to get addicted to opium poppy hotpot, especially now that he would be there on his own. The thought was exhilarating. Having made sure that the Wednesday fight was still on, he put away his vocabulary book and hurried to the street around the back of the college. His vocabulary lists made him feel like a walking corpse. Only poppies could rouse him, and he was desperate for some.

It got dark early in winter, and the air of M City was thick with smoke and fumes, even more so than the dirty old town he came from, though it was hard for Li Wen to make a judgement. He was increasingly unsure whether he had a clear memory of his hometown. What he was sure of was that the winter in M City was colder and darker, and there was an unaccustomed dampness that seemed to invade every crevice of his body. The road from the middle school to the teachers' compound had always been brightly lit, apparently because a third of the teachers who lived there were retired and elderly and afraid of tripping at night. Li Wen went to look at the lights again. Their relentless beams seemed to have the stubbornness of old folk intent on dispelling the ignorance of the younger generation. Right now, half the lights on the streets behind M City University either flickered because of fluctuations in the voltage, or were off altogether. There were long gaps where the lampposts had broken bulbs or none at all. The streets where the students hung out were full of all kinds of people, whether they were kids still wet behind the ears, or had grown up and thrown in their lot with society on the outside.

When Li Wen arrived, he saw Peddler Wang was back selling knockoff goods from his cart, and was opening up the cardboard boxes. Another consignment of clothes must have arrived. Li Wen had brought one or two things from Wang, along with the rest of them. He always felt that they were not warm enough in winter and not breathable enough for the summer heat, but he had never said anything. The monthly allowance his mother gave him did not allow him to go after the genuine article, but, in any case, he did not regard himself as a serious sports student. In his favour was the fact that for visits to the English department, a practical, respectable-looking shirt was fine. You usually could not tell the brand, or even if it was a winter or a summer shirt. Peddler Wang had been around for years, and had quickly sniffed out that Li Wen was not a loyal customer. So they never talked much, and Li Wen was not going to go out of his way to greet him.

A November frost had made the ground slippery, and Li Wen almost lost his footing at the entrance to the hotpot shop. As soon as he was through the door, he was enveloped in warmth. The room was stuffy and dimly lit, and he felt his every pore expand and suck in the cheap aroma greedily. He finally managed to order a bottle of Xuejingying, a locally made fizzy drink. On its bright blue label, he drew a silly face, a grinning doll. This fizz was sweeter than Coca-Cola. In fact, it was only carbonated water and sweetener, with blue colouring added. He had not had any for far too long, because every time he came with Big Brother Chen's gang, they all had to drink Yanjing beer. He did not like beer. It tasted sour, it had a bad smell and it came back on him when he burped. Heaven in M City in winter was opium poppy hotpot washed down with blue fizz. The shop owner looked hard at him, at first speculating that he was alone because he had broken up with a girlfriend, but then realising that the look on his face was not grief, but self-absorption. So, in spite of the fact that it was not good business to let one person occupy a table by himself, he cut him some slack and reluctantly let him be. Maybe he had money, he thought, maybe he was going to become a regular client. There were always some students with enough money to splash out on food.

Li Wen had no idea why the hotpot shop owner first stared at him and then walked away. He had always been a sensitive child, very concerned about his image. Now he was worried that the boss might turf him out. So he ordered three dishes of meat and a decent serving of vegetables, and finished the lot. The sports students never did that; they always ordered a full table of dishes and made sure to leave plenty of leftovers, because it made them look good. After the last sip of fizz, he burped just like Chen would do, comfortably ridding his belly of the gas, and paid the bill. Then he went back to the self-study room for a while. He had just discovered it, and it was a great place, because there were no sports students there. It was open all night from six in the evening to six in the morning and there was no danger of being disturbed, except possibly by the occasional couple snogging in the back row.

After his hot meal, Li Wen felt cold when he stepped outside and hurriedly pulled the hood of his fleece over his head. Whether it was the effect of the poppy pods or the gas in his fizzy drink he did not know, but he immediately turned right and slipped into the alley that ran down the side of the hotpot restaurant. He felt like a naughty kid sneaking away on his own, to the hidden treasure on which he had put his mark. Just then, he saw two figures, their shadows intertwined with his, standing quite still by the recycling bins. It gave him a jolt. All he could think was, 'I'm finished! I'm done for!'

One of the two was Peddler Wang, and the other was Big Brother Chen. Chen was pale, and his forehead was covered in beads of sweat. He had on a sports fleece – as if he had slipped away from the boxing at half-time. He pressed some folded one-hundred notes into Wang's hands: 'Same as before, I want some Modafinil. It really works.'

Wang took four foil strips from his battered bum bag, each with a dozen pills. 'I broke a carton apart. Easier to carry. It'll keep you going for a while.'

Chen took the foil strips.

'I took four today. They really fired me up. I was flying, the others were just walking. You too, Wang. You look like you're in slow motion.'

Peddler Wang smiled. It was a guileless, innocent smile. Li Wen's mother had forgotten to warn him that people like that were really crafty. Mother and son were middle-of-the-road folk themselves, neither very simple, nor very sly. Li Wen's first reaction now was, *Wang's a deep one.*

When the other two sensed Li Wen's presence, the three of them stood quite still, Chen with the foil strips still clutched in his hand.

'Shit . . .'

He spat a gob of phlegm. Even though the alley was dark, Li Wen could tell that Chen was trembling from the cold. If Chen came over and whacked him, just like he hit out at the chengguan officers that day, Li Wen would have let him, would even have volunteered for a beating. Violence was the best way to solve things. It showed that there was a genuine bond between them. It suddenly dawned on Li Wen that the precious thing that the chengguan were after was not the boxed-up knockoff clothes, but the pills Chen was holding; that what Big Brother Chen and the others were really against was not the chengguan in their uniforms, but the sporting spirit of fairness and justice that the head of their department had been dinning into them since their first day of college.

The three of them confronted each other warily. They were like cannibalistic Mormon crickets with bodies the colour of rotting meat, their antennae questing like radar for some hidden, sinister signal. In the endless winter night, the only street lamp over the recycling bins suddenly came on. Li Wen could see Big Brother Chen's face flood with a mixture of feelings: embarrassment, bitterness and mockery. He twitched, from the effects of the Modafinil or possibly from dislike of Li Wen. After a moment, Chen walked over to him. Li Wen knew that he had nowhere to hide. He waited to be punished violently; he would not fight back.

Peddler Wang stood alone in the shadows. He knew there was always a boxing champion among the sports students, every year. He steered clear of the college students' business. They had a mutual understanding: they were linked not only by the sportswear he flogged, but more importantly, by the limits imposed by the sport itself. To these young people, Peddler Wang was a magician awarding them the fruits of the poppy. So when Chen just glared at Li Wen and walked past him, Peddler Wang kept a tight grip on his bum bag. He was used to fighting and knew that silence was much more destructive than violence.

As Chen passed by, Li Wen sensed the true meaning of hatred, and he hated that knowledge.

I'm finished, he thought. He stood rooted to the spot, all alone, he had no idea for how long, until eventually his whole body went numb with cold.

9

For a whole week, Li Wen was oppressed by a sense of impending doom, though he had no idea what form that doom would take. Everything that had happened that night around the back of the school was crystal clear one minute, and a hazy blur the next. The fact that Chen hadn't meted out immediate and brutal punishment did not make him any happier. Prolonging the agony wasn't Chen's style. It could only mean that he had taken a real dislike to Li Wen.

Li Wen had been to one of Big Brother Chen's boxing matches: back then he had been at a loose end on Wednesday nights, as he was on nearly every one of the roughly one thousand nights and counting that he had spent at M City University. The whole building, and the surging heat that arose from the sports students' bodies, both stimulated and repelled him. He could feel how intensely alive they were, but at the same time, he was painfully aware that he did not belong to their world. He had never seen a boxing ring until now, and it struck him as bigger than he expected, like somewhere you'd corral wild animals but made of blue and red foam. The first man to challenge Big Brother Chen was a scrawny, swarthy specimen, who looked as if he wanted to give Chen, the triumphant winner of three fights in a row the previous week, a run for his money. The pair of them held their gloved fists high in front of their foreheads, darting lithely to one side, then the other, eyes fixed on each other, neither giving the other an inch for a whole minute. They were evenly matched, and landing a killer blow involved finding each other's weaknesses – that was the essence of combat sports. Li

Wen saw Chen's eyes begin to blaze. In their depths was a dead zone where he could not read any emotion. He had seen a look like that on *Animal World*, the look of a jaguar when it was about to pounce on its prey. Then Chen spotted the instant when the man's movements slowed, and without a moment's hesitation, he swung a right hook. His opponent made more and more missteps and misjudgements, and Chen battered him relentlessly, until his nose ran with snot stained pink by a trickle of blood. After that fight, all the sports students got the message: Wednesday's matches were a proper showcase for a champion.

When Big Brother Chen was with his mates, whether in the dorm or at the hotpot restaurant, he never talked about what happened in the ring. Most of the time, he talked about himself, his childhood, his aspirations and his girlfriend. Once or twice he brought up his time at the sports school. Li Wen remembered very clearly that Chen started to shiver from head to foot as he talked (just like when they'd encountered each other by the bins), the sweat pouring off his forehead. The two other dormmates, whose names and faces Li Wen could not remember, had a lot to say about their experience at sports school too, and Li Wen was left on the sidelines. When he did try to chip in, by mentioning his own middle school or the long-distance running team, he sounded like a stuck-up primary school kid.

One night, he had a dream: he saw a body – it must have been Big Brother Chen's though he couldn't see the head, only a well-muscled, toned physique – hanging in the middle of the school gym like a pig in a slaughterhouse, while a boxer in a helmet yelled hoarsely and rained punches at the body's belly, doing what Li Wen now knew were called punch resistance exercises. Li Wen's eyes shot open, and his heart began to pound. The dormitory was in darkness. It reverberated with snores and stank of bodies. He was sorry he'd told them that he had been in the school long-distance running team, and sorry, too, that he'd had to listen to them talk about their training. He breathed in and out, his nostrils inundated with the body odour of these male athletes, wondering, *How can I get out of here? What will I do if I can't move dorms? I never want to come back here again.*

For a whole week, Big Brother Chen made no move. In fact, he made sure never to catch Li Wen's eye. For his part, Li Wen spent the time in the study room, waiting until the lights went out in the dormitory to creep in and grope his way to his bed. Effectively, they became like creatures of two different worlds, one living in the light, the other in the dark; one venting his fury by trying to bite the other's neck, the other unable to figure out where this hatred had come from, but doing his best to stay out of the way anyway. Li Wen felt like a zombie, no different from the faceless body in his dream.

The study room was another world of smells – hot and cold food, books new and old, and perfume, which could have been cheap or could have been pricy, he had no way of telling. There was one person here who didn't smell of anything at all – the girl who had appeared in the study room for the first time this week. He remembered that she always sat in front of him in English lectures, and now she sat alone two rows behind him and a little to one side. She was unbelievably skinny.

Impelled by some urge he could not resist, Li Wen got up and moved quietly backwards, so he could see what this skinny, odourless creature looked like. The girl met his gaze calmly, as if waiting for Li Wen to speak to her. Her straw-like hair was pulled tightly back in a ponytail, except for some fluffy wisps that fringed her forehead. Her eyes were huge and sunk deeply into the sallow skin of her sockets, Li Wen noticed. They were just like his mother's eyes; his mother's were a bit more delicate and pretty, but they shared the same expression: puritanical, blazing, not the sort of eyes you would forget in a hurry.

The girl was the first to speak.

'You're the one who sits in on our English classes, aren't you?' Her voice was expressionless, and so low you could hardly hear her.

'Er, yes,' said Li Wen, scratching his head and wondering whether he should sit down, as a few of the others in the study room were already looking their way.

'My name's Zheng Xiaowei.'

'Li Wen. Er, I'd better go back to my seat.' He pointed to where he was sitting. As he went back, he glanced at the stainless-steel thermos on Zheng Xiaowei's desk. It was exactly the same as the ones they had at home. They had two, but he didn't like hot water, so he never used his. His mother took hers with her every day, adding a few dried chrysanthemum heads and a handful of goji berries to the water.

Zheng Xiaowei was the first girl he met at M City University who had spoken to him of her own accord. He was not immediately attracted to her – perhaps she had become too familiar a figure – but at the same time his ambivalent feelings drew him towards her. She was from the English department, he thought, there was no harm in hanging out, at least that made one more person he knew. Their meetings fell into a pattern: Li Wen made a point of arriving at the English lecture room five minutes before the start of class and automatically slid into the last row. Zheng Xiaowei was already sitting in the row in front of him. They never said hello to each other there, and in fact, looking at them, it was impossible to tell that they had met before. But he ran into her every couple of days in the study room, where they would say hello from where they sat, two rows apart, and then get on with their work. There was a strange rhythm to their meetings: they knew each other's names, but not who the other was.

Li Wen was relieved that this scrawny girl did not attract him physically. He never mentioned her to Big Brother Chen. Sometimes, when Chen spoke about the girls he picked up around campus, Li Wen would feel hot all over and, later, have the sort of wet dreams he had had in middle school. He hadn't the faintest idea what Chen's girls looked like, but imagined them to be alluring beings with perky breasts and creamy-white, floral-scented skin. Anyway, he wouldn't be hearing many more of Chen's stories. The term was almost over and after the summer holidays, he hoped to get into the English department. Last time he went home for the winter break, his mother had given him an expensive box of ginseng for Dr Yao.

This particular night was no different from any other. It was midnight. Li Wen had stayed in the study room as usual until it was time for the dorm lights to go out. He could not stop yawning, probably because he had pigged out on rice noodles in the canteen. They were somehow chewier than the wheat lamian noodles he was used to at home, and sort of slippery; he had to plaster them with chilli oil to make them taste like pasta. Every time he went looking for the greasy, sticky bottle of chilli oil, it was always to be found stubbornly peeking out of a mound of detritus on a table, almost buried by dirty plates and bowls stained with leftover rice and vegetables, as if it were playing games with him.

If Zheng Xiaowei didn't show up in the study room by eleven o'clock, it meant she wouldn't be coming *Everyone plays time games*, Li Wen thought, half-asleep.

It occurred to him that he had a very practical reason to be looking out for her. He had attended English classes for almost a term now, but he would not be able to take the final exams with Zheng Xiaowei and the others because he was not formally registered. (How could he have forgotten?) However, he was desperate to find out what Zheng Xiaowei was revising for the exam that only the English students would take. Was it to satisfy his own curiosity, or out of jealousy? He wasn't sure. He waited for two evenings, but Zheng Xiaowei did not come to the study room. Even if she had and he had absorbed every scrap of her knowledge, it would not have made any difference. The fact was that he wasn't registered. He was a ghost in the English department, just as he was a ghost now, wandering along the path from the study room back to his dormitory.

At this time of year, the paths across the campus were dotted with either small groups of friends or couples welded together. Once, he even saw two girls in an embrace, one of whom looked like a sports student. In the gym, he had always ignored all the women athletes with their cropped haircuts, even though they teased him mercilessly him for his running times – not even as good as theirs! Nothing that went on there had anything to do with him. He didn't understand the love and friendship that bound these athletes together, and he didn't want to.

The early summer evening was hot and humid. The air above the path was thick with midges that dive-bombed his face, so he had to keep batting them away. The weather was so muggy, all he wanted to do was get into bed and have a good night's sleep. Sure, the dorm stank of sweat, but as long as he was asleep, he wouldn't be able to smell anything. He thought he saw a figure hovering in front of the dormitory building, as if someone was keeping an eye out for him, but surely he was mistaken. He saw himself simply as a wandering wraith, not worth spying on.

As he went up in the lift, he decided he wouldn't bother having a wash. He kept his toothbrush on the right side of his bedside table, so he could reach it, brush his teeth in the toilets and creep into bed without making a sound. He walked down the brightly lit corridor as quietly as he could – even though the sports students were all dead to the world and footsteps late at night were as unlikely to disturb them as a leaf blowing off a tree. Li Wen hated the snoring that he could hear coming from every room. It sounded brutally and uncontrollably hormonal. He tiptoed silently past, counted off the tenth room on the right and stopped, wiped the sweat from his hands and pulled the key out of his sweatpants. He put his ear to the door; it sounded eerily silent within.

Without thinking, he opened the door. Not that there was anything else he could have done. The silence was deafening. Li Wen shut the door behind him, and suddenly half a dozen arms lunged at him, pinning him to the table beneath Big Brother Chen's bunk. He struggled, the table dug into his back, and he gasped in pain. Judgement Day, so long postponed, had finally arrived. Only he hadn't expected it to happen at night. At least in daylight he could have seen the blood running down his face. He stopped struggling and breathed out, hoping he wouldn't have to wait long for Chen's fists to fall, and for it all to be over.

Ten seconds passed, and he felt what was unmistakably Big Brother Chen's hand. No one else's felt half so murderous. Four or five round pills were shoved into his mouth. He tried to raise himself and spit them out, but an arm around his neck pinned him down. Then he felt Chen shove the mineral water bottle into his mouth. *Just as long as I don't swallow them, I'll be fine*, he thought. He had a sudden vision of the pills, their colour and size – they must be the same ones Peddler Wang had sold Chen, the Modafinil.

Li Wen attempted to hold his breath as his mouth filled with water, but found himself choking and had to swallow the mixture of water, snot and spittle that covered his face. Someone turned on a mobile phone and the bright screen shone in the darkness. Fear, dread and hatred overwhelmed him as he groped his way to his bed amid a chorus of jeers and cheers, his face screwed up in distaste. There was a roaring in his ears and he could barely hear what Chen was saying, or maybe the roaring was Chen's voice.

'You're gonna get hooked!'

Like an automaton, he crawled into his bunk, though his mind didn't seem to be instructing his movements, and he fell flat on his back. Trying not to make any noise, he tried to force himself to regurgitate the pills he had just swallowed, but it was no good. They had turned into a bitter-tasting sludge in his throat and quickly dissolved. He began to shake all over, and he could hear his blood pounding through his body. He stared unblinking up into the darkness, but not a murmur, not a sob or a cry, passed his lips.

For the whole of the next day, Li Wen looked and felt like he was at death's door. His every sense quivered. He had never felt so stimulated, and it reduced him to despair. He couldn't even control where he was pissing, his urine spurting all over the tiled floor of the toilets. Apologetically, he got some loo paper to wipe it up, watched in amazement by a curly-haired youth who came in behind him. Li Wen mopped obsessively, not caring whether he was wiping up the other students' piss along with his own, wanting only to get it all clean and dry. During his morning run, his nose and throat filled with snot and spittle, so that he had to keep sniffing and swallowing. The trainer gave him a quizzical smile, as if to say, *So it's your turn now.* Or maybe Li Wen was being paranoid: did the trainer really know about the pills? He ran with great bursts of energy that scared him. He felt like a dog panting in the sun to try and cool down, but the heat inside him came and went in surges: sped up, slowed down, sped up again and slowed down again, his heart pounding all the while. What terrified him was not the thought of becoming addicted, but the loss of control over his body. His willpower had no control over his physical energy any more. He made a huge effort to rein in his body against an unassailable force that was driving it forwards. The struggle was mentally exhausting and desperately painful.

The worst time was that evening. He went to the study room, but Zheng Xiaowei did not appear, and he only stayed for a few minutes. His heartbeat had calmed, but he felt completely spent, as if he had just had a high fever. The only place he wanted to be was back in his own bed. He had never been so completely focused on his own body; everything else around him seemed to be happening in a dream. He would reach out to touch something and find there was nothing there. He was trapped in a world where his very self had become infinitely, terrifyingly huge. Surely they wouldn't do anything else to him, would they? This already seemed like Chen's ultimate punishment: forcing him into a nightmare in which he was bonded to their group. He was exhausted, though not at all sure whether this was his body's reaction to the drugs or his mind's looming fears. He wanted to lie back and carry on dreaming, like a boxer in the ring, oblivious to everything around him.

In the dorm, the electric light was still on, and Big Brother Chen and his mates stared at Li Wen. This was the first time in months that he had arrived before lights out and they could see him. Li Wen looked back at Chen and saw the excitement in his dead gaze, and something like dread in the emptiness of his smirk. It dawned on him that they both feared the exact same thing: that they had been bonded together from the start. Without speaking, Li Wen and Chen stared at each other for almost ten seconds before Chen averted his gaze, turned to the other two youths and carried on playing the game. Li Wen realised that his thirty-year-old persona in *The Sims* was officially dead. He would never be able to pick up where he left off. Even if he got another game emulator in the future, things would never be the same again.

Their amplified shouts sounded like they were coming from a parallel universe, and the smell was overpowering. Li Wen lay flat on his back, eyes open, until the lights went out and the dormitory was plunged into darkness. The chemical effects of the pills may have passed through his system, but they lingered in his senses the way the poppy pods in the hotpot did. Li Wen jabbed a fingernail into his palm, where his mother had said there was an acupuncture point that stimulated the heart. *They might come back for me again one day*, he thought to himself. A few rays of yellow light from outside leaked through the gaps in the dormitory's cheap curtains, not the sort of thing you'd notice when you were asleep, but luridly bright if you were not. To Li Wen, the yellow beams felt like a shocking revelation. He could almost convince himself that he had no idea what substances the sports students had forced into him.

At their last class, the English lecturer set Edgar Allan Poe's 'The Tell-Tale Heart' as holiday reading. Li Wen put himself through some exercises and went back to the dormitory. He had decided to stay on there through the holidays. The summer sun shone directly into the room. He stood in front of the bunk bed ladder, a lone figure, his shadow sliced in half by the bunks opposite. He shivered in spite of the warmth. Then he opened his bag and retrieved a green cigarette lighter from the right-hand zip pocket. It was a cheap one, just one yuan, from the student shop below the canteen. With the right kind of fuel, this little lighter could set the whole building ablaze, Li Wen thought, though he actually quite liked M City University. At least he had a bed here and felt more like an adult, a fully weaned grown-up.

He tucked the lighter into his jogging bottoms and made a beeline for Chen's bunk, where a blue-checked quilt lay crumpled, giving off a strong smell of testosterone-laden sweat and feet. Very gingerly, he picked it up and, holding it away from him, carried it to the toilet. The dormitory building was quiet at this time of day, especially on their floor, because the sports teacher recommended three in the afternoon as the best time for physical fitness and endurance training. He threw the quilt down on the tiled toilet floor. A sports student's determination only lasted as long as a boxing match, but his was life-long. He knelt down, flicked the lighter and held it to the quilt. The first time, it didn't catch. He tried again, and a long tongue of flames set a corner of the fabric alight. The lighter the material, the faster it burned. Finally, the cotton blazed, beginning to smell like a spirit lamp in a middle school chemistry experiment. Li Wen stood up, his head swaying a little, and watched as the quilt sent up big plumes of black smoke. He was keenly aware that he wasn't the virtual Li Wen of the simulation game any more. This was the real Li Wen's Last Judgement on Big Brother Chen in the real world. For the first time, he despised himself. He was only capable of hiding in the shadows of the afternoon, burning other people's quilts. He lacked the courage to do anything worse, like punching or stabbing his enemy in the face. He felt empty. All his former elation had drained away.

That brought him to his senses with a jolt. He reached under the sink and grabbed a plastic basin that someone had left there. He slammed on the taps, filled the basin to the brim and hurled the contents over the half-burned quilt. The flames had been disappointing, not nearly as bright as he thought they would be. The smell of burning cotton had wafted out into the hallway and he heard the cleaning lady shouting. It took him back to his childhood, hearing someone shout, 'Stop thief!' when he was with his mother on the bus. He knew he was in trouble now.

10

THE night train ride seemed to go on forever. It had been almost impossible to get a ticket before the Spring Festival, when everyone was heading home; he had been unable to get a sleeper ticket and had to put up with a cheap hard seat. He had talked to his mother three times on the phone about it, but all she said was, 'You need a break, you've been working too hard, Son. Come home and I'll soon set you to rights.' In his mother's eyes, a gruelling twelve hours in a hard seat was a necessary evil. Li Wen and his mother had not taken many trips together, and as far as he could remember, they had always travelled in sleepers, certainly never hard seats. They never indulged in first class nor did they expect any special treatment, but they weren't going to punish themselves just to save a hundred yuan. Hard seat passengers had no self-restraint or sense of decency, especially at this time of year when the train was conveying what seemed like hordes of refugees back to where they belonged. Almost everyone took off their shoes and travelled in their socks or bare feet, making sure to occupy every inch of the cramped space, with its worn, grimy seat covers, that they were allotted. Nothing in his upbringing had prepared him for this. His mother had done her best to inculcate in him a desire to get on in life. His head spinning from the stuffy air in the carriage, he groped in his bag for his hoodie to cover up with.

Something rustled in the right pocket. He paused and patted along the pocket seam. It was still there. He investigated, and found another train ticket. It seemed to carry all the clamorous expectations of a lottery ticket, the kind with red letters on a white background that he'd seen on the greasy dining table at his grandparents' house. You just circled a few shiny numbers in pencil and waited for the reveal, convincing yourself that you'd stood a chance to win the jackpot. (Though the odds were slim, to say the least.)

Right after coming out of the director's office, he had taken a gamble and gone and bought an extra train ticket. A pane of glass – fogged with heavy breathing and smeared with fingerprints – separated him from the ticket agent, whose face he could hardly make out.

'Where's this one to?' she asked.

'Beijing.'

He hardly recognised his own voice.

The woman slipped him the ticket, apparently deaf to the tremor in his words, or perhaps she had witnessed too many such spur-of-the-moment decisions and was impervious to them. People used trains to leave their old lives behind and start new ones. For Li Wen, that extra train ticket was a tiny thing, but made anything possible, rather like the knife he had hidden at the very bottom of his bag.

He had no particular plan. He pulled his jacket over his face and closed his eyes. He would try to get as much shut-eye as possible. His mother was still in blissful ignorance.

But sleep would not come. The hours passed by, and he felt like he was floating over the Karamay oil field, the sky so blue it seemed about to tumble down on his head. Although he had never been there, he was determined to go one day. He spent three days in a row with his head hunkered down on his desk in the back row of the study room trying to sleep, the drops of sweat from his hair leaving his arms and the table beaded with moisture. He felt as if all the other students were lined up in their seats like a jury in an American film, grimly condemning him: 'Look at that guy! He's the one who burned his dormmate's quilt!'

Not long before, and with some hesitation, he had presented the ginseng that his mother had given him to Dr Yao. She had told him to put the box in a plain paper bag, because it was too showy. After much searching, he could only find a bag that Peddler Wang had given him when he bought a knockoff designer sweatshirt, which he had wanted to keep, but it would have to do. As he went to Dr Yao's office carrying the black bag with the triangular logo, he kept looking around him, terrified that people would spot the big red box of ginseng poking out. Just like the first time when his mother had taken them out to a meal, Dr Yao made a big impression on him today; he was wearing a grey suit despite the heat of high summer. His office was air conditioned, so he obviously wasn't too hot. He went in and put the bag on Dr Yao's desk. Yao stolidly gave him a little lecture on doing well at his studies. Li Wen almost confided in him that he was sitting in on English classes, then bit back the words. He had seen immediately that there were several rectangular boxes just like the one he had brought sitting under the coat rack against the right-hand wall of the office. He felt like the barber in the fairy tale 'King Midas and His Donkey Ears', burdened with a secret he could only whisper into a hole he had dug. The world certainly was a dangerous, confusing place.

The next time he saw Dr Yao, he was with Mr Cao, the deputy head of the physical education department. Up till now, Li Wen had not had much to do with the head of his department. Cao had shiny, smoothed-back hair and a mild expression; he was a solidly built man who had reportedly run the Ironman three times. He had dropped in a few times when they were doing group training, but did not appear impressed by Li Wen's prospects. Unsurprisingly so, Li Wen felt. Today, Cao's first words to Dr Yao were, 'What are we going to do about this boy, Sir?'

For the first time, Dr Yao looked annoyed, taken aback, even – though Li Wen might have been wrong. It might have been fear.

Yes, fear. At some point in his university career, Dr Yao had found himself taking on the role of a nursery nurse. The university students got taller with each passing year, but they also got more childish. Every year he would have to 'fix' things for those who found themselves in difficulty: some were about to flunk their exams; some came in and said they wanted to change their majors; a few simply dropped out halfway through their studies and went abroad. All of them had one thing in common: when they first met him, they all kept their heads down and skulked behind their parents, as if rendered mute by a cloud that hung over them.

Dr Yao had been impressed by Li Wen, however, because of his resemblance to his father (though his complexion was fairer), with whom he had been friends at university. Yao had done very well for himself, and this made him feel like he had to take Li Wen under his wing and do something for him after his father's untimely death. The higher up he went in the education system (and he had been working in it for twenty-odd years), the more Dr Yao felt that he was not teaching, but giving out favours with the limited powers at his disposal. When Mrs Li first invited him out for dinner and introduced her son, Dr Yao noted a certain wilfulness in the boy's eyes, which he interpreted at the time as probably due to the loss of his father. Now, Dr Yao sensed something lurking beneath the stubborn exterior. He had seen countless acts of violence at this university, and in his experience, the more uncommunicative a student was, the more capable they were of doing terrible things. As soon as he learned what Li Wen had done, he thought of the look on the boy's mother's face and wished he had never met either of them or decided to help them. He had seen that look on the faces of other parents, but Mrs Li's expression had brought him up short. It was a curse to place all one's hopes in one's child. Soul-destroying, in fact.

'The quilt he burned belonged to Liu Chen, the student we recruited specially because of his boxing,' Cao finished.

Dr Yao grunted and said, 'There must have been a reason. I heard they had an argument.'

'That can't be true. Li Wen said that Liu Chen forced him to take stimulants, but Liu Chen said he didn't.'

Li Wen was standing on the other side of Dr Yao's desk, but Cao and Yao were talking over his head, as if he were not there. He spoke up, as if he were talking to himself, but louder.

'He did force me to take the pills.'

There was a pause. Cao gave him a look, and Yao said, 'I'm going to record it as an argument in the dormitory. This horsing around is getting out of hand, and it can't go on. The physical education department must keep control over its students. Otherwise, they'll get a bad name in the other departments.'

Li Wen was nonplussed. Was that the end of the matter? Was no one to be held responsible? Looking at Dr Yao, he sensed that although he wasn't at the end of the road, the end was definitely in sight.

Later that afternoon, he went back to Dr Yao's office again. He stood outside, waiting for a woman teacher with permed hair to leave with a stack of files in her arms before knocking on the door. Dr Yao gestured to him to come in and close the door behind him. Li Wen said, in a voice that no longer seemed to belong to him, 'Does this . . . does this mean I can't switch to the English department?'

Dr Yao stared into Li Wen's eyes, as if willing the flames of craziness that lurked within not to ignite, and slowly nodded his head.

Li Wen felt himself start to shake, just as he had after swallowing the pills. He acknowledged he had done wrong, but at the same time he was overwhelmed by the feeling that the wrong others had done him had just been skimmed over. They were even casting doubt on whether it had really happened. Again and again, he swallowed convulsively, trying to fight his nausea and feeling of helplessness.

He heard Dr Yao say, cautiously, 'You can still graduate with a degree in sports management, you can get a good job with that major. But you mustn't take drugs, that stuff is really bad for you.'

Dr Yao's words seemed to be coming from further and further away. After about a minute, Li Wen finally forced himself to swallow very hard, and the shaking stopped.

'Dr Yao, please can you not tell my mother?'

He was not so much speaking as begging.

He could not actually remember whether Dr Yao agreed or not, and he had no way of telling, because he sleepwalked through the rest of the day. If Yao had said yes, that would be one more secret between them, a fragile secret to be stripped bare and exposed to the bright light of day when it came time to graduate.

The school found a way to cover up the scandal. Chen was given a token warning; the following year he was sent to compete in a college boxing tournament and won, and no one ever mentioned the pills again. Li Wen was kept in the sports department but was switched to sports management. Everyone in the department knew him. He was the one who burned other people's quilts.

He found himself plunged into a yawning abyss filled with their whispers. If he ever closed his eyes, stinking, roiling black smoke and leaping flames engulfed him. As he struggled to fight his way out, his mother's face emerged into view, her expressions of love and hope peeling away, layer after layer, then distorting and turning to despair. It struck him that the only way that this would stop was if his mother disappeared.

*

'Make sure you keep some nice fish for me next week, my son's coming back on holiday,' Mrs Li instructed the fishmonger. The woman was about her own age, or so she seemed. Mrs Li had long ago arrived at the stage when you could tell someone's age from their wrinkles. She knew she looked her age – she had crow's feet at the corners of her eyes and had to dye her hair once every six months to cover up the grey roots. She didn't know many people in the town where she lived, and hardly got out of the house nowadays. When she did venture outdoors, she usually stayed within the confines of the staff housing compound at the teacher training college.

She had been to the old Catholic church behind the teacher training college again last month. The truth was she was a bit fuzzy about the difference between Catholics, Protestants and other denominations, but she was convinced that the One up in heaven that she believed in could read what was in her heart. Before Li Wen went to university, she had only been to one or two church services, during the month after Li Wen's father died. It was then that she had taken the lemon-yellow leaflet from the women who handed them out at the entrance to the market and become a believer. Religion made her feel that she had regained some long-lost dignity, because it promised that glory lay ahead. She had never spoken to Li Wen about her faith; she couldn't find the way to tell him that she believed in the Lord, so she hid it from him. She tucked the Bible into her bedside drawer along with her bank passbook, in a silent admission that they both served her as begging bowls.

Sometimes she wondered if she was really a true convert. She could not bring herself to say grace before meals, although she did give silent thanks as she served the food. She hardly ever attended a house church or went to church services, although she knew that there was a historic Catholic church no more than twenty minutes' walk from where she lived. She had no close friends among the other parishioners, and the few times she did meet them in the street, she simply nodded in greeting, just as she would have done with any other locals she vaguely recognised. What worried her most was that she was always asking the Lord to do things for Li

Wen, rather than praying for His protection. She felt her prayers did confer some mysterious power, but at the same time she could not help questioning whether her faith was genuine. Occasionally, she wondered if she would ever have the sort of romantic, mysterious Damascene conversion she had read about in foreign novels at school.

After Li Wen went to university, she kept up her faith in secret, just as before. The rituals remained unchanged: she still said her prayers silently at mealtimes, though she added a few extra visits to the Catholic church on Sundays. She even felt that keeping her faith secret from Li Wen made it more real. It became her strength, her anchor, her friend, her lover. She remembered the first time she attended worship as a believer. The priest in his white shirt and black overcoat had said to her, 'When you believe, you will see the Lord.'

So when Li Wen pushed her to the ground in a frenzy, she thought he must be possessed by the devil. This was her time of tribulation; she was suffering like Christ on the cross.

*

Li Wen did not sleep a wink all night, and the instant the train pulled into the station, a wave of fatigue assailed him. And yet he had never before managed to confront the dirty old town where he had been born and raised so calmly. It wasn't that the journey from M City was especially arduous, but extreme familiarity made it feel further and further away. Li Wen was travelling with just a backpack and a duffel bag. He had cautiously crafted a plan: if he sensed his mother saw the seams in his story, he would come up with some excuse and return to school early. He had purposely packed a few extra English textbooks in his bag to lend credence to his story. He spotted her right away in the crowd at the station exit. His mother wore a mid-length pea-green down jacket and had dyed her hair back to black. As he observed her, he felt an unfamiliar pang of grief. He could see her, but her eyes were watching something further away. As she drifted on the sea of people, heaving to and fro, Li Wen hunched one of his shoulders, lifting the bag and trying to claw it back from the current, cursing himself mercilessly, but softly enough that no one else could hear. He watched as his mother shrivelled up again, ageing before his eyes, and realised there was nothing he could do to rescue her from this place where her dreams and her time had evaporated. The crowd pushed him forward, leaving him not an instant to pause or breathe, and spat him out at his mother's feet. The hand Mrs Li had extended shrank back. She caught a brief glimpse of Li Wen as a boy, cute, clever, always making funny faces, and then there was another flash, and she had to crane her neck to see his face. He was thinner than she remembered. She knew it – away at school, he hadn't been eating right.

Li Wen returned to his room and fell asleep without even changing his trousers. He slept for a while, how long he wasn't sure, and that vague sensation returned: his mother was standing just outside the door, eavesdropping on everything. This sensation was mingled at first with the fragrance of hongshao braised fish, but the scent soon dissipated. Then he thought he heard himself say to himself, *You have to get up*, but he drifted away and dozed a while longer. Like a soldier drawing on his last ounce of strength to crawl back into a trench as a hail of bullets flew overhead, only by sleeping in his own bed could he make everything go quiet – nothing at all had happened, and nothing would. He realised 'home' was a colourless, odourless, soundless laboratory flask. Back in this place where they had lived in long-term symbiosis, he smelled only the scent of his mother, which reminded him of home. Every other smell, no matter how piquant, acrid, or pungent, was foreign. When he woke, it was already evening, and his body was covered in sweat. He realised his mother had turned on his electric blanket, likely hours earlier. He got up and went to the kitchen, finding his mother sitting at the table fiddling with her phone. The silence smothered even the sound of breathing. Before, she had read the paper, but now, she had swapped it for a phone. Li Wen had always scorned this habit of hers, one he had managed to never pick up: he eagerly consumed all types of information, even falsified concoctions of contemporary events and corporate schemes, and advertising drove him out of his gourd with ecstasy. Mrs Li never told him about the news stories she read. Like her religious faith, it was a matter which should not be allowed to distract him.

Li Wen's future was unfolding just as she had planned, no deviations, no mishaps. She had faith that once the path was laid, Li Wen would stride down the bright, broad avenue of freedom and love and leave this place behind. She knew Li Wen would find happiness, and as for her, she would stand staunch by his side, and their glory would never fade. There wasn't a living person who truly understood his or her own predicament, Mrs Li believed. She was strongly suspicious of the idea that people's souls returned to drift about the places they had lived in life. She had never seen or heard the spirit of Li Wen's father, not even that day in the old cathedral, not one time. Once, she had been lying in the bedroom when she heard, as she drifted amid vague semi-consciousness, a slight stir, a kind of *kathunk, kathunk*. After Li Wen left for M City, every evening, she recited a secret incantation, repeatedly checking the window and door locks, making sure all the light switches were off like a night watchwoman doing her rounds, fearing that at this midpoint of the plan which had yet to come to completion, there could be some unforeseen mishap, such as a burglary, or a carbon monoxide leak. That day, when she heard the *kathunk, kathunk*, her first thought was, *It's the ghost of Li Wen's father*, but she didn't move, she simply lay face-up in the blackness, because the sound soon went away, and she was seized by the sensation that someone had slid a door open and was about to slip away. And so, out of an abundance of caution, heeding her intuition, she stayed stock-still and tried to restrain even her breathing, reflecting that just living in the world was a more dreadful fright than any ghost could give.

The next day, Mrs Zhao (yes, another woman named Mrs Zhao, this one a former literature teacher who had retired from the middle school a few years earlier) of the administrative committee of the teachers' building knocked on the door. She wore her hair drawn up in a bun with a precisely defined circular shape, and the middle of her right brow sprouted a mole so large it prevented her eyeball from spinning freely, further intensifying the fierce glare in her eyes. She also wheezed a little when she breathed, but she was a decent person, thought Mrs Li. Mrs Zhao reminded Mrs Li that a theft had been reported in the neighbouring apartment building the evening before, and Mrs Li told Mrs Zhao about the *kathunk* sound she had heard, noticing only then that cold beads of sweat had broken out on her back.

Each year, Li Wen arrived before the Spring Festival and stayed a few days at home. It was the longest span of time he and his mother would spend together throughout the entire year. They had always kept to the same rhythm, taking vacations and starting school together at exactly the same time, neither lagging behind, neither vying to be first. They ultimately settled into separate spaces in the home: Li Wen in his room, his mother in the sitting room – occupying these deliberately disparate zones, they achieved a kind of spatial harmony. As they drifted apart, neither one knew what to say to the other any more. Like an alarm clock ringing at the appointed time, Mrs Li merely performed the predetermined functions of reminding Li Wen to eat, study, and sleep. Li Wen didn't even know what he was doing, having failed to seclude himself in a sealed world as he had wished. When the time came, he yearned for school to start again. He longed to become simply another student wearing the same uniform as the rest of the crowd. It seemed to be the sole way he might regain freedom. This year, the tension between Li Wen and his mother felt thicker than ever.

None of the windows in the home faced the main road. The scenery consisted only of another anonymous residential building, and further up the street, the school playground. No matter how long he stood at the window, the vapour in his brain did not disperse. He took the knife and train ticket from his bag and crammed them into the deepest recesses of the armoire. The date on the train ticket moved backward on its own: ten days, eight days, three days . . . like his purpose, there had been no rhyme or reason to his choice of date. He was just reflecting that dying meant losing everything, when his mother's shrill insistence that he deliver a new year's gift to Mrs Zhao, the retired teacher, halted his train of thought. It struck him that anyway it would be a waste to use up two bottles of oil and two bags of flour (which his mother had calculated would be necessary for the batch of New Year's Eve dumplings) and keel over.

Finally, by the time his mother began scrubbing the floor not just once but twice a day, antiseptic fumes had infiltrated Li Wen's room, making his head spin. The smell made him think of the deaths of his father and grandfather. Death was a sudden onslaught of degeneracy – with this thought, a wave of panic washed over him, leaving his palms slick with sweat. For the first time outside of M City, he yearned for the sense of transcendent acceleration that the stimulants had given him. He tried his best to sleep during the day, and to keep sleeping through the evening. Continued sleep brought a tingling satisfaction his mother could not fathom, and he realised that true pleasure was always drawn from clandestine sources. Some days later (or was it minutes, or hours?), in the afternoon, a middle-aged woman he had never seen before knocked twice on the door, and Mrs Li rushed to open it, at which point a church calendar and a wooden cross changed hands. Neither of these things was ever seen again in the sitting room or the kitchen; godly items were stashed in a secret hiding place. Only later, on that decisive final day, did Li Wen catch the tiniest fleeting glimpse of her secrets, but to tell the truth, he didn't care by then.

Li Wen couldn't even count how many days it had been since he had gone out (seeing as he had no friends or classmates to go out with, there was no reason to set foot outside). Every day was exactly the same – eat, sleep, sleep, eat. He was immersed in a lingering funk, wallowing in a swill of lethargy, doing little but waiting for the sun to set outside the window. He seemed to have no other choice. What he couldn't see, what he had no way to know, was that his mother conscientiously cancelled out each day on the church calendar, another day, another check mark. She enshrined the calendar on the headboard of her bed, believing that finally, a few days before the new year, she had detected a sign from God, some holy stirring. The days before the public holiday began were dominated by gift-giving rituals. His aunt had found a set of imported cosmetics somewhere, and he watched as his mother accepted it, seeming to be thinking of something else. Gingerly, one by one, she pulled out the glimmering glass bottles, then put them back without opening them. While retying the bow on the gift bag, she muttered to herself, 'Excellent quality, I'll send it right on to Dr Yao.'

That morning, he woke with a start to the sound of his mother pacing in the kitchen, stepping so lightly he thought of the white willow catkins that drifted in the air in early spring, but it was this lightness itself that agitated him. The lightest things were always the most aggravating. It was finally time – at eight o'clock this evening, he could permanently break free from this horrible pacing sound. He had to make a decision. He could invent some excuse, claiming, for instance, that he was going to buy a tub of yoghurt, or that he was going to the bookstore to fetch a book, but it might not ring true. Or he could await an opportune moment – it would take no more than a minute – to fling open the door and take flight. Even at lunchtime, he pondered what sort of story would best buy him his freedom. His pulse continually accelerated, until he worried his mother might hear. His covert escape plans thrilled him limitlessly. The train ticket was in his pocket, where he had put it that morning, right under his mother's nose.

As he savoured this endless array of escape fantasies, fatigue overtook him. In the dream, he was in Beijing, and the streets were filled with young men and women with faces like flowers, chattering in delectable Beijing dialect. He longed to acquire this accent his mother had failed to hand down to him. At five in the afternoon, he became flustered and restless. He was tempted to make a clean break, knowing his mother couldn't stop him; alternately, he could take the knife from the armoire and cut through every obstacle, no one would ever find him, but he didn't even have the guts to fit the knife handle in his grip. Then he heard his mother talking to Dr Yao – yes, that time they had had dinner together, she had taken this same toadyish, picayune tone. Dammit, even now, Dr Yao still had the power to determine their destinies.

This was his true Last Judgement.

The time is now. There's no turning back, Li Wen thought to himself, repeating the words over and over like an oath, but at the same time, he was filled with an unprecedented tranquillity. He could hear his mother's footsteps outside the door. She was on the verge of entering.

Her gaze pierced his backbone, meeting no resistance. She looked at the young man with his head bowed before her, beginning to suspect she had never really understood her son. She had tried to mould him into the best possible version of himself, she had given him everything, but still there had been a mishap, he had taken a detour. It must be a mistake, it must have been someone else's child – she couldn't believe that the wicked, wanton act she heard described over the phone had been committed by her Li Wen. But then, when she lifted her head slightly and her gaze skidded quickly across his, she saw without any doubt the self-satisfaction brought by an act of vengeance. She could see also that he had not the slightest shred of reverence for the omnipotent Lord who held their destiny in his hands. Li Wen admitted to himself that he was definitely evil, and he knew he could never atone for this evil, the evil of rejecting the sacrifices of others and becoming the master of his fate.

He watched as his mother stepped into the room, mouth turned down at the corners, forming the shape of a mountain ridge, eyes filled with a mix of fear and suspicion. As he pulled the quilt from beneath his bottom and shoved it to the side, he was fairly certain he heard his mother shouting, her voice fluttering rapidly from loud to soft, near to far. He heard his name being called repeatedly, but it was as if he were listening while someone called for a stranger who happened to share his name, 'It's all over! You used to be such a good little boy. But now our world has ended!' He also heard his mother repeatedly demanding a response. He watched as the words 'good little boy' shot through space, weaving through the tongues of flame that had consumed Big Brother Chen's quilt, continuing on to darkened corners he had never known existed, and he realised he was nothing but mummy's good little boy, and despair swallowed him. He couldn't manage any response, anyway he didn't have a reason. He prostrated, flinging himself at her feet, and said nothing.

Mrs Li didn't hear any response from Li Wen. She just couldn't understand the boy. It was as if a landslide had washed out a road between two mountain settlements, or perhaps that road had never really existed, maybe the freely flowing communication between mother and son had been a flimsy fantasy. Sending Li Wen to school in M City had been her final gamble. In ten more years she would retire, and according to her calculations, she had no further capacity to aid his ascent up the ladder of success, now that their world was crumbling around them. They were just what people said they were, skeletons of a mother and son clinging to each other for dear life. She knew that she had overdrawn from the sympathy they had saved in their shared account. The part of the phone call from Dr Yao that shocked her the most was, 'Li Wen set fire to his classmate's quilt.' No matter how she pictured the scene, the face of the perpetrator was a stranger's. The Lord had never warned her of such a terrible eventuality. The Lord had promised to protect Li Wen.

'And then I took some stimulants.'

Li Wen tried to muster up a lucid, solemn tone, delivering an abbreviated account that omitted the cause of the incident, transposing passivity with active initiative. In the story, Li Wen came across as a problem child, a creature of a world utterly apart from adults like his mother. He watched her reaction carefully as he spoke. He couldn't deny that he drew great pleasure from what he saw. Evil, he now realised, could only be conquered by more subjective evil. Now there was nearly no time left. Let his mother believe he was incurable and incorrigible. Maybe then she would give up on him, and that would be the end of it. He suddenly realised that the evil act of shattering his mother's dreams was his first act as an adult, a kind of merit badge, a sign he was no longer a child. He stood on the brink of an abyss, watching as his mother waved a fist at him (or was she reaching out to hug him?). Subconsciously, he pushed.

With a thud, his mother landed face-up on the floor. The floorboards still smelled of the antiseptic solution she had cleaned them with that morning, the smell of Li Wen's father's deathbed. Her withered, straw-like hair broke free from her broken ponytail clip and splayed chaotically across the floor.

'Hideous bitch.'

Li Wen wasn't sure if he actually said the words out loud. In his imagination, he crumpled her up like a piece of wastepaper and tossed her to the floor. But his mother began to sob and shriek, and he sensed her mucus and saliva hardening on his arm and rapidly putrefying. Her sharp, shrill cries percolated through the stench:

'Son, you're all I've got! How could you do this to me? You're our only hope!'

Li Wen didn't hear what she said next. He wasn't anyone's only hope. He grabbed a fistful of her hair and smashed her head into the wall, again, and again, and again, until her face was completely caked with a crust of blood and sweat. Once he started, he didn't let up, beating her face in, leaving her mangled, repugnant and filthy. She made no move to resist as the pool of urine beneath her spread. Only by smashing her to smithereens could he staunch the flow of this hateful liquid, severing the ties of blood and flesh that bound them. He had to keep going until his strength was spent. Waves of stomach acid washed up his throat. There was a hum in his ears. He went limp, sensed he was on the verge of sobbing. He looked down on this woman slumped on the floor like a sack of potatoes. He bit his lower lip hard, drawing blood.

Then he saw only himself, an isolated figure in a darkened room.

He wasn't sure quite how he made it onto the eight o'clock train, which was nearly empty, barely half the seats filled.

Their world of two had ended. The Last Judgement was complete. He remembered only that as darkness inched down, she seemed to make the sign of the cross, up to down, right to left – it was the first time she had ever let him see her make this holy gesture. In the end, she had surrendered them both to the Lord. He was a demon damned to darkness, and her last act was a blazing beam of light. He covered his head with the white blanket from the train, but still the light blinded him. He heard only his breathing and his heartbeat. He huddled beneath the quilt, shivering, as if with a fever. His mother was dead. He had killed her.

11

THE rubber ball in his mind ricocheted continually through imponderable time: it was all over, it hadn't happened yet. Free will seemed to drive every action, but at the same time absurd coincidences led to limitless deviations. Half awake, half in a dream, he watched as his mother's body, still lying in the corner of the bedroom where he had left it, dried in the wind, turning ash grey and rock hard, and recalled a news story about the Iraq War he had watched years ago with his mother – swirling grey smoke, soldiers carting bodies from the battlefield. The bodies were like morsels of putrid meat, and strangely, they all seemed to have the same face. A crowd of people watched from the side. Only the dead walked alone.

He couldn't remember how long he stayed by his mother's side. Lying lifeless on the floor, she radiated light, just as she had in life. Now, amid absolute silence, she was pure and clean. He remembered that once as a boy he had come down with a fever, and his mother had remained by his bedside, towelling off his entire body repeatedly, starting again at his head when she finished at his feet. He had slid his small, fevered hand into hers, finding inside a soft, comforting ocean, and all his fears vanished.

I didn't do it. She just died, Li Wen told himself.

He cut through the arid, oppressive train station and came out on the other side. The enormous station was like a nightmare, a bizarre, inescapable whirlpool. The instant he arrived in Beijing Station, they started pushing, people whose faces and genders he couldn't make out, shoving him left, right, back, and forward. In this way, he passed through an enigmatic underground tunnel and, back above ground, countless broad avenues that all looked the same, shoved through life, whittling away interminable time. He knew just one thing for certain: it was never a good idea to strike up conversations with random people in train stations. They would drive you places in their sinister fake taxis with no plates, dump you in caves you'd never manage to crawl out of, cram you into barrels filled with substances that would vaporise you in seconds.

He had enough in his bank account to pay next term's tuition. Now, that money was all he had left. He had no luggage, only a black backpack crammed with useless crap. Yet to return to ordinary consciousness, harried by guilt and fear, in his haste he had grabbed only the buckwheat pillow his mother had made for him and the blue electric toothbrush sitting by the sink. He seemed to recall darting into the toilet to brush his teeth and chucking his mother's red plastic toothbrush in the bin – it was yet another example of her always giving him all the best stuff.

Li Wen went round and round until he ended up back where he started, and realised he was doing circles around the train station. He always found somewhere to sleep, but never stayed any one place for long, deliberately choosing cheap fleapits deep in the bowels of alleys. Big, bright hotels like the express hotel he had stayed in with his mother hurt his eyes. He held his breath as an old man who seemed on the verge of nodding off scanned his ID card without ever looking up. The old man spoke in Beijing dialect; on hearing this, he let out the breath he had been holding. In fact, it seemed he couldn't be bothered to look the old man in the face. He observed the wide-open eyes of the policeman on the advertising card atop the table, sensing the officer could leap off the paper at any moment, grab him and drag him home, back to the lifeless body he had left lying on the floor – by now, that body must have putrefied, seeped into the floorboards like fertiliser into soil.

Sitting in bed in the 150-yuan-a-night hovel, Li Wen realised he was surrounded by real silence: the cheap resin table, the white disc-shaped plastic alarm clock, the dust fluttering before the green window screen, the ineffable, foul, smoke-like odour that blotted out the scent his mother had left on him the day before. Later, within this poorly lit room like the interior of a medicinal capsule, he thought everything over and realised he couldn't recall whether, when he ran into Mrs Zhao, the teacher, in the courtyard, he had been trying to tell her that his mother had died, or that he had killed her. He had repeatedly gesticulated at the ground, tracing a closed circle like the gesture his mother had made before her heart stopped – right, left, up, down.

When he left the guesthouse in search of food, he was unspeakably weak, white like an albino, drained of vitality, so overcome by fatigue that he barely remembered his mother's death. He commanded himself, *Keep your mouth shut.* He had exchanged a few words with the girl selling boxed lunches at the corner market and realised he barely recognised his voice. The timbre and diction seemed utterly alien. He sensed he had stepped into an extraordinarily vapid world of unrestrained freedom.

Nothing about that year was normal. He no longer set any goals for himself, and his mother's alarm clock no longer rang to remind him of the time. He slept the days away in the rundown little hotel, but rarely fell into a deep sleep; he sensed he was hovering above himself, doing the backstroke through the ether. His mother, his grandfather and his father were there too, but they all seemed more substantial than him, somehow more real. He learned to take his temperature by exhaling warm vapour onto his hand, just as he had gauged his pulse by feeling his wrist on the running track.

He believed in ghosts. The day after his grandfather died, Li Wen was sure he saw him in a dream. He couldn't make out the figure's face, saw only a slightly hunchbacked silhouette moving its lips; he couldn't make out the words either, couldn't even guess what they might be. He firmly believed that his consciousness had strangled his grandfather's words. He avoided any news that might mention the name of his hometown (in fact, no story ever appeared), and before long, even his mother's ghost mysteriously vanished. Until then, he had seen her ghost twice, sometimes three times a day. She had no body, no fixed form. There was just a beam of light, but when Li Wen saw it, he knew it was her. In life, his mother had strictly fixed his waking time. The alarm clock would ring and she would turn it off, then pull the white plastic pin again in an eternally repeating cycle. A few days ago, his phone rang, even though he had set it to silent, and the frequency of the cellular waves snapped him awake, but when he picked up, nobody said a word. The caller ID read 'FOOD DELIVERY', but he never sent out for food, so he was convinced his mother was sending him a secret message from far away. When he hung up, it suddenly struck him that his mother was truly gone, had returned at last to her real place of rest.

Several times, after devouring a few cups of instant noodles, he thought of Zheng Xiaowei.

She was the only living woman he ever thought about during this time when day bled into night, and he was secretly proud of this. He imagined that that day, everybody, including Dr Yao, had busied themselves cleaning up the aftermath of his heinous act (to them, it was like fixing a stoplight smashed in a traffic accident, they simply restored the mechanical functioning of the device), but then a long period of forgetting had begun, a forgetting abraded by everyday existence until its meaning was worn away.

The day after Li Wen returned to the dorm from Dr Yao's office, Big Brother Chen's bunk was empty: his computer, his quilt and his games console were gone. Some sports drink bottles were scattered on the table, and the blue bedroll, which was so threadbare that the bed base showed through, hadn't moved a millimetre. Li Wen poked around, found that the liquid in the sports drink bottles hadn't changed at all, nor would it change when the bottles were pitched in the bin. The commercials claimed the stuff rapidly replenished electrolytes, but in reality, the drinks consisted of preservatives on top of preservatives. One time, Big Brother Chen returned to the dorm to ask the rest of them out for hotpot, but Li Wen said nothing, didn't even turn his head to look, and therefore the peace between them held. It seemed that, as Dr Yao intended, they had smoothly, fully forgotten one another.

What Li Wen didn't know was that, during all his days as a student, Big Brother Chen never returned to live in the dorm.

When his thoughts turned to Zheng Xiaowei again, he got the sense he was looking back on the previous century's events. A deviation is a blank spot on the calendar of daily events, but when you reflect on the past, you find everyday life continues to move forward in its everyday way. People aren't accustomed to looking back, though. People like to beautify stagnant time, deeming this history, mourning history by forgetting.

That day, after buying two tickets at the train station, Li Wen left the canteen and, screwing up his courage, strode rapidly toward the study room, refraining from running so as not to lay bare the full extent of his purpose. Today, he had brought a copy of *Sports Management*. He was now a full-fledged sports student; worse still, he was a sports management major. He could imagine himself squandering the prime of adulthood in some small neighbourhood fitness centre, returning in the evening to a newer, even more nondescript teachers' housing compound where he would eat, sleep and wake again, living out a vapid monotone life, tripping over his tongue when he tried to speak because he had nothing to say, wearing a moustache slicked with detestable white grease.

The hot noodle concoction from the canteen roiled in his stomach. Only once he excreted every last bit of this steaming substance was order restored to his bowels. On returning from the lavatory, he found Zheng Xiaowei sitting in her regular spot: frail and wizened as ever, two eyes drooping from a jaundiced face, she seemed not to have changed at all, though her ponytail had been exchanged for a gently swaying braid. He sensed everyone in the classroom was staring at him, whispering in each other's ears, 'It's him, the one who burned the quilt, run while you still can.' They had once again dug open the hollow he had carved in the tree, but it didn't matter. He would bid them a stoic farewell like a warrior, never to return. He saw himself leaving the study room, head held high, shoulders squared, leading Xiaowei by the hand.

That night, they ended up in a little hotel behind campus, ensconced still deeper in the maze of alleyways than the building for professors' families. It was Li Wen's first time, and he imagined that in this regard, he and Xiaowei were equals, deriving a practised air from this mistaken assumption. Following the instructions he had looked up online, after attaining an erection, he mounted her and began stroking her back and hair. According to the internet, this was supposed to calm a woman's emotions and secure her trust. Xiaowei slapped his hand away, pulled off her tee-shirt and giggled.

'It's your first time, isn't it?'

Li Wen said nothing. He stared at the gums exposed behind her half-open lips, nagged by a not-quite-definable sense of shame. Xiaowei picked up his hand back up and began sliding it smoothly all across her body.

'Never mind, I think we both know the answer.'

Face flushed with shame, countless glib lines flashed through Li Wen's mind, but he stayed silent. Zheng Xiaowen's hands steered his hands toward a copious vitality he had never before known, followed by abrupt release – her skin no longer seemed desiccated but slick, smooth and scorching hot; in the guttering light of the little hotel, her face no longer looked jaundiced, and her movements and her voice guided him through the necessary procedure, like a practised mother guiding a nursing child.

When it was over, Xiaowei's body rapidly detached from his. Her sticky sweat cooled on his skin, and her bony wrists jabbed him.

'What made you want to sit in on our English class anyway?' Xiaowei's voice had regained its former feebleness.

'I just love the language.'

'I've never liked PE. When I'm running, I feel like I could drop dead at any moment.'

'That's because you're breathing wrong. Breathing is the key – to running, boxing, football, everything.'

'I've always been good at English. Being an English teacher wouldn't be so bad. Tell me, why did you decide to major in PE? Do you actually like it?'

'I burned someone's quilt.'

Zheng Xiaowei giggled again. She seemed to think Li Wen was poking fun at her in some way, cracking an insipid joke prescribed by the online instructions.

When they left the hotel, rather than the sense of having completed a coming-of-age ritual, Li Wen felt only fatigue and ravenous hunger. He knew his mother was watching him from far away, watching another woman guide her son, that other woman with whom she had shared her son in life. Li Wen grabbed Xiaowei's hand tightly, thinking that having breakfast at a little neighbourhood place ought to sober them up. In the small restaurant next to the hotel, the patrons were all student sweethearts who had spent the night together, or hook-up partners who had met online. The streets around campus were all geared to this purpose, providing every sort of service from sleeping to eating to sex within a compact radius. At this time of morning, students staying on campus didn't come here, so if you saw someone you knew, you knew what they were doing and kept quiet about it. Everyone stayed out of everyone else's business. No one spoiled anyone else's fun.

He shovelled the steaming xiaolongbao into his mouth, gulping them down dry, without any vinegar or soup. Just then, he lifted his gaze and saw Big Brother Chen barrel through the door, leading a girl by the hand. She seemed to be attached to his side with superglue, face flushed crimson, dependent and ashamed. Li Wen subconsciously lowered his head, but at almost the same moment lifted it again and turned to look directly at Big Brother Chen. After all, he wasn't alone, he was with Zheng Xiaowei, a fully developed girl, so he had confidence. Li Wen and Big Brother Chen exchanged a look, like two wild buffalos eyeing one another on the Great Plains of the Amazon. Chen snuck a glance at Xiaowei, and the corners of his lips lifted a little. In a booming voice, he called out, seemingly to Li Wen, 'Six deep-fried dough sticks and two bowls of jellied tofu. Make that to go – we're having breakfast in bed!'

That sense of shame that had assailed him the previous evening flared back to life. Li Wen swallowed the final dumpling, grabbed Xiaowei's shrimp and seaweed soup and took a gulp. The other boys had long since lapped him on the track of life experience and now stood by the sidelines jeering, 'Have you heard? It's his first time. His mummy doesn't let him go on dates.'

*

He saw that Zheng Xiaowei had sent him several messages over the past couple days, just a small handful. He never wrote back. Should he tell her he had disappeared? Should he thank her for officialising his entry into adult life? The messages explained that her father had found her a middle school teaching position in her hometown. After graduating, she would go in for an interview, and she asked whether he wanted to keep hanging out after they graduated. It was then he realised he had nowhere to go. Having fled to Beijing, he had left behind the teaching position at the middle school.

For about a week, he felt like a proper posh kid. He didn't have to pick his dirty knickers up off the floor, he had flunkeys to clean up after him – holed up in the hovel, his only responsibility was to go out and buy a boxed lunch when he was hungry. When he came back, the bedsheets would be folded, though from time to time the room exuded the stale odour of age, suggesting the presence of many people over an extended time span – but he never saw a single other person and remained absolutely isolated from the outside world, undisturbed by anybody. He bought a notebook computer, learned to play the online game *League of Kings* but gave up after three days, confounded by the endless upgrades and lack of fixed goals, finding he didn't have the patience to ascend to the king's throne. In his memory, this time period was like a spring nut, simultaneously indispensable and barely worth mentioning, an illusion of the future and a funeral for the past.

12

GODSLAYER was a pro gamer who lived in the east-facing room with the large balcony and rarely emerged during daylight. On meeting GodSlayer, Li Wen learned for the first time that there was such a thing as a 'pro gamer'. Since he moved in, the two of them had spoken only a handful of times. Li Wen had finally found a proper job at the front desk of a gym in a shopping centre on the periphery of the Third Ring Road. His room faced west, so he never saw the morning sun. Finally, like his mother, he again allowed the hands of a clock to regulate his concept of time.

When he first saw the for-rent ad on the mobile game site he had started to fiddle around with, he shivered with fear, suspecting it could be a front for a human trafficking operation. He had never dreaded so deeply that a city could catch him unaware and swallow him whole. That afternoon, he pulled on the bright orange tee-shirt with the gym logo. For some reason, he wasn't sure why, advertising swag always came in bright colours – perhaps brightly coloured items were cheaper to manufacture. He picked up a stack of flyers and headed directly for the room with the number 901 on the plate, the one with slips of paper of every colour crammed beneath the door handle – takeout places, fitness centres, massage parlours, even some small cards with escorts' numbers. It was the same wherever you went, the vacuous exterior of contemporary life smashed into pulp, philistine listlessness promptly laid bare. Li Wen pressed down on the doorbell for a good while, he couldn't remember exactly how long, and finally someone opened up.

When he first laid eyes on GodSlayer, Li Wen reflected that he was as emaciated as a monkey, his eyes lined by inflamed black rings. He seemed to have gone an awfully long time without sleeping (or was it that he had gone a long time without waking?).

After Li Wen moved in, the two of them never discussed their initial meeting. Li Wen suspected GodSlayer never realised that the boy pretending to hand out flyers had been him. Such crude tactics were his sole means of self-defence.

GodSlayer occupied two rooms of the three-bedroom apartment, and Li Wen moved into the west-facing bedroom. He had an inkling GodSlayer had rented out the room because it faced away from the sun, but he never really understood what difference sunlight made to his flatmate. In the end, GodSlayer made a good flatmate, and he was reasonably sure the other man felt the same about him, though they discussed personal matters only a pitifully small handful of times.

'What do you do?'

'I'm a personal trainer.'

'What do you do?'

'I'm a pro gamer.'

They had exchanged a scant few lines of dialogue, and already Li Wen had lied. In Beijing, high-class fitness centres, ones that cost fifteen thousand yuan a month and up, only employed coaches who had trained in America and the UK, graduates of Beijing Sports University and Capital University of Physical Education and Sports. They did not, in fact, refer to themselves as fitness coaches, but as 'personal trainers'. This seemed to lend their every act an air of scientific professionalism, as if only in this way could they gain the city's trust. Li Wen determined that GodSlayer was telling the truth, and the somewhat dubious grounds for this determination were as follows: people who were good at games deserved to be trusted a bit more than normal people, because after all, they lived apart from the everyday world. It was a crude, juvenile logic.

The game GodSlayer got paid to play was *League of Kings*, the one Li Wen had given up on. They rarely ran into one another during the day. They also rarely ran into one another at night. Every day, Li Wen left home at 9:45 a.m. on the dot, exited the apartment complex, and navigated two narrow alleys, passing a nail salon, a hair salon, and a Shaxian snack shop. According to his calculations, it took precisely fifteen minutes to reach the rear entrance of the shopping centre. Sometimes, in his memory, the road to the shopping centre was superimposed upon the road to the middle school, as if the two were actually one and the same. Only in the second month did Li Wen gradually begin to expand his sphere of activity. Here, it was difficult to accurately grasp the workings of the public transport system. In the city where he was born, he and his mother had always taken the bus, though most of the time there was no need to take public transportation at all. In M City, he was generally either running around on campus or on a round trip to someplace nearby. In Beijing, he was a bat flitting about in a series of blackened caverns, be it his dimly lit room or the multi-storey shopping centre absolutely devoid of natural light. In that tiny sliver of time when he wasn't working, he was in the subway, which was the same – artificial light lit him day and night. Only the commute from the apartment complex to the shopping centre reminded him that he lived beneath the sun.

In this sense, Li Wen and GodSlayer definitely made excellent flatmates. Li Wen had finally found someone with whom he could share a space, a completely invisible person made of a translucent substance. They were two peas in a pod. They were both acclimatised to their own lives. They knew nothing of one another's comings and goings in the day or the night, and there was no need to scramble to monopolise the toilet: GodSlayer had an ensuite in his bedroom, so the one outside belonged completely to Li Wen. Neither GodSlayer nor Li Wen ever had friends over, but as in his university days, Li Wen kept his toothbrush and soap and so on in a little plastic basket which he placed neatly by the sink, as if he were merely a lodger staying the night, which in fact he was.

*

Li Wen worked for a short while in many different fitness centres. On leaving one, he had no trouble finding a position at another. Dr Yao had been right: a sports management major could always find work. When he bought an ID online, he bought a diploma, too. He wavered for a long while over whether to put a different name on the fake ID card, but in the face of endless options, he ultimately chose to mingle truth with falsehood – he really wanted the diploma, and he also wanted to begin his new simulated life in Beijing under the name 'Li Wen'. He inwardly matched wits with the wide-eyed cartoon cop. When he settled the hotel bill, he didn't dare turn his head, fearing if he let his eyes slip downward just a little, the policeman's gaze would gore him.

The fitness centres all had names like 'International Uplift' or 'International Inspiration' or some such thing that consistently communicated the idea of peppy upward motion. As far as they were concerned, a hardworking, dependable young man with a bachelor's degree was quite a catch. He worked at the front desk, in sales, as a health consultant, even as a private coach. He quickly learned to gain the trust of the men and women who lurked day and night in fitness centres – he sold various types of protein powder to men covered from head to toe in swollen egg-like muscles; he explained to women in skin-tight pants that they needed to work their buttocks more to get that sleek, sexy look; from time to time, he dredged up new forms of flattery to convince them that whatever they were doing was working. Everyone was the same, both men and women, dying inside from loneliness. And among the women, he learned to scout out the most likely prospects – that is, the ones who would sleep with him – and take them to a three-hundred-yuan-a-night business hotel. At some point, his life had veered off onto a new path, he couldn't pinpoint exactly when, but what was certain was that, among all these lonely people, he was racking up experience points at a respectable rate thanks to his salary at the fitness centre.

In fact, during his first week living with GodSlayer, he went out among the machines and pretended to be just another gym junkie, and no one was the wiser. He silently sneaked into the office of the study abroad organisation on the floor above the fitness centre, asked roughly how much it would cost to apply to an American university and discovered his entire savings would barely cover the application fee. He instantly forgave himself, just as he had when he had gone to the bank intending to take out a new debit card (linked to a Beijing address) and realised he needed an invisibility cloak to hide himself from the world. There was barely a mao left in the account that had once belonged to the old Li Wen, and the new 'Li Wen' couldn't open a new one. Tightly clasping the number he had been assigned by the computer, seated in a row of metal chairs with no distinguishing features whatsoever, he passed the time by counting the number of banking products offered by the advertisements on the walls – who knew there was a VIP Card, a White Gold Card, and a Black Gold Card? Finally they called his number, 'Number 21', once, twice, then three times, at which point he crumpled the slip of paper clutched between his fingers, stuffed it in his pocket and left.

Li Wen soon learned to drink. He taught himself to recognise the subtle differences between various types of liquor – his favourite was XO. The gym girls would take him out to bars or karaoke parlours, and he would deliberately emblazon the flavour of every drink they drank upon his senses. Every time he fumbled with a bottle under dim lighting, groping its shape, squinting to make out the words written on the label, the girls laughed, said he was a goody two-shoes who knew nothing of the world. He didn't confirm or deny it, he just laughed along, knowing nobody really cared about these boring details or the bumbling impression he made. He got what he paid for at the bars and the business hotels, and they extracted the full value from their private lessons. It was a fair and square arrangement.

Only Gym Junkie Chen was different.

Gym Junkie Chen had an extremely round face, the kind with no protruding lines at all. When they first met that day at the gym, Li Wen deliberately underestimated her age, because she had bought a package of ten classes and he knew there wasn't a person on earth who didn't relish little white lies. She informed him that his flushed face inspired special confidence. Li Wen learned for the first time that the sheen of a woman's skin was derived not from youth but meticulous care and costly upkeep; she was almost forty, but there wasn't a single wrinkle on her face. (In fact, it was as smooth as a crystal ball and sparkled in the light.) On the first day of class, Gym Junkie Chen declared that she didn't like exercises that left her sweaty, all she wanted from Li Wen was a fascial massage and stretching exercises. Li Wen had had encounters with many such women before, there was no need to instruct them in strength training and functional exercises like an actual fitness coach, it was better to be like a clockwork soldier with the spring wound tight, fondling them, stroking them, maintaining a gentle touch, keeping the goal in sight but never getting hasty, and soon they were satisfied. There was nary an agglutination of muscle to be found in her shoulders or legs, she was light and fluffy as a cloud, and the first time he took her to the three-hundred-yuan-a-night business hotel, he reflected that maybe there wasn't enough substance to her to merit the expenditure. He noticed that after following him into the room, she sniffed at the hotel's indelible musty odour. She wrinkled her brow, but didn't comment. He saw her a few times after that, in a chic hotel she booked, his first true five-star Beijing experience. The room did not stink of damp, a standardised fragrance suffused both the lobby and the room, and the hotel staff would deliver food and alcohol to your room whenever you wanted, even in the dead of night. She taught him to drink cognac, telling him, 'Drinking drinks no one else understands, preferably ones that aren't too popular, is the way to convince others of your importance.'

His first swig of XO left him choking, but soon his naïve olfactory sense settled upon the liquor's unique wood and fruit fragrance. With Gym Junkie Chen, he felt unexpectedly comfortable and at ease, even mixing XO with cola right before her eyes – he didn't comprehend these artefacts of her daily existence, but she placed them in his grip, one after another, teaching him their feel. In her presence, Li Wen felt like a child, but he wasn't the least bit ashamed. He learned to savour the liquor by swishing it around in his mouth, coating his teeth and gums, rather than swallowing straight away (the more expensive the liquor, the longer you paused before gulping it down); he learned to overcome the giddiness he got from drinking, to let the high lift both him and her from the ground and sweep them toward freedom. He saw that he had once again entered the world of *The Sims*, that game from so many years ago. He stood on the exterior of an eggshell peering into a skyscraper window at the virtual 'Li Wen', realising then that he was nearing the brink. He would have been happy to spend the rest of his life in the chic hotel, reclining upon the silky sheets, waiting for Gym Junkie Chen.

One evening not long after, she announced she was leaving.

'He has bought me an apartment and invited me to join him overseas.'

Li Wen didn't have any idea who 'he' was, but immediately inspiration struck – perhaps it was the virtual 'Li Wen' guiding him from afar – and said, 'Funny, I've been wanting to see the world myself.'

As he spoke, he boxed his ears inside his mind. He realised his words were merely a juvenile pretext, an awkward fumble at a love that had already slipped through his fingers.

Gym Junkie Chen didn't smoke, but the look in her eyes said she desperately wanted a cigarette.

'Are you sure?'

Li Wen had never nodded so vigorously in his life. He recalled only that she never asked him out again after that. When she left the room, she said, 'I'm almost certain we'll never see each other again, but I guess there's a tiny sliver of a chance, so in case we do, pretend you don't know me.'

*

Beginning the second Sunday after Gym Junkie Chen left Beijing, Li Wen invented a secret game, which he called Subway Surfing. He became obsessed with getting on the subway and seeing where it took him, riding it with no aim or direction in mind. Sometimes he would randomly pick someone to follow – it could be a man or a woman, old or young. He would stick to them as they changed to another line, and then get back on the subway and ride on, or retrace his steps, he didn't care. He began to prolong the game from half a day to a whole day, from the first train on Sunday to the last one, but still it left him feeling empty.

On the subway, the instant chemistry he had with women seemed to dissipate; they didn't see him, and he didn't see them. One Sunday, he got on the subway train and sat down. There were always plenty of empty seats on the first train, no matter which of the local stations he started from. By midday, it was getting crowded and most passengers were standing. A young man in a white shirt with a black shoulder bag was standing in front of him. Li Wen thought he looked familiar, but couldn't quite place him. The man pulled his right hand free of the crush, and Li Wen could see he was holding a book, exactly the same as the one Li Wen had borrowed from the university library, an old edition of Edgar Allan Poe's short stories with a dark green cover. Li Wen finally remembered where he had seen this fellow passenger before. Three more stops passed and he got off. The way the air wafted towards Li Wen now told him that the women were here. So it must be around one o'clock – that was the time they came. There were two of them, one with a blue headscarf rolled up and tied around her head to make a hairband. She was not much to look at. There was a lot of grey in her hair, and it was easy to imagine what a hard life she had had. Her Chinese was not fluent, and Li Wen guessed she was Korean – there were a lot of Koreans in this part of Beijing. The second woman might have been a university student. She had curiously square features, and her eyes were so small they looked like two lines sewn onto her face. She wore a pair of round, black-framed glasses, and had an awkward, timid look about her. They were always here, doing the same thing every week at the same time, like marionettes popping out of a music box; they floated down the train aisle packed with strap-hangers as if the crowds were invisible to them, each carrying a white canvas bag with the words 'Mutual Aid Society' printed in bright blue, gently pressing leaflets into the hands of the passengers, smiling no matter whether it was accepted or rejected, all without saying a word.

The first time they had offered Li Wen a leaflet, he had been drawn in by the sincerity of their gaze and felt strangely gratified that they had picked him. But he didn't actually take it, and when they turned up the next Sunday, and the next, Li Wen shut his eyes, folded his arms across his chest and pretended to be too tired to take any interest in what was happening around him. This time, however, before Li Wen had time to look away from the man with the copy of Edgar Allan Poe, there they were. As the student type with the glasses held a leaflet out to Li Wen, her eyes lit up in a way that reminded him of the time he pushed his mother to the ground. Just that once, her eyes had given off the same glow. Li

Wen took the leaflet, and the student type smiled at him, though he was only one of the crowd and she had no way of knowing whether he was a believer too or whether she was wasting her smile – but in that brief moment, Li Wen felt that he knew what his mother's secret was: she was one of *them*, she had answered the call.

When he got back to his flat that night, GodSlayer had just eaten a takeaway and was ready to start his day. Li Wen was still clutching the leaflet. Now, he consigned the sacred text to the food waste bin, where it joined a stack of takeaway food containers and somehow absorbed the gravy like blotting paper. Then he had a change of heart and fished it out again, shaking the liquid off it. He needed to make a serious effort to dig himself out of the sand dunes, to extricate this version of Li Wen from subway fantasies and dreams of five-star hotels. He switched on his phone, typed a few search terms into Taobao. He felt like he was groping through cobwebs, but he was confident he would find what he wanted. He just needed to choose the right one from the eye-catching adverts, just as the student on the subway had picked him out, though he was conscious that what the web offered would never share the light of day with reality.

A week later, Li Wen was the proud possessor of another bespoke graduation certificate. He grabbed the desk lamp and held it over the embossed paper in its blue card cover so he could compare it with the other one. Identical. Dr Yao would have been surprised to know that Li Wen now had both a certificate in Sports Management from M City University and a graduate degree in English, so brand-new that the smell of cheap ink still wafted off it.

*

It was the first time that Dr Zhong had given such explicit advice to Mrs Luo, and it had taken her by surprise. She imagined that he and Dr Pei were one of a kind, people who did not like to interfere, especially when it involved upsetting the applecart. So she hesitated for a couple of days. She had taken for granted the carefully created equilibrium in their lives: Mrs Zhao's silence, Dr Zhong's steadiness, and the harmony imposed by Dr Pei surrounded her and Suwei like an unbreakable triangle. She could not imagine what bringing in another person would do. Nor was she much taken by Dr Zhong's blandishments of the 'positive effects' an incomer would produce. All she cared about was total stability.

When Suwei was still learning ballet, he had shared a desk at his middle school with a half-Japanese girl who looked like a kimono-clad doll from a Kyoto tourist shop, right down to her neat, jet-black fringe. They were a chatty bunch, these mums waiting to pick up their children from school, and would always exchange a few words if you met them at the school gate. Not that they usually hung around there. Once, when Mrs Luo had finished her work and stopped by to pick up Suwei, she arrived a bit early and asked her young secretary to park in the huge public car park next to the school. It was always full of shiny BMWs and Audis, lined up as if they were in a car showroom, and when she looked over at them, she saw the children's mothers lined up as neatly as their cars. Some of the women carried crocodile leather clutch bags and wore diamond-studded sunglasses. They strode towards the school entrance, making an even bolder display of wealth than their cars. Mrs Luo spotted the half-Japanese child's mother, whom she had met at the parents' meeting. She was a fair-skinned Chinese woman with beautiful, slanted, peach blossom eyes. The woman told her that she had hired a French teacher, a piano teacher and an art teacher to give Leafy (or whatever the girl's name was) home tuition.

'It's so dangerous out there. She's safer if the teachers come to our home. I'm always reading stuff in the media, I worry myself sick!'

'That's because she's your daughter, girls are always a worry,' said Mrs Luo. 'Suwei goes out to classes with his ballet teacher, no problem.'

'Well, the only time I stop fretting is when I've got her at home,' said the woman. 'As for sending her to a foreign university when she's older, I just can't make up my mind.'

Mrs Luo smiled and glanced sidelong at her. She had had the same worries, and still did. The thought that her child might disappear was the stuff of nightmares. She really did have bad dreams like that – they used to jolt her awake in the dead of night. Suwei came out of the school with the half-Japanese girl. The two of them seemed to be getting on well, and Mrs Luo imagined the pretty girls he would bring home with him when he was older. Looking at these two children side by side, she noticed how fair he was compared with the girl. He was wearing the polo shirt she had just bought him, and it showed off his long, straight neck. He was walking with his toes slightly pointing out, and looked like a graceful white swan against the setting sun. *He's a superstar in the making*, thought Mrs Luo. She was amenable to letting Suwei go to ballet classes because Mr Pan, his teacher, had been an eminent principal dancer in his day. She had to admit that she trusted ballet dancers unconditionally. To her, they were all good people. It was also true that, deep down, she was incredibly envious of anyone who could fit into the same size leotards year after year.

Before she married Mr Chen, Mrs Luo had only one criterion for judging people – they were either good or bad. That was the way her parents had looked at life, and she had simply inherited their worldview. They had lived and worked at the Second Artillery Arsenal, her father in the factory union and her mother as a nurse in the health clinic. Her father was a tall, thin, handsome man with a hawkish nose. The factory folk were always commenting how much she resembled him, especially in her fine facial features. She remembered him arriving home every night at six o'clock sharp, whistling some tune whose name she never knew. She imagined it must be one of Teresa Teng's songs. (Her mother had a sweet Teresa Teng smile, which made her eyes narrow into crescent moons.) So when she buried his ashes in the exclusive Cloud Mountain cemetery, she bought all the old Teresa Teng tapes she could find and laid them on his gravestone.

When she was at the dance academy, she would sometimes sneak home and drop in at the health centre, where everyone knew her. They all reckoned she was going to be a great star, and showered compliments and snacks on her. She accepted them graciously but never touched them. Instead, she took them home and put them in a big glass bowl on the living room table. To her, their gifts were a reward for her beauty, something to be appreciated but not indulged in.

All the girls were weighed every day at college, and it was strictly enjoined on them that they must not put on weight. They were adolescents, and the smallest intake of sugar would make them grow full breasts and round bottoms overnight – something they could not hide from the teachers. After she and Mr Chen married, they went to Moscow on their honeymoon and saw the Bolshoi Ballet. In the darkened theatre, she found her mind wandering: which pyjamas should she pick to wear to bed back at the hotel? At that moment, it dawned on her why there were no voluptuous ballerinas. The extra weight made their dance moves look heavy and erotic, and physical desire entirely eliminated the weightless quality that a wiry frame could embody. So when she thought of her mother's body, which was as sweetly fulsome as her smile, she felt an odd disgust. Even after her mother had left them, her father continued to say she was a good person, and so was the head accountant who had taken her away. But Mrs Luo knew that her mother's lovely, plump body was her original sin. Her father used to bring home bottles of cheap alcohol. He did not smoke, so he would sit there in silence and drink all night long. The booze eventually destroyed his liver, and he died of liver failure at the age of sixty. The day he died, Mrs Luo had just gone to Beijing to join the music and dance troupe. She could admit to herself now that her anorexia back then was not only a typical ballet student's fear of getting too heavy. It went deeper: she was actually terrified of developing a curvy body like her mother's. She would stand naked in front of the bathroom mirror every night before going to bed, touching herself all over and vowing to stay skinny for the rest of her life. Her father drank in the kitchen, however, and when she noticed that her breasts were starting to grow, she began quietly to lock the door every time she went into the bathroom.

Now she was looking more and more like the mother she remembered. She had many dreams of her plump mother and her father (all skin and bones before he died), especially around the time she went back home to see the new cemetery. Cloud Mountain was said to be their city's 'dragon vein', and the civil engineers had brought in a feng shui master to look at it. As a result of that inspection, they developed half of the mountainous area into a tourist area and the other half into the most exclusive cemetery in the city, in the belief that locating it here would confer 'yin' blessings and smooth the path to success for the city's leaders. Mrs Luo could not make up her mind whether she believed in all that feng shui stuff.

'This place is a good place for the departed to sleep because it has a ridge behind it and it's shaded by big trees,' the feng shui master declared when she went to see him about a plot for her father, and she felt that, on this occasion, there was some truth in his words. That afternoon, she forked over the full amount, 450,000 yuan, thus giving her father a good place to sleep. When the factory folk heard, their reaction was, 'That young woman's done her father proud.'

They also said, 'She's given a good man a final resting place.'

Thinking back now, she wondered if she could still call her father a good man. At the end, he was drinking so heavily that he seemed to have a skeleton's empty gaze. She only found afterwards that he had been retired early by the union because he was always befuddled and sometimes paralytically drunk. He began to wander around the house like a dark wraith, stinking of alcohol and despair. She had to get away from home. So she auditioned for a place at a dance academy as soon as she could, and left. Her first day at the academy was hard. The freezing bunk beds and the girls caked in makeup made her feel like she had been trafficked into some prostitution ring – which was indeed how the mums and dads at the factory talked about city girls.

However, now that she had spent so long in Beijing, living among a select one percent of the city's population on an estate where the villas were spread out around an artificial lake, Mrs Luo had almost forgotten about that simple dichotomy between good guys and bad guys. She was often surprised at how fast she forgot things – like the years she had lived in the dance students' dormitory, a four-storey building, its hallways plastered with adverts that fluttered in the draught and so jam-packed with bicycles that it was hard to get in or out. Right opposite was a forty-storey life insurance building, and a sparkling-clean new-build estate shiny with green glass, called something like 'Golden Years'. When Mr Chen first started courting her, Mrs Luo would always get him to drop her at the Golden Years entrance and make sure he had driven away in his black Audi before crossing the road back to her dorm block and walking in through the rusty iron gate on which hung a wooden sign reading 'No Motor Vehicles Allowed'.

He sounds like a good teacher, Mrs Luo thought when she saw Li Wen's CV pinned up in the Estate Management Services office. She knew how ridiculous Estate Management Services sounded, when really it was just an outfit supplying the residents with nannies, housekeepers and tutors. People like Mrs Luo could go and look through their files and pick out the ones that looked suitable.

'Mr Li graduated in English and has a degree in sports

management, too. We've interviewed him and he seems honest and open, just the kind of tutor children take to,' the middle-aged manageress told her.

'That's what one needs nowadays,' Mrs Luo agreed. 'Someone who's healthy and sunny-natured.'

13

ONE of the things Li Wen disliked most about the fitness centre was the uniform. He had to wear a jogging top all day long, long-sleeved in winter and short-sleeved in summer, with matching bottoms that were the same all year round and always stank because he forgot to wash them. He felt like a secondary school student in a uniform like that. Then there was the familiar smell of the plastic they came wrapped in, reminding him of the knockoff sportswear that Peddler Wang used to sell off his cart in that gloomy back alley. Finally, in the very last gym where he worked before officially finding a tutoring job, he got a uniform that didn't smell of plastic. It was made in China, like the ones his mother used to buy for him in high school. She always maintained that this old-style stuff was good quality, and he had quickly learned what real cotton smelled like.

Li Wen saw Beijing as a city made up of islands in a swamp. There was no common ground; the residents were condemned to live forever as disparate, alienated individuals, glued to invisible floaters, some head-down, others head-up.

He took off his new uniform, which was blessedly odour-free, and stuffed it in his bag. He had bought himself a new canvas duffel bag instead of the backpack he had had to use before. The canvas bag looked classless. He had figured that out at the last gym, where he had longed to be one of the young men who strolled in and out, dressed in stylish shirts and carrying their sports gear stowed away in a canvas bag or gym bag slung over one shoulder. In that fitness centre, he never saw the boss until the day he handed in his notice, though he had heard that the man was the son of the owner of the shopping centre. Apparently, he had returned from studying in the US with a passion for sport and had opened what was reputed to be the most expensive fitness centre in Beijing. Somewhere in the deepest recesses of his memory, a ball bounced back and forth over and over again, making him oddly curious about the owner of the fitness centre, as if meeting him was the only way to make sense of what had happened to Shuisheng after he went to America. Shuisheng had been so secretive at school. Perhaps knowing the boss would help him understand his friend. He told himself that Shuisheng and the owner could be friends, that they were the same kind of people.

Back at their apartment, GodSlayer didn't notice any change in him at all (no surprise there), even though Li Wen ditched his gym-issued sweatshirt (he kept the odour-free tracksuit though) and switched from trainers to a pair of brown suede shoes he bought online, and went to the local barber to get his hair cut short at the sides and spiky on top; it didn't look as sporty as the buzz cut he used to have and gave his forehead room to breathe. At home, there had been a framed photo of his mother and a seven-year-old Li Wen on the sideboard in the living room and, in it, he had a thick fringe, just like his mother. She cut his hair herself until he was seven, because she was convinced that barbers always had their minds on something else and might nick him with their careless hands. She was very gentle, and she used a nice-smelling shampoo as well. She used to say he had inherited her hair, coarse and black. Li Wen, however, had soon learned to pull stray hairs out using just the right amount of force without hurting himself, in the hopes that he'd end up with nice, soft, fine hair. In spite of this, he loved the bristly feeling he got from her hair when she put her arms around him and held him tight, and really missed this as a grown-up. In any case, his hair never changed, it still grew incredibly fast. Later, he abandoned his fringe because it reminded him of the picture his mum used to keep on the chest of drawers, the one he had turned face-down just before running out of the flat to catch the eight o'clock train.

At the fitness centre, he always felt like someone was watching him. And yet there was no chance that either the gym users or anyone who came to the front desk to ask for the toilets would remember his face, especially when he shed his uniform. After Gym Junkie Chen, he went on to have sex with just two or three more women. It was purely sex, none of them got sentimental about it. It was as if physical urges were a way of keeping fit. Beijing's most exclusive fitness centre required the trainers to be on the premises even when there were no classes, so that the users could always find one. For ten hours every day, he felt like countless eyes were on him, as he skulked among exercise machines that looked like instruments of torture, weaving in and out of the toiling bodies. When he left work, he was convinced that everyone was still watching him – in the passages underneath the shopping centre, in the cafes selling takeaways, and in the subways with their roaring trains. He knew he had to keep out of sight to avoid being caught. Discovery would be disastrous.

At least now he was a tutor, and he did not have to go through the same regime day after day like he did at the gym; tutoring was a highly creative career for Li Wen, at least at first. Behind the front desk at the gym, he had only been able to guess who the customers were from their clothes and their appearance. He sometimes even made up backstories for them. But as a tutor, he was an intruder, he could really get inside families, people and stories of a kind he had never imagined before. Not that any of them were going to volunteer the truth. The residential estates where he found work were further and further out from the city centre, the houses were bigger, and the echoes he heard were emptier. *The best way to deal with people like them*, he thought, without specifying to himself who 'people like them' were, *is to keep your mouth shut.*

He started by making his lessons into a bit of a performance, broken up by fitness exercises like open and closed jumps and plank holds. He knew that the rush of oxygen would ginger his students up. The first one he tried out this routine on was a short, pimply-faced boy whose name he had forgotten (all he could remember was his mother calling him by his English name, Sam something). This was his first job as far out as the Fifth Ring Road. Even after taking the subway line to its northern terminus, he still had a thirty-minute taxi ride, so the boy's mother always gave him an extra two hundred yuan each time to pay his fare. Then the same woman introduced him to another mother with a daughter, then the mother of another boy, and the mother of another girl. He had so much work that he almost stopped tutoring kids who lived inside the Fifth Ring Road; he figured his lessons were popular beyond the Fifth Ring Road because the kids were on their own so much that their mums saw some value in these exercises. It was still hard to find his way around Beijing – the roads were always petering out when you least expected it, running into a cluster of old-fashioned one-storey shacks sandwiched between towering skyscrapers, effectively creating a slum in the middle of a rich neighbourhood, or landing you up in a collection of luxury villas plonked down in the middle of nowhere. There were times when he thought he was seeing a mirage, before he realised that all these places looked alike. Like the children who grew up in the villas, they were all equally cool, standoffish, introverted, and cautious.

These kids and their mothers trusted him completely; not one of them questioned who he was or bothered to check whether he matched the Li Wen on his ID card. And so he felt a great silence descend on him again, as heavily as a falling scythe. What really got him down was not being able to play Subway Surfing any more – it was a daft game, but had given him so much enjoyment. Though there was no one to stop him (possibly a deterrent in itself), the fact was he had become completely indistinguishable from any other traveller on the subway, one of millions who used it just in order to get where they were going. Then one evening – though it was impossible to tell whether it was evening when you were underground – he stepped through the barriers and almost bumped into half a dozen people standing in a circle in front of him. Most of the crowd were rushing past them, with the occasional busybody craning their neck to get a quick look. He heard a voice say, 'We're not a pyramid scheme, we're just here to wake people up.'

Li Wen was sure he had heard the voice before. Up close, he recognised the girl in glasses who had once given him the leaflet and the woman in the blue patterned headscarf. Of course! It was the weekend again. Nearby, he saw two men in hats and navy blue shirts and trousers and made a point of looking at the labels on their breast pockets. So there were traffic police in Beijing. It was at that moment that he realised there were law enforcement officers everywhere, all the time, in this huge city, circling like eagles over places he could not see, judging the best moment to land. The two men spoke with thick Beijing accents.

'We've had reports about you, and we've seen you giving out leaflets. We'd like you to come with us. Nothing to worry about.'

Li Wen could not bring himself to take a second look at the girl and the woman. All officers of the law scared the hell out of him. He was suddenly afraid that the two men were about to vault over the brand-new railings and arrest him, or that behind them a man in police uniform was lurking, waiting to launch an ambush. It was only as he walked away, head down and almost jogging (he would not run), that he realised that he had merged so well into the crowd that no one was interested in who he was. Back in his flat that evening, Li Wen retrieved the leaflet from the drawer he had stashed it in after retrieving it from the bin, carefully smoothed it out, and for the first time felt safe enough to give it a proper read from beginning to end. 'The Lord will come down to the oppressed and tell them that all suffering is a blessing.'

*

There had indeed been an old policeman in a navy-blue uniform lurking at the back of the crowd. Officer Wang had come looking for someone, and thought he had just spotted them. He tried to move forward to make sure, but the milling crowd got in his way. This station was always extremely busy. To the west was a demolition site, and to the east a new housing development. Their police station sat bang in the middle. This particular Officer Wang, from Miyun on the northeast outskirts of Beijing, was deputy station chief. Before the Beijing Olympics, he had been busy arresting people for drinking and fighting, and after the Olympics, when there was a boom in construction projects, he had fought constant battles with residents whose houses were up for demolition. In time, new communities, the sort that the young and affluent dreamed of, were built, and gradually his station had become a forgotten backwater. His juniors dealt with the minor cases, and any major cases were passed on to his superiors.

Officer Wang had grown old at the police station. His promotion to deputy station chief came to him through seniority, rather than any special talents (of which he had none), but he did become ever more proficient at cooking hongshao braised pork. He needed this skill because his old lady taught at Langfang Normal University between Beijing and Tianjin and only came home once a week. Officer Wang needed to make sure his daughter got a proper dinner, so he learned a few dishes he could rustle up without much difficulty. Last year, the girl had been offered a place at a top university (as good as Peking Uni) in Shanghai, and when her father took her to the airport, he had made sure to press a box of hongshao pork into her hands so that she would not be homesick.

His daughter refused point blank to take the offering. She said that carrying food onto the plane was much too embarrassing, and besides, the reason she was going south to study was to get away from home.

So this year, Officer Wang taught himself to play *League of Kings*. There were five officers at the police station, including himself and the station chief, and sometimes a couple of trainee officers fresh out of college. In the corner of the duty office there was a TV left over from the Olympics (the designer of that particular brand had gone into hiding in the US the year before), but no one watched it any more, except occasionally when the chief got them to watch a football match with him. They'd agree out of kindness, but when the match was over, the chief would be left sitting there holding a cup of instant noodles that he hadn't had time to add water to. Eventually, even the chief taught himself to use an iPad, and found stuff to entertain him and to get him through the night shifts, though he could never remember the next day what he had watched. As for Officer Wang, his fierce battles in *League of Kings* ended up frying his mobile phone, so he went back to his iPad and used it to watch replays to get him through the night.

At his age, less than six months away from retirement, most men were either coasting along or going through painful divorces. Only Officer Wang still had ambitions to beat old age and achieve something before it was too late.

At first, he was curious to see how GodSlayer would make use of the new hero in *League of Kings*. GodSlayer didn't say much, but he had all the right moves, and Officer Wang was learning a lot from him. He was perfectly happy to learn from youngsters like that. His only fear was that the youngster might one day turn into an old codger like him. Today, he turned off his phone halfway through the game and got a bottle of Beijing Beer from the boxes he kept stacked in the kitchen. He loved drinking beer, and this was the only brand he respected. An old guy like him could only drink half a bottle of beer during the day before he got uncomfortably bloated. *I'm a stupid old git*, he thought to himself.

Before joining the police, Officer Wang had been fascinated by criminal psychology and used to devour the police procedurals he could borrow from the library of the university where his wife worked. He imagined himself having a career like the hardworking detectives in Seichō Matsumoto's novels; he knew all about concepts like the Oedipus complex, the Antigone complex and Stockholm syndrome, one of which always seemed to tie in neatly with every fictional death in Matsumoto's work. Yet, as he was to find out, in the real world more than half of all murders were either random acts of violence or accidents, or at least such was the official verdict.

'I could try looking somewhere else, but I just have this feeling that this is the right area,' Officer Wang muttered to himself. He was on his own – he had no reason to involve the chengguan in the search. In any case, they were busy catching the church leafleters. In Officer Wang's experience, no matter what the young did when they arrived in Beijing, they'd end up passing through this station.

*

Suwei was the first of the kids to speak to Li Wen when he arrived on the estate. The others saw Li Wen just as one more activity that their mothers were pushing them into, whether he was listening to them recite English or putting them through those mysterious fitness exercises. They didn't differentiate between adults; to a child's mind, grown-ups represented a force they didn't understand, one that kept driving them forward.

In the pitch dark, Suwei sat with his back to Li Wen. Beijing was not a humid city, but right then, all the moisture in the room seemed to have coalesced into invisible crystals, and the smell churned out multiple memories for Li Wen. There was something very familiar, even nostalgic, about it. It transported him back to a house run by women, redolent with women's sweat, a smell that underscored the male animal's inadequacy and subordinate status. There was something else too, something that anyone who encroached on Suwei's world would immediately recognise: there was never any ventilation or natural light here, so that the water vapour had turned from air to water and back again countless times.

'Hello, I'm Li Wen. I'm your new teacher.'

Suwei still refused to turn around. Li Wen was wondering whether to repeat what he had just said when he saw a flash of light – blinding in the pitch dark – coming from Suwei's screen, a PS2 games console he had once been very familiar with. The screen was slim-line and so big it seemed to proclaim that today's fast-moving technology had ambitions to create a parallel universe the same size as the real one. But the black games console that sat beneath it was an old gent, a refined oriental version of Rip Van Winkle complete with imperial queue. Hardly anyone played these games nowadays – everyone preferred online games where all you needed was to repeat simple logic and then extend this logic to increasingly complex, interconnected worlds. But here the connection between the game device and the screen was a dead zone; there would be a definitive ending, like a novel. There was no need for humans to communicate, the souls in the game understood each other without a word being said.

It occurred to Li Wen that he believed in souls in games, otherwise he would not have named his character in *The Sims* 'Li Wen'. The boy in front of him, whose face he had not yet seen, sat in the only light corner in this dark cave of a room. He hunched his back, but his shoulders stayed level; his limbs were long and slender, and he looked somehow like a warrior armed to the teeth, or a beetle with a hard carapace, perched motionless on the cold marble floor. He seemed to be summoning white ghosts to swoop down and launch a systematic attack on the red-eyed, red-bodied demon on the screen. Its head was covered in sinister antennae and its body glowed with the red light of death. It stared straight at Suwei like it wanted to carry him away.

As the white ghosts, under Suwei's command, delivered the killer blow, the demon burrowed down into the infinite earth, and a deep voice roared (in English) through the stereo, 'REVENGE!' Almost at the same moment, Suwei turned his head and said to Li Wen, 'This is Diablo, the devil that can never be killed.'

Li Wen had begun to wonder whether the light in Suwei's eyes was a sign of the aloofness that his mother Mrs Luo had talked about downstairs, or a kind of absolute purity that he had never seen before. The lines between the two were easily blurred, as they could both verge on frenzy.

'I think he's your friend,' said Li Wen.

Suwei shot him a sidelong glance and said, 'You're not my new teacher. We've never had a teacher in our house, only the doctor. Mum says we only need the doctor.'

As Li Wen was to find out, that was practically the longest statement Suwei would ever make to him. Like an old man who knew he was reaching the end of his life, Suwei eked out his breaths and the words he spoke with precision, usually indicating his answer with a nod or a shake of his head or, more often than not, no reaction at all, although he always kept his eyes open, even when he was in Diablo's world of darkness.

Actually, Li Wen didn't need to teach Suwei anything, Mrs Luo had explained. All she wanted him to do was stop him sitting in front of that huge screen all day. She was worried it would ruin his eyesight. Li Wen understood her words to mean that his sole task was to keep Suwei from harm. So he bought him some books from an online bookshop, all classics. That took very little effort, as sophisticated algorithms gave you intelligent recommendations and put the whole lot in your basket. To the classics he added some books in English, mostly fiction. After all, his diploma said he had majored in English and he didn't want to be found wanting. No poetry, which always contained a lot of words he didn't know and didn't want to bother looking up. However, as he was to discover when he read these books to Suwei, no matter what they were, Chinese or English, crime novels or stream-of-consciousness, horror stories or historical sagas, Suwei always had the same expression on his face: he kept his head bent and seemed to be listening intently, yet his body seemed oddly disassociated. As Li Wen read on and on, he sometimes paused, and his voice was the only sound to echo through the deserted house. It actually sounded like someone else's voice.

Every hour and a half during their lessons, Li Wen would make Suwei get up and move around, shake his shoulders or stretch his legs, and every afternoon he gave him half an hour of exercise – press-ups, jumping on the spot and so on – designed to stimulate the blood flow from the soles of his feet upwards. However, they did not seem to stimulate Suwei. Li Wen figured that he must be a natural dancer because his muscles were so flexible and he could stretch his legs out straight with no effort at all. He saw in Suwei none of the stubbornness of an athlete, but rather the detachment of a trained dancer. Body language was often more reliable than words, a truth that Li Wen had already learned in his brief career as a private tutor. Mrs Luo had instructed him never to mention ballet, although it seemed to him that Suwei had immediately read everything from his expression. He knew the mothers in these villas. They did not waste words; if you poked your nose in when they asked you to be quiet, they would attack and destroy you.

It was as if time had stopped in this house. Li Wen carefully carried out Mrs Luo's instructions, including what she had told him about the basement. In fact, during the daytime, when she and Mrs Zhao were out and it was only Li Wen and Suwei, he felt as if they were trapped, as if they were stopping each other from growing. Li Wen did not mind this feeling at all. The slow stagnation made him feel totally relaxed, and Suwei gave him a strange sense of security, as if the boy's presence formed a protective barrier between him and those terrifying eyes that hid in the shadows. Li Wen sometimes napped on the living room sofa in the afternoon when he got sleepy, although the white leather stuck to his skin and squeaked when he moved. Suwei never took a nap, nor did he sleep in the first half of the night, as Li Wen was to learn from the portable recorder, which was always on till two o'clock in the morning.

Suwei paid no attention to the rest of the house, which was too big, in Li Wen's opinion. Mrs Luo said they could use the AV system on the first floor to show films, but when Li Wen mentioned this to Suwei, the boy just frowned. One evening, Mrs Luo took him up to see a film called *Pulp Fiction*, which she said had been recommended by a friend who was an actor. By the time they were three-quarters of the way through the film, Li Wen almost felt like the man of the house as he sat next to her on the soft sofa, his glass of single malt scotch on the rocks sitting on the glass coffee table nearby.

Surely, Suwei must have felt he had been betrayed, he thought. The boy must have smelled the countless young men who had gone into that AV room with his mother and then into her bedroom, and now he was one of them. Dr Zhong had described Suwei as akin to a small boat setting off to float downriver in willed solitude. The boat could only go with the flow, any attempt to alter its course was futile; safety lay in the river. 'He has refused to grow up,' was the doctor's verdict. Li Wen saw himself in a small boat too, struggling to navigate through the river gorge. In his case, no matter whether he rowed fast or slow, the boat went with the current, floating into the void. Unbeknownst to him, the relationship between Suwei and Diablo was being mapped onto him and Suwei, enveloping him completely and inescapably.

To begin with, he had found it hard to understand how Suwei never had any problem finding his way in the dark world around him, especially when he heard Suwei's voice coming from the black box saying that he couldn't actually see what was on the screen, none of the virtual flowers and grass, or the huge buildings looming up in the middle. Yet it was always Li Wen who got lost. Every time Li Wen played as the Priest of Light, he got stuck in the reeking swamp of the Maze (when two people played the game, the other could not move forward alone, so Suwei always had to come back and get him out). To Li Wen's surprise, Suwei's Necromancer actually said, 'I don't want to be alone,' and grabbed his hand. The pair of them stood looking at each other by the boiling lava for a long time, or maybe it was just a minute, neither of them moving. It seemed to Li Wen as he looked at Suwei that the boy was staring at the screen so intently that he might have become one with the lava. This time, Li Wen's Priest of Light charged forward and met the snake-haired demoness who could turn people into stone, with Suwei's Necromancer hot on his heels. He realised that Suwei had been talking to him the whole time. He didn't need to see what was on the screen, he just knew where he was.

*

If he had never known the shape the truth could take, perhaps he would have embraced Mrs Luo's version of it without hesitation. But narrative is often unreliable, especially when the narrator tells a story face to face. The power of the spoken word is far less persuasive than that of a story that has been recorded.

Li Wen had a sense of foreboding. He knew that the version this woman would tell him would not match what he knew, and would not lessen the sense of guilt he felt towards Suwei. What really panicked him was that the guilt came not from sleeping with Suwei's mother, but from the fact that he had found Suwei's story. Perhaps Suwei had deliberately baited the trap, putting the recorder where he was sure to find it, and he had rushed onwards like a lemming and plunged into the abyss, through to its multiple layers of secrets.

Every time the manikin in his ear jumped out and said to him, 'You're done for!', he saw hope and despair intermingling, bewitching him, jolting him out of his stagnation and making him take another step forward. Perhaps it was Suwei and his mother who gave him the illusion that he, like Suwei, was absolutely safe here. Li Wen decided to use Suwei's secret as a threat. This was his last chance to go completely under the radar and stay put.

Fuck it, I'm as despicable as she is, he thought to himself. That day, he had downed two cans of Coke one after the other, the only two he could find in Mrs Luo's fridge. She and Suwei didn't normally drink it, probably because people of their social class tended to avoid consuming anything that made you burp or fart. Li Wen hadn't told Mrs Luo that he used to drink Coke with brandy. He knew her sort never mixed their drinks – they felt it was vulgar. He was careful to present himself to Mrs Luo as an adult who knew his drinks. He had not forgotten that look of smug disdain she once gave him. When he started going to Mrs Luo's bedroom, Li Wen found that he had become the house wraith. It was only when he stayed the night that he realised it was Mrs Zhao who helped Suwei bathe once a week, and that Mrs Luo never went into Suwei's room when her son was asleep or getting dressed. If she did go there, she knocked three times, something Li Wen used to long for his mother to do, but which he now found unbearably cold.

No, not cold. Cowardly.

The way Mrs Luo told it, Suwei had bloomed and then withered like a day lily.

'You know how cruel girls can be!' A tremor ran through Mrs Luo. Then she stopped herself immediately and, rather than gazing into the distance, fixed her eyes on the completely dust-free floor.

'They copied his movements and laughed at him. They said boys shouldn't swivel their hips like girls do.'

If he hadn't heard the voice on the recorder, he could almost have believed everything she said, or at least part of it, because at that moment she was pure mother. The fishy smell that clung to her was gone, and there was only the aroma he had been familiar with long, long ago.

Suwei had been the only boy in the ballet class, Mrs Luo told him. None of the neighbours were going to send their sons to ballet; they wanted them to learn golf or horse-riding. But Suwei was born with an instinctive grasp of the body's rhythms. His limbs were as supple and straight as a girl's, and he loved to show them off. As their ballet teacher said, while the others were figuring out what dance was, Suwei embraced and became one with it. Mr Pan said he had not seen such a talented male dancer for many a long year. Most of the boys in his class who went professional did so because it was an easy route to a steady job and a decent salary – there was always a shortage of male dancers. He knew that the only way he could hope to produce the perfect male ballet dancer was this combination of Suwei's purity and his mother's determination. Mr Pan had repeatedly tried to persuade Mrs Luo to move him to their ballet school as a full-time trainee dancer, but she refused. He was at a top high school and she wanted him to stay there for two more years and then leave without going to senior high school. She had a plan: when he was old enough, she would send him to a ballet school in the UK to study dance. In her imagination, he was going to become China's Nureyev. She conveniently forgot that the more elite the troupe and the younger the students were, the more shut-off their world was. A boy like Suwei faced constant ridicule; it was a gruelling battle. The local boys called him 'sissy' behind his back and jeered at the way he walked with light, prancing steps and his head held high. They said he wore girls' tights when he danced. The girls, too, snickered and insulted him. They could not see the beauty that transcended gender.

'I had to protect him,' Mrs Luo went on. 'He had shut himself off. He was growing up in a vacuum. Imagine how hard it must have been for him to stop dancing.'

Li Wen was tempted to believe everything she said. He could no longer disentangle truth from fiction. When she said she wanted to protect Suwei, he was reminded of the way his mother's hands had clawed the air before she died. Mrs Luo's voice and his mother's gestures had both come from deep inside them. Mothers like these could not bear it when their children were ostracised, but their attempts to protect them simply hastened their descent into social exclusion. Still, as long as the mothers lived, their children could cling to them and stay alive too. Li Wen focused an almost despairing gaze on her and said, 'None of that is true.'

After a long pause, Mrs Luo looked up at him and stared back. It was a tactic she had learned long ago from Mr Chen, designed to probe into whether her opponent was telling the truth, and also in some small way to intimidate them. She did it now not because she believed that Li Wen knew the real reason why Suwei had turned out like this, but because right now she wanted to believe that Li Wen was all-seeing. Once she had told him her version of Suwei's story, she felt as if a weight had fallen from her shoulders, even though it was peppered with lies. All these years, no one had been willing to find the truth, not Dr Pei or Dr Zhong, not even Mr Chen. They only saw objective pathological causes. She was aware that since he became her personal secretary, Li Wen had felt oddly guilty about Suwei. She had seen it the day that Li Wen had met Mrs Zhao coming out of the bathroom. Though mostly what she saw in Li Wen's eyes gave her the mysterious feeling that Li Wen had merged himself and Suwei into one being.

'What you're saying isn't true,' Li Wen repeated. 'Suwei is damaged, but in my dreams, I want to turn into him. You didn't know that, did you?'

'He's got problems with his eyes.'

Mrs Luo suddenly shifted her gaze to one side, but there was only a metal vase there. Then she went on slowly, fatalistically, 'Can you tell me your story?'

In layer after layer of buried memories, Mrs Luo's shame and despair scalded her like the tongues of flame around a demon. Sometimes, she even suspected that she was being haunted by the giant red demon king in Suwei's game, the one that they kept killing and resurrecting. Li Wen was edging closer to her secret, but her instincts told her that this young man might have something in common with her: they were both trying to protect Suwei out of inertia rather than high moral principles.

'Yes, I can do that.'

In fact, Li Wen had decided not to tell the truth (his own story and Suwei's story as he knew it) to Mrs Luo. It was enough to know. Contempt. That was what he felt for himself, more strongly now than at any time since he set fire to Big Brother Chen's quilt.

14

THE fiery beams of light brought new life, Mrs Luo knew. After Mr Chen disappeared, she had been recommended the photorejuvenation therapy by the ladies in the social club, whose skin always glowed like light bulbs. She had been having it for so many years that she couldn't remember the exact name of the procedure – IPL something. It was applied by a machine mounted on a trolley, rather like a mechanical street cleaner. Every time it boomed, her face burned like the sun's core and she had to cover her eyes with a soft blindfold to protect them from the light. But it was worth it: that light gave her a new lease on life. She came in for the treatment every three months, and every time, without fail, the soft-spoken Dr Wen would repeat as she put the blindfold on her eyes, 'Don't touch the blindfold. The light rays could blind you.'

Dr Wen also used to hand her a green silicone stress ball which fit in the palm of her hand, telling her to squeeze it if she found the procedure getting too much for her. This toy worked remarkably well at relieving any tension. She lay on the comfortable hospital bed in a cubicle decorated like a ladies' tea room and squeezed it in her hand when the pain was bad. The ball reminded her of the dogs that people kept on their estate; they always had the same green ball in their mouths or paws. It seemed like humans and dogs dealt with distress and desire in the same way: dogs used a ball to appease their hunger, humans used one to dull their feelings. Anyway, she only had to put up with the procedure for half an hour, and after that she emerged with a bright, glowing face. Sometimes she even forgot how old she was, but what did it matter anyway? Time flowed downstream like water, but the clock could always be turned back.

It was two days since Li Wen had returned the car keys to her and she had a premonition, of the kind she had had after Mr Chen disappeared. She still had a month to go before her next procedure was due, but she called Dr Wen all the same to see if she could fit her in. The doctor told her to come on in. She need not worry, bringing it forward once in a while would not speed up – or slow down – the ageing process. Reversing the effects of time was a lifelong treatment.

After she was finished, Dr Wen gave her an ice pack that fit like a mask and instructed her to ice her face at home for two days. It might have been retribution for getting the treatment a month early, but Mrs Luo felt like her face was on fire. Suwei was behaving oddly today. He came down to say hello to her, but there was no flicker of a reaction when he saw the ice pack mask. She was unsure how much her son knew of her secrets and her life. When Suwei was doing ballet, she had told him that his dad was working overseas and would be home soon. Then she told him that he was 'far gone'. She felt that this was the right phrase to use in relation to his father, because it encompassed silence, the unknown, pessimism and possibility, as well as disappearance.

But this time she hesitated, wondering if she should use the same words to describe Li Wen. At least she and Chen had come to an understanding, whereas she didn't think she and Li Wen had struck any kind of mutually beneficial deal. Until now, she hadn't been sure how much Li Wen knew about Suwei. One of the many important things she had learned was that if someone held their knowledge of your secret over you and demanded payback, that secret was at least safe with them. The greediest people were often not very scary. The day when Li Wen came over for the last time and spilled out that rather muddled story, it reminded her of when she first came to Beijing. She and her friends used to hide their ID cards right at the bottom of their bags as a way of cutting themselves off from any memory of their places of origin. But try as they might, the street names had a habit of dragging them back down memory lane and trapping them there amid the mud-filled potholes. In her mind's eye, she saw Li Wen standing there stark naked in the shadows, out of the glare of the sun rays leaking through the window, telling her he wanted to become Suwei because he had nowhere else to go. Mrs Luo saw herself and Li Wen as fellow travellers: Li Wen clearly wanted to burrow inside the perfect eggshell she had created for Suwei, because he knew that this was the only way to combat his terror of the unknown.

She also remembered that on that same day, an old policeman had dropped by to ask her about a kid who had had an accident on the estate. She had told the policeman that she had never seen the boy. The old man had that earnest look on his face, typical of people of his generation. They stared into your eyes, no matter how routine their task or how unrewarding. She remembered too that the policeman had asked Li Wen a question, and Li Wen had answered almost inaudibly, 'I don't know,' and might even have flinched, though she was not sure if she had imagined that. Mrs Luo had keen intuition. It put her on high alert, and she began to fear that beneath this young man's very ordinary appearance there lurked a kind of madness that could annihilate her son. She was so frightened that she even checked all the doors and windows again to make sure they were closed before nighttime.

As the evening and night dragged on, she lay on the sofa in the living room waiting for her face to cool down. Her reflection in the ceiling mirror looked like a different person. Meanwhile, she had plenty of time to think. She found herself in love with her own newly-rejuvenated skin, but full of loathing for teenage girls. They reminded her all too painfully that she too had once possessed youth that was more than skin-deep. She wondered why men could relive their youth with young girls, and could even find peace with them, while women vented their hatred on teenaged girls, as if this was the only way they could turn back the clock.

Before Mr Chen left, the management company had found them an eighteen-year-old, Xiaojuan, to do some work around the house. Although Mrs Luo's face had not yet been old enough to require the photorejuvenation therapy, she found herself resenting Xiaojuan's vitality. The girl's exuberant energy seemed to fall on them like a spell that trumpeted FERTILITY! loud and clear, as if she was a doe in heat. Mrs Luo was not the kind of person to fire her housekeeper for no reason at all. She was both more forbearing and more open-minded than folk who were born wealthy. Her patience was rewarded, and one sizzling afternoon Xiaojuan told her that she had just found out she was pregnant by her boyfriend, a hotel manager. She had decided to have an abortion. Mrs Luo had seen the boyfriend once, from an upstairs window, when he brought her home. *He doesn't love her. Look at the way he's touching her buttocks and not her hands*, she said to herself. Looking down at his head of slicked-back hair, she was sure that he wouldn't stay long with Xiaojuan. So that afternoon, she bundled the girl off to a nearby private clinic where she filled in all the forms and ticked the 'Pain Relief' box. Fifteen minutes in the waiting room and the nurse came to tell her that it was all done. She booked Xiaojuan in for a three-day stay and paid all the fees, including her travel fare back home (although admittedly, after a moment's hesitation, she got Mr Chen's secretary to buy her a hard sleeper ticket, not a soft sleeper).

By way of parting advice, Mrs Luo told the girl, 'Find yourself a good man to marry. Don't let anyone treat you like that again.'

The young girl thanked her through a flood of tears. 'My three days at the clinic were as good as a five-star hotel, I've never been anywhere like it. All that food and drink and people to wait on me!'

She went back home with the words 'Mrs Luo is a good woman' on her lips. But the next time Mrs Luo went looking for a housekeeper, she made sure to stipulate, 'Someone older, who's been married and already has children'.

It was easy enough to make a baby vanish, just like that. When Xiaojuan had her abortion, Mrs Luo didn't inspect any of the scans. Her stomach lurched at the thought that the poor infant might have been gotten rid of even before it had time to take shape.

And before Mrs Luo realised it, time had raced by, and now was now.

Mr Chen had been her first boyfriend, but she knew what men's physiological reactions were like. All the girls in the dance troupe learned that pretty quickly. When the male dancer lifted the female dancer, or when the female dancer did fouetté turns between their partner's hands, they felt 'it' growing and rubbing against them. They got used to it and were eventually indifferent to it. Their bodies were not their own, they were sacred vessels that embodied the dance. When Suwei was almost ten, Mrs Luo had stood watching him through the glass door at the back of the dance studio for a long time. The boy seemed born to dance. As yet he showed no signs of physical maturity, for which she was profoundly grateful. She had heard too many stories about teenage dance students being told they had no chance of becoming professionals. It didn't matter how hard you worked, if you got to puberty and developed hips that were slightly too wide or breasts that were a little too generous, no matter that this was a perfectly normal development in a healthy male or female, you had no future in ballet.

As Suwei's mother, Mrs Luo would have liked to keep him forever in that divine moment that was the cusp of adolescence. In her imagination, Suwei would never pass through his teenage years. Instead, he was destined for greatness as a dancer. But now all her dreams had ground to a halt and were wallowing in stagnation. Instead of new life, that stagnation had brought with it utter darkness. She imagined it as countless bats hiding in a silent cave, clumping together in terror and forming a huge black mass whenever the smallest gleam of light found its way in.

*

At the end of each week, what seemed to be a funeral procession passed silently through the swath of vacant land between the lawns. Clad in black jackets and white dress shirts, they had a stern, solemn air; the children followed behind the adults, cautiously measuring their pace. With every step, the American children seemed on the verge of tripping over their own long, pointed legs. 'There they go again, off to sing the praises of the Lord,' Mr Chen said to Mr Song, whom he called 'Old Song'. Old Song wasn't old at all – he looked about the same age as the fourth young man in the procession, counting from the back, maybe not quite a quarter of a century old. Mr Chen and Mr Song had been living in the hundred-square-metre Boston apartment for almost five years. Mr Song said he just couldn't get used to living in such a large apartment, he had the sense of unidentifiable particles flitting about chaotically in the deserted cavernous air, and all transparent substances raised his hackles. The longer he lived there, the more Mr Chen was soothed by a sense of ingrained comfort – often, he read one book in the sitting room while Mr Song read another in the kitchen, or vice versa. But still more often, Mr Chen stood at the window looking out, as he was doing now.

It had struck him that the best-attended churches were those in either rich neighbourhoods or racially mixed downmarket districts. Everyone was equal in the eyes of the Lord. The white people in the neighbourhood were friendly with him and Mr Song, because interacting with them was rarely necessary, and other than a clear separation between what was needed and unneeded, fixed distance was the main foundation of a stable friendship. Mr Chen admitted that one of the main reasons he had chosen this apartment was that, as the agent had pointed out, the majority of the residents were professors and researchers at nearby Harvard University. Outside the apartment, the white people called them Chris and Song. Some of them mangled the pronunciation of Mr Song's name, calling him Sam, and Mr Song called him Chris. Mr Chen had become so accustomed to this that he barely remembered his own name any more.

When Dr Pei rang Mr Chen, Mr Song was in the midst of recounting the details of a viral social media post as the final churchgoer was straggling past the window frame, clutching a bouquet of white flowers.

'Who would've thought it? 21 North Street, the next street over from ours. They say when they found her, she was still in her tutu.'

'Oh. Who would've thought it?' Mr Chen repeated as he stirred sugar into his coffee, but his shoulders were slightly hunched, an obvious sign of tension. Something Mr Song had said had made him recall a buried episode from his past.

'They say the kidnapper had a doctorate in anthropology from Harvard. Never met the man myself. According to the story, he struck everyone as the shy, sheepish type. No one ever expected this from him. But luckily, the girl is still alive. She went on beating a water pipe in the basement until somebody heard . . .' Mr Song continued, attempting an exhaustive account of this crime that had occurred on the very next street, but looking out from the apartment building, he could see that the children still occupied the communal lawn. They lifted their little faces to the sun, pinpricks of light coagulating on their eyelashes, utterly unaware that one among them, the disappeared girl, had faced the gates of heaven in a putrid black basement.

'Kids – they have a strange affinity for people who hurt them.'

Whipping milk into a froth with a small spoon, squinting to distinguish the tiny white soap-like bubbles, Mr Chen realised his vision was misting over. Eye problems ran in the family. His father had died blind in both eyes, his grandfather, too. He knew that one day he would die blind in both eyes, and so would Suwei. He went on, seeming to be talking to himself, 'Apparently, they're better at eavesdropping on children than we are.'

'Hey, at this time of day, that must be Dr Pei calling for you, right?'

Mr Song handed him the phone and went downstairs to take out the rubbish. Mr Song knew that, in addition to checking on the condition of Mr Chen's eyes, Dr Pei probably used these weekly calls to feed him bits of information about Mrs Luo and Suwei. On deciding to leave with Mr Chen, Mr Song had learned of the 'disappearance pact' between Mr Chen and Mrs Luo. He had in fact never met Mrs Luo, but had nonetheless in some way participated in their tale of disappearance, and so whenever Dr Pei rang, Mr Song kept his distance. Appropriate distance was the foundation of the trust that he and Mr Song had maintained for many years, a foundation built atop a crevice shot through with airholes.

When Mr Chen hung up the phone, Mr Song was just returning from taking out the rubbish.

'He says Suwei's eyes are acting up,' said Mr Chen.

Mr Song squinted for a very long time and managed to make out Mr Chen's expression. It wasn't helplessness, and it wasn't shock. He sensed Mr Chen had been waiting for this day, and he watched as a shroud of destiny descended over the other man's face.

'I'm going home and bringing Suwei back so they can have a look. Dr Pei thinks maybe there's a way to treat him here in America. He says it was playing games in the dark all day that did it. We have to get him over here.' Mr Chen's voice gradually grew softer as he spoke. Since Suwei was born, Mr Chen had known he would someday face this fate. He had known Suwei would one day leave his mother's side and enter a world of darkness, the bleak inheritance of all Chens.

'Go, then. Maybe it's just temporary eye strain. Surely they can help him here.'

Mr Song knew this was a lie. He believed that at least, rather than face a derelict, disastrous world at some incalculable moment in the future, Suwei would choose to burrow into the bottomless black holes in his eyes. He understood Suwei, because he had once been the same kind of boy. He had joined a special gifted class at the age of fourteen, imagining back then that time in the world rushed ceaselessly forward, and so he sealed his lips and stopped speaking to people, which in fact did partly solve the problem: when you refused to speak to others, they ceased invading your time. He went on this way until the day he met Mr Chen on the introduction of the laboratory supervisor, who explained that Mr Chen knew all the smartest people here and would surely prove useful to him in the future. What he didn't know was whether, at any point in the past, Mr Chen had glimpsed the workings of fate in the world that was invisible to the naked eye. In fact, he had spent a long time staring, becoming more and more convinced that the stories of microorganisms were much vaster and longer-lasting than human stories, even believing that just maybe, when humans observed microorganisms under infinite magnification, they observed us in return through infinite belittlement. Later, when he was with Mr Chen, Mr Song realised he had no actual interest in science, so he merely eavesdropped on gifted people, knowing clearly that what Mr Chen derived from him was an illusory youth like a flower reflected in water – for ten years now, they had slept together almost every night, but sleeping was really all they did. It had been a long time, and Mr Chen had never made a pass at him. Also, he believed that the essence of human communion was not sex, that was merely the clumsiest method of ensuring two people fell peacefully asleep. When Mr Chen moved out, Mrs Luo cursed him, calling him a 'stomach-churning queer'. They both knew the chemistry had been stamped out of their romance, and they saw in each other their past and future selves.

Mr Song recalled that, just before he left Beijing, Mr Chen took him to Fireworks, a nocturnal establishment secreted two storeys beneath the giant shopping centre. He had been to the shopping centre a few times before, bought some clothes and eaten some food, never suspecting that a recondite world of twinkling neon lurked beneath. Mr Chen led him across the dance floor, which was crowded with people who spasmed and flailed like overheated perpetual motion machines, and he watched many men and women shaking their heads and arses, seemingly unaware of the existence of tomorrow. When they reached the VIP area deep within the club – in Beijing, wherever Mr Chen went, he seemed to miraculously home in on some secret space from which common folk were excluded – the male receptionist with red polish on his fingernails swivelled his hips through the exit, and a pair of scantily clad young women sidled in. They wore tight silver and white miniskirts. The slightest movement bared their lithe bodies, and their eyes betrayed bleak fatigue. They ingratiated themselves into the gap between his seat and Mr Chen's, one followed by the next, and then began to wriggle, their short miniskirts shortening still further, hands groping for the warmth of any protrusion. Mr Chen and Mr Song both spent the entire evening enjoying private shows, and when the two young ladies at last departed, Mr Song snapped to his senses: he realised he had been given a glimpse through a peephole at the decadent predicament Mr Chen was in. 'Welcome to my world. Their imaginations are so barren that physiological stimulation is all they can see.' Mr Chen informed Mr Song that, as he certainly already realised, the night was a kind of parting ritual. Earlier that year, 'Old Song' had turned twenty.

*

Mrs Zhao took Mr Chen to the kitchen. A half-hour earlier, she had ridden the small lift to the underground car park and spun in redundant circles around the vacuous spaces marked with ringed numerals. Mrs Luo had told her only that she was to meet a 'Mr Chen', but her sense of smell, sharpened by many years of interacting with her female employer, told her that this 'Mr Chen' was the very Mr Chen who had disappeared years earlier. She watched as Dr Pei's car pulled in, saw the squat, middle-aged man in the driver's seat, brow rumpled like a mountain ridge, and her suspicions were confirmed. Mrs Zhao had always had the sense that in this family, Dr Pei was like the clasp at the end of a necklace, a metallic device that closed with a snap, fastening a string of disparate, slippery pearls. Face to face with Dr Pei, renewed respect filled everyone's eyes, even Mrs Luo's. Mrs Zhao had been a housekeeper in the gated community for a number of years and had worked under many women – some who lived with husbands, some who didn't; some who lived with children, some who didn't. She knew all rich people had a common failing: they disappeared at the slightest provocation, and every one of her employers in the gated community seemed to have been born with an innate disappearance reflex. These disappearances could mean they had killed themselves, committed crimes, gone bankrupt, gone into hiding, were pulling the wool over everyone's eyes, or nothing at all, and once the women were done crying, magnanimous monetary compensation often conveniently showered down from the heavens. Thus, a 'disappearance' was no longer an alarming nadir of desolation, but an everyday occurrence, and as long as they had some money, the people in this place were perfectly willing to live out their lives without complaint. She knew that all she had to do was keep control over her mouth and her eyes, saying nothing, hearing nothing, seeing nothing, and she just might be the only one in the home who didn't disappear without warning.

'Suwei is upstairs.'

Mrs Luo lifted a finger and pointed up, a signal for Mr Chen and Dr Pei to keep their voices down. It had been several years since she had seen Mr Chen, but he didn't seem like a stranger. His eyes were just as they had been back then, twinkling beneath a sylvan brow, and he still stood with the ramrod-straight bearing of a former soldier, gripping his right wrist with his left hand. His dangling right hand held a white paper sack. Experience told Mrs Luo that the plainer the package, the more valuable the item inside. She had spent a great length of time preparing, to hide her aged timidity from Mr Chen, digging deep into drawers, finally selecting a form-fitting black wool turtleneck that concealed the lines on her neck.

She glanced at Dr Pei, who held her gaze. She had known from the beginning that Mr Chen had planted Dr Pei to keep an eye on her. The entirety of the funding for the dental clinic came from Mr Chen, that had been part of the agreement from the start. For nearly ten years, back when she was Mrs Chen, she had called him 'Old Chen'. A guardianly, fatherly name, and the name that had given her the greatest comfort as she faced down a bewildering new life in the city with every pore in her body gaping. With Old Chen by her side, she discovered the city's friendliest, most flattering aspect, gyrating at great speeds and simultaneously spiralling down, until she lost the baby, lost Old Chen, and lost Suwei. And then, Old Chen became 'Mr Chen'. Maybe, over all those years, she had never really understood Old Chen – where his money came from, what his life was really like, his inner thoughts and feelings, his vision of the future.

Spinning in a centrifuge, her memories of Old Chen were soundproofed, snagged one after another on unexpected hitches or wedged into obscure crevices. Now, like Old Chen, she told other people she was an investor, and she always seemed to be vaguely grasping new mysteries – the annual profit from the snarling clinic with the contemporary façade wasn't worth even half the dividends from the stocks and bonds Old Chen had left when she agreed to let him go. For the rich, interpolating surface and substance and orchestrating charades were essential survival skills. Now, for instance, under her instructions, they were trying their best to keep quiet, forgetting that the purpose of Mr Chen's visit was to take Suwei to America and fix his eyes.

'I've been telling him all along that his dad disappeared.'

Mr Chen wordlessly dropped the paper sack he had been holding into a dining chair where no one was sitting.

Mrs Luo went on, 'I'm not sure whether he understands disappearance the same way we do.'

'But you have to tell him, let him prepare himself.'

Can his eyes even be fixed? Mrs Luo didn't actually ask the question out loud, but deep down, she believed it was safest for Suwei to stay the way he was. As long as he remained eternally stunted and paralysed, like the juvenile Suwei she had glimpsed through the classroom window, his suffering would never come to light. There was no need to speak the truth. Here in her home, the truth was not important, and on top of that, she would always be his mother.

'I don't want him to die in darkness, like his grandfather did.'

15

Mrs Luo and Mr Chen agreed that first of all, she would go upstairs alone, in hopes of softening the shock of Mr Chen's sudden reappearance. Dr Pei said he was going to fill up on petrol and might be gone a long time. Mr Chen couldn't find his way around Beijing any more, could no longer gauge how much petrol it would take to get from one side of the city to another. The roadways spiralled continually inward like intestines, neither lifting up nor dropping off. If you missed an exit, you wouldn't even think of going the rest of the way around on the same ring road. People were always coming up with intricate excuses to conceal the last lie they'd told, and it often happened that by the time one story crumbled to dust, the plot of the next was already thickening. Mr Chen pulled open the refrigerator door, rummaged around inside and found a bottle with some white wine left in it. To make it look like he was waiting, a drink was an indispensable accessory.

On getting out of the military, he'd had a combative thirst for alcohol. He seemed to be saying, 'Come at me, let's see who ends up emptied out.' A bottle of wine and a young man made outstanding sparring partners. He seemed to know that it hadn't been Mrs Luo who had left this half-bottle of chilled, flat white wine in the refrigerator. By the time he declared himself 'far gone', he had already tacitly consented to the invasion by the wine and the young men. In Boston, there had been so many things he couldn't remember. Destiny seemed to have turned a corner, and the difference in time zones walled off the past. Here and there belonged to utterly different dimensions, but now that he was back, there was nothing he couldn't recall, as if an invisible current electrified everything again.

Mrs Luo didn't like taking Suwei to Mr Chen's hometown. The year Mr Chen's father died, they had paid him a visit, and Suwei had come along. Mr Chen's hometown was in the north, but strangely, humidity seemed to descend upon the place in winter. She was forced to roast her clothes atop the radiator, as no amount of airing would dry them. They said that centuries ago, the city had flourished thanks to the silk trade, and many businessmen from the south had settled there. Mr Chen had always believed that these southerners had brought the damp with them. As time went into decline, the glory of the north evaporated, and if the construction workers hadn't accidentally excavated the grave of a northern general a year or two ago, the city's heritage would have been cleanly forgotten. He didn't visit often – his father lived in a retirement home for cadres, and though the city was small, he could never remember which street the retirement home was on. Time after time, young cab drivers reacted to the words 'cadres' retirement home' by flashing bewildered looks, as if the term had been stricken from the dictionary. Finally, he decided to simply text himself the address of the place, so that he could recite confidently to these young people, 'Number 12 North Xinhua Road'.

He remembered the first time Suwei had seen his grandfather. Not knowing what to call the old man, Suwei had stroked his shrivelled hand and tentatively said, 'Grandpa'. In Suwei's eyes, the old man before him was as big as the grandfatherly tree in their nursery teacher's stories, and seemed to exude the odour of decaying wood.

'Grandpa, what do you do every day?'

In fact, clutter covered almost every inch of the old man's room – Mr Chen never again saw so many wooden ships in one place. He always believed this was the only reason why his father remained

– to watch over the room. As long as he had his sight, he had been able to make model ships; now that his eyes had given out, he could only take the ships in his hands and caress them one by one. Each day he took inventory, confirming each ship was still there.

'I build ships.'

His father had spent his whole life around ships, and believed earnestly that he was contributing to his country by crafting ship parts. Some years ago, Mr Chen had been planning to bring his father to live with them in Beijing, but the old man always insisted that the state had given him a room in the cadres' retirement home, and he was set on doing what the motherland said, they could have Beijing with its hustle and bustle. Mr Chen constantly heard his mother complaining about his father. Back then, he was still young and had believed his mother was simply disgusted by the way his father buried his face in a bowl of noodles and hoovered them up in two or three brash slurps. It was only as a grown-up that he untangled his father's story.

As a boy, the phrase 'colour-blind' (he had learned this disconcerting term from his mother) scared him out of his wits. He barely heard anything but the word 'blind'. Sometimes, Mr Chen thought his father was too stubborn. He saw at some point that his father was taking longer and longer to build each ship, yet still continued repeatedly polishing every identical part, remaining as fixed in this routine as in his meal habits, inhaling the same egg and noodle soup day after day. His father said he was old now, and everything tasted about the same and felt about the same. It had always bothered Mr Chen that before his father lost his sight completely, there would someday be a single model ship he would fail to finish, and this ship now sat on the headboard of his father's bed, apart from the completed ones. The cast-off ship crouched awkwardly, bereft of mast and sail, exuding the same smell as his father. (Or perhaps it was his father who had absorbed the smell of the wooden ships after all this time.)

'But the ships have nowhere to sail to.' Suwei gripped the unfinished wooden ship, longing for it to come to life.

His father laughed, reached out and stroked the back of Suwei's head.

'The boy's got a dent in the back of his skull, a sign of luck.'

His father was not a lucky man. According to his mother, the reason his father hadn't been able to get work in Beijing was that the certificate he had obtained from city hall stated, 'Comrade Chen Weiguo suffers from colour-blindness.' Mr Chen recalled that he had asked his mother what colour-blindness was, trembling with dread, believing it must mean complete loss of sight. Every few days, he would fling himself before his father, fearing he had never been clearly seen. In fact, his mother never explained to him what colour-blindness was, not until she scrounged up a hundred thousand yuan to take him to Beijing on the overnight train. In the damp, poky, half-underground rented room, she grasped his hand and whinged for the whole evening that his father had no such affliction, someone had written those words to claim for themselves a bureaucratic post that was rightly his, and if he had sought out a certain official, pressed a piece of fruit into his hand and said the right things, there would have been hope, but his father's scruples had done him in. He saw recrimination and unbent determination in his mother's eyes, reading into that smothered, inwardly directed look a love he had never before seen. Mr Chen now had a clear view of every detail of his father's story. Like the wooden ships that filled the room, it proclaimed the message that death would win in the end.

Beginning with his father's father, every man in the family had suffered the same fate, dying in darkness. Without any warning, one day, they simply couldn't see. When his father complained that he had lost his sight, Mr Chen had a presentiment – his father wasn't long for the world. He had taken Mrs Luo and Suwei on this trip believing he could go at any time, and this could be their last chance to see him; also, he wanted to take his father to stay for a few days in the home they'd just bought in Beijing, though he understood that he would certainly be unwilling (and lacked the energy) to leave the tiny room at the cadres' retirement home. The room was barely bigger than the guards' booth at their new villa. Since boyhood, he had always remembered, 'Comrade Chen suffers from colour-blindness.' This had served as his entire motivation for studying hard to get into university in Beijing, and then for staying on in the city.

It was unfortunate, thought Mr Chen, that his mother had died just a few years after he went into business for himself. He and Mrs Luo weren't married yet back then, and he spent his days ricocheting frenetically through the city. When his mother came to Beijing, he could only take her on a tour of Tiananmen Square, then retreat to his rented room. He had nothing to his name. His mother had longed to hold a grandson in her arms, but to tell the truth, Mr Chen wanted a girl. He harboured a secret hope that a daughter could disrupt the Chen family legacy of blindness. Later, he bought a big, brand-new home, paying completely in cash, but by then his mother's vitality was rapidly flagging. She was so shrivelled they were all taken aback. In her last few months on earth, harassed by lung fatigue, she heard Mrs Luo was pregnant, but just a few days later, she slid into the next world, taking her hopes of holding a grandson with her. The doctor said she had choked on her own breath. Mr Chen still wasn't certain whether letting his mother die in a hospital in Beijing had been the right decision. That day, when his mother's eyes closed, she looked unexpectedly peaceful. The doctors and nurses at Union Medical College Hospital had done everything they could. They said her lungs were already completely dead, and all the air in the world was of no use to her any more.

A few months later, at the same hospital, Mrs Luo gave birth to a baby. It was a girl.

*

Countless days later, on a Monday, Mrs Luo finally regained her grip on the regular flow of time.

More than a week had passed without word from Li Wen, not even a phone call. The keys he had handed back still lay on the tea table in the sitting room. Each day, Mrs Zhao picked up the keys, wiped off the table, and put the keys back in their place. But time was no longer muddled and bleary. Before, she had had no idea how many days had passed due to extreme fatigue, and because time flowed in one direction only, abandoning her to the past. Now she remembered that she was supposed to wait for Dr Pei, who had promised to bring her a progress report.

She dreamed of Manman again – her waxy yellow body spinning continually in a giant metal box; curled up into a miniscule, naked ball, scarlet and scorching hot; eyes squeezed tightly shut, breathing evenly – Mrs Luo never clearly saw the girl's face, and she never told Suwei about this older sister who had died before he was born. She had survived for just nine days, and Mrs Luo wasn't sure whether she had ever really, truly existed in their world. Before Mrs Luo went into labour, she and Mr Chen had agreed that if the baby turned out to be a girl, her name would be Manman, because they wanted her to move through the world in a slow, leisurely way. The doctor who delivered the baby had said that dancers had open hips, easing the birthing process, but Manman seemed to resist coming into the world. No matter how forcefully Mrs Luo bore down, the baby just wouldn't come out, not until the pudgy nurse wrenched her open with a pair of forceps, baring the tip of a small head, and finally Manman slid out of her belly. Mrs Luo felt for the first time that she had been carved into bits and divvied up, and she watched as the same nurse shovelled Manman into a giant oven. When she came out again, she wasn't breathing. She lay limp in Mrs Luo's hands, light as a cloud.

In an instant of hopeless exhaustion, a new life came into the world, and Mrs Luo became a mother for the first time.

She and Mr Chen were in almost complete agreement from the beginning. They talked it over and signed the consent form to donate Manman's body to medical research, not out of any high-minded motive, but because the feng shui master they had hired to do a reading on the house said the baby had never become a person, and if they didn't get rid of the body, it would be bad luck for their next child. In matters of yin and yang, Mrs Luo trusted feng shui masters, convinced they could see more than she could. Or maybe she gleaned psychological comfort from spiritual self-deception. For a long time afterward, she forgot all about Manman, even in her dreams, until Suwei was born. Mrs Luo believed Manman was immersed in the warm enclosure of her subconscious, silently spying on them, ultimately switching places with Suwei. Each time Mrs Luo awoke, the dream remained tangible and terrifying, as if she could reach out and touch Manman, run her fingers along the gentle pleats of her wrinkled skin – newly-born babies were like elderly people on their deathbeds, their bodies softened and hollowed out, as if the instant they crossed the threshold to death, they sloughed off all the weight they had carried while alive. When Mrs Luo took younger men to bed, Manman stayed in hiding – she must be scared to be seen, thought Mrs Luo. When Manman was carved out of her, she was convinced she had caught a glimpse of limbs that were long and slender, just like hers, and it had occurred to her how pretty the baby would look curled up into a ball.

*

Mrs Luo didn't have a key to Li Wen's new flat. Intuition warned her continually that this young man could pose a threat. She knew that, for the rich, a home in Beijing was like a green silicon stress ball. She had seen too many of Mr Chen's friends use such tricks to evade potential interpersonal risks, since people respected you more when forced to forget about you, and on top of that, people who put up capital for housing were always rich, and rich people hated risk. Mrs Luo discovered only later that they in fact had no ability to adapt to change and shattered under pressure. During this period, Mrs Luo went out only two or three times, returning on each occasion to find Dr Pei waiting to deliver a report. Dr Pei said he had just bought a cutting-edge ultrasonic scaler, the only one of its kind in Beijing, it completely took the patients' pain away. Dr Pei had hesitated for a moment, then added that Mr Chen was coming to see Suwei. Maybe, across the ocean, there was a way to fix Suwei's eyes.

'Mum, there are holes in my eyes.'

In Mrs Luo's memory, since releasing that monster that spurted red tongues of flame into the darkness, Suwei had never again called her mum. After losing Manman, it turned out to be almost impossible for Mrs Luo to become pregnant again. Manman's brief life began and ended in early spring of 2000, a time when swirling chaotic emotions consumed the world, and everyone was saying the turn of the millennium meant they were on the cusp of a completely new time-space. No one had any idea what the future would bring. Mr Chen was always telling her it didn't matter, in spite of everything, they would eventually hold another beautiful baby in their arms. In the second half of the first year of the new millennium, Mr Chen installed a brand-new home theatre system for her, with surround sound, and the two of them watched many American science-fiction films. Mrs Luo was seized by the strange sensation that she had completely lost her innate physical faculties, and vine-like metallic tentacles, the kind often seen in sci-fi films, were sprouting continually from her belly and growing longer and longer, wrapping her up inside. She was convinced she had completely lost the physical ability to become a mother.

Before making the final decision, she and Mr Chen tried for a full five years. During this time, she became both sensitive and numb: lovemaking was reduced to a revolting rote procedure meant only for procreation. In her eyes, Mr Chen was no different than the stud animals on *Animal World*. They completed the task quickly and accurately, but never managed to produce new life. Mrs Luo believed staunchly that Mr Chen had gone impotent over these five years. She knew better than anyone, in fact, that what this man had lost was an interest in other people's bodies, female and male alike. Later, only she knew that she heaped such scorn on Mr Song because it was the only way to win back a bit of respect – it was much easier to admit that one man had been stolen by another man than to admit that her husband had gone impotent because of her.

What struck still greater dread into her was that the hormone pills she took made her blow up like a blimp. She panicked over this, more so than her sudden tearful breakdowns in the evenings. An accumulation of fat encircled her abdomen, and she imagined layer after layer of cloudy yellow oil bubbling beneath her skin. Worse, the oily folds of flesh on her belly made her think of Manman writhing in the oven-like incubator: her arms and legs were so little, and she was as limp as a Barbie doll. Mr Chen tried to console her, but there seemed to be no passion in his voice. Constantly repeating a scripted daily ritual, they had exhausted all their feelings and hopes for the future. It was as if only time itself recorded each passing day, while the two of them continually regressed; it was as if the future were an empty box suspended in the air, remaining eternally out of their reach.

Lifeless toy dolls with gaping eyes always made Mrs Luo think of Manman. She was grateful at least that Suwei didn't seem to know of Manman's existence. After Suwei was successfully conceived, there was no need for him to uncover any of her memories of Manman. She managed to convince herself that the feng shui master's advice had been effective. Suwei instinctively had no interest at all in any manmade toy. From the moment he was born, he was interested only in listening and appreciating, as if he had emerged into the world for the sole purpose of staring at it with wide-open eyes. Mrs Luo never made any record of the passage of time: she remembered that the first time she gone to extract her eggs, the doctor had explained to her that many women tracked the entire fertilisation cycle in a 'cultivation diary', and at the time, Mrs Luo was determined to absolutely never allow herself to keep such a record. Later, she repeated the mechanical steps of extraction, insemination, transplantation, cultivation and confirmation countless times. It was crucial not to miss a step, and to start again from the beginning on coming to completion: if it was determined during the first step that her eggs could not be implanted, then all the work up to the cultivation step would be a waste. Mr Chen only accompanied her the first time. People tended to think of both science and hospitals as temples, wrongly assuming that they could get whatever they wanted by lighting incense sticks and earnestly praying. But when the reality of science bared its cruel face, wishes were beaten into the depths of despair, wrecked by repeated rounds of data analysis. Knowing this deep down, she never asked Mr Chen to go with her again. She requested only that the young chauffeur who drove her to the clinic be dismissed from duty before the final day when the transplant succeeded.

It struck her sometimes as incomprehensible – by some opaque, mystical process, the sperm and eggs, stored in a sterile box, pierced by ice-cold syringes, ultimately either agreed or refused to combine, and when they did form new life, the infant itself seemed to belong to some utterly alien species. They simply weren't the same – when Manman was born, she knew the baby was her own flesh and blood; but with Suwei, she was never sure. He had taken so long to arrive, and more than his mother, she felt like an observer to the entire interminable, uncontrollable scientific process that at some point slammed to a halt in either failure or success. She tallied up the days, months, and years, counting in fortnightly intervals, until in the end she nearly forgot why she was coming and her entire motivation was reduced to extremely regulated, inertia-bound drudgery. She realised that pain struck men more hastily than women, so deep down, she didn't blame Mr Chen when the new baby was born and their marriage started to lose its shape and flavour. For years now, their viscous bodily fluids had sickened her, and when she reflected that this same stuff was about to be put into a sterile test tube and swished around, like a middle school science experiment, and it was from this that new life arose, she wondered if her lost eggs would end up like Manman: botched, destitute, living out a lost existence in her dreams.

The instant Suwei was deemed a success, Mrs Luo gingerly cradled her bulging abdomen, as if the seed of the entire world was inside. She was determined to give this child all the most beautiful things in the world – or so she said to herself then.

16

Like Mr Song, Mrs Luo barely made a sound when she walked. Mr Chen only knew she was near when the fruity scent of her drifted in, carrying with it a strange sour undertone. But all fruit begins to rot sooner or later, and true to form, she too had begun growing old. Suwei followed behind Mrs Luo – while he was away, the boy had grown taller than both Mrs Luo and himself. He now had long, lanky limbs, but the thing that hadn't changed was that his chin was still lifted a little in the air, as if to say he wasn't curious about anything and nothing in the world could harm him. Suwei's eyes stared directly at him, flashing with an impenetrable, inscrutable glare. As far as he could see, there were no holes in the boy's bright, piercing eyes. Mr Chen had no way to know whether Suwei had recognised him, or even seen him. He remembered the look in his father's eyes as he lay dying, a bleak clouded sheen, as if his eyeballs were wrapped in a shroud of grey muslin. On this screen, his father watched visions of almost feral joy, and in the end had been unable to break free from things he couldn't see. He still recalled the tear-like secretions mingled with pale yellow eye gum which had streamed from the corner of his father's right eye, and the fear of losing his sight before declining into old age struck him for the first time.

Mrs Luo pulled out a chair for Suwei, and the three of them sat down at the marble dining table Mrs Zhao had polished earlier that morning until it glistened in the light. Mr Chen propped his elbows on the table, then dropped his arms back by his sides. He didn't like things made of stone – gleaming stone material seemed like something the previous century's nouveau riche would choose. He had extracted Mrs Luo from behind the rigid iron gate of the Beijing dance troupe and sat her down at many a dinner table beside monied socialites. He remembered dancers and troupe leaders lurking determinedly on the sidelines of their business negotiations. He had definitely been in love with Mrs Luo's forward-driving vitality, believing in the illusion that this woman could break the family's bizarre, longstanding lineage of sudden blindness and stunted growth. In their family, his mother stood half a head taller than his father, but seemed even taller because she was always standing (she loved wearing heels), and his father was always squatting, fidgeting with a model ship or some part that had broken in the factory.

He still wasn't sure whether his consistently shrewd mother had made the right choice for him, or if the image of his cowardly father, seen through his mother's eyes, had watched silently as he swaggered into disaster. He was also unsure whether he had truly made a success of himself. When he went to the sales office in the gated community to pay, he seemed to see images of himself reflected in countless mirrors – when he sat down among the other men, all waiting for the same thing, no one could tell any more who was who, nobody had any identifying features – they weren't all that young or all that old, had middling physiques and looks of fatigue and exhaustion in their left eyes, while their right eyes were filled with unconcealable pride; at their sides sat beautiful women, as resplendent as flames that threatened to come leaping out at any time. Strangely, after paying his money and securing his apartment, he never again saw, anywhere in the compound (which was so big it seemed to have no borders), any of these men who looked just like him. Beneath the small, dilapidated company housing building, unfamiliar men seemed to be drawn together by a collectivising power, making fast friends among the rusting communal exercise equipment, smoking up four packs of cigarettes, guzzling ten bottles of liquor, and ending up devoted to one another ever after, and this is how he got into the business he was in.

Behind his father's back, his mother had gone around gathering money from friends and family until she had scrounged up a hundred thousand yuan, which he had used to start his financial consulting business. At the time, his mother, like any other person, had absolutely no idea what finance or consulting were, knowing only that all of a sudden, a large number of people they didn't recognise were driving around in imported cars and moving into luxury homes. He was hesitating, thinking of asking his mother for yet more money, when he saw tongues of flame shooting from her eyes, flashing out to singe his father who, like the 'damn fool' he was, had failed to seize the chance to move to Beijing, and he saw also in those eyes an innate feminine spirit of adventure.

'Mummy's on your side! Together we will sprint into the jaws of victory!'

Mr Chen still had no idea how many people his mother had pestered to rustle up the funds, how she had managed to piece together a bank account balance big enough to send him to Beijing in just a week, but she had. He suspected his father had known from the beginning, had even had a vision of his future fortune, as well as the premature death of his first granddaughter. From the day he began doggedly imploring his father to come to Beijing too, he had become even more reticent, submerging himself in the world of model ships.

'In our family, daughters die young, and our wives are too ferocious for our own good,' his father had said to him as he lay dying.

When his business first turned a profit, money was still money. By the second time, the twentieth time, and the two hundredth time, bank deposits were like glistening crystals imbedded in the limitless night sky, eternally unreachable, transforming into strings of numbers when hauled back to earth. Once, he heard Mrs Luo telling the newborn Suwei a story. The story went like this:

A long time ago, there lived a poor, elderly man and woman. One day, a monk came looking for lodging, carrying a hefty cloth sack, and they served the monk the only food they had, a stew of radishes and rice, and the monk gave the sack to the old man and woman, telling them the riches inside would never run out. The first time, the old man and woman took out just enough for a simple meal, but later they grew greedier, taking enough for a sumptuous banquet, enough for a plush bed, and finally enough for a house. They took more and more, until they had everything they had ever wanted, but they found themselves wanting more than they had ever wanted before. Wouldn't it be wonderful, they thought, to fill the house with riches? And so they took and took, until the stack of riches grazed the ceiling, and they forgot to eat and they forgot to sleep. Much later, the monk returned to find the old couple dead, crushed flat beneath their riches, wearing sweetly satisfied smiles.

He couldn't be sure whether the sleeping Suwei heard the story, but he thought he saw the boy's small, soft lips making subtle movements. In any case, when the story ended, Mr Chen got the sense that he was that elderly couple. At first, he too trembled with fear, not knowing how a graduate of a military school with a degree in foreign languages was supposed to transform himself into a financial consultant. Later, like all Beijingers who hoisted themselves up by other people's bootstraps in the late 1990s, the scales fell from his eyes, and he realised riches welled up effortlessly from gaps in time and information. Making money seemed a limitlessly profound mystery as well as a sordid affair where nothing was secret. Any disparity in time or information was an opportunity to make profit – back then, they called it 'snatching opportunities'. Only later, on learning the principles of economics from the intellectuals, he realised what he was doing was 'investing'. He was the type of person who loved being around doctors and professors, sensing that from them he could glean the secrets of life. He loved listening as they stripped away the secrets of how to live and how to tell stories, the twin lifelines of doctors and professors. He didn't enjoy having friends over to his place.

In the new millennium, many 'old farts' of his generation were swallowed up by shadows. They called such people 'far gone'. They slunk into the distance until every trace of them vanished.

All profitable activities carried risk. To make money, you had to lay your own life on the table as a bargaining chip. Take pearl divers, for example, or Himalayan honey hunters. Suwei eyed him studiously. In fact, Suwei's gaze had hardly wavered since landing on him, but he detected no trace of doubt in those eyes; Mrs Luo, meanwhile, seemed lost in thought, at a loss as to when to open her mouth or what to say when she did. Mr Chen wanted to face Suwei in a completely sincere way, hoping that in Suwei's eyes, he didn't look as if he had just stepped out of a Hollywood movie, futuristic laser beams boring a giant hole into his body; but his hand instinctively sought out the white sack he was carrying, containing the two jars of Himalayan honey Dr Pei had given him, explaining that it was the most expensive honey in the world. He knew he must seem unfamiliar to Suwei. He had been repeatedly rehearsing this act almost every day since even before his 'disappearance'. Suitable presents in tow, he would burst onto the scene and puncture the vacuum of unspeakable silence between them. The presents had to be sufficiently extravagant, displaying both material wealth and unconventional taste, and they had to form a natural part of his social play acting. For people who made money with money, it was best to make friends with everybody. Only then would people open their eyes to the brilliance he cast on the curtain, willingly take the stage and play the role of the clown, bouncy, vivacious, and utterly phoney. Even in his son's presence, it was important to stay in character. After many aimless years spent 'far gone', he had finally reappeared before his son, taking the form of a clown.

'It's honey. Mr Gong's company makes it. It's pretty good, apparently.'

'Big Boss Gong, the one who was obsessed with sailboats?' Mrs Luo had grown accustomed to sorting those friends of Mr Chen whom she had met into groups by their hobbies. As far as she was concerned, they were all in the same business, and only their hobbies distinguished one from the next.

'The very one. Dr Pei says he's been in the health food business for the past few years.' Mr Chen wanted to linger on this topic. In fact, he hadn't seen Mr Gong in years. When Mr Gong and the others walked away, they had taken with them the previous century's hubbub and tumult, leaving only a strip-mined no man's land in the space that separated them from one another. As far as he could remember, Mr Gong had always had many different hobbies: before sailboats, it had been golf; before golf, tennis; before tennis, bridge. Mr Gong had goaded him to join the golf team, and he had in fact gone along on several occasions, but quickly discovered he was a hopeless ignoramus at golf. Mr Gong found him a coach, a member of the Chinese national team. He learned that angles were everything, including the angle of one's protruding arse, extended arm, and swinging club. A pair of binoculars dangled from the coach's neck; it was important to peer slyly into the distance at a precise angle too. In the end, he just didn't like this slavishly imitative, pernickety sport. He lacked that innate thirst for victory.

What he *did* enjoy was chatting with the doctor and the professors who were also in the golf club, the philosophy professor especially. In fact, he was completely unfamiliar with many of the names they casually dropped into conversations, but this unfamiliarity itself exuded inexpressible wonder, and he liked to listen as they rattled off names like Foucault and Derrida, and from time to time prostrated themselves at the altar of Kant and Hegel. The jaggedly astringent Chinese translations of these names tumbled awkwardly from the tongue, but like guavas and unripe papayas, with the astringency stripped out, only simpering sweetness would have remained.

Mr Chen rarely said a word around these intellectuals. It gave him greater pleasure to entertain them, spending his money taking them to the best places. Finally, he simply began booking a suite in a hotel where, rather than sleeping, they would eat and drink all day and all night. Mr Chen would sometimes glance at them and think to himself that someday, Suwei could be like them, gorgeous languages spilling from his mouth. Surely, Suwei would accumulate a large fortune and donate it all to build China's largest library.

From the first day Mrs Luo sent Suwei away to ballet academy, maybe even before that, Mr Chen was buried alive by desolation. He once heard the intellectuals say that the year 2000 would be a year of revelations: like a rubber ball, the world would hit the wall and come bouncing back, and the world itself would enter a parallel time-space. Their ramblings never reached any definitive conclusion, and their tangled words and metaphors turned right and wrong on their head, so Mr Chen could only see the year 2000 as, crudely speaking, a new beginning of some sort. When Manman's brief life ended, he began thinking again about death. His mother's death was like a swaying lamp sputtering a final gasp of light, and the contorted coils of Manman's little body made him think life itself was phoney, and his father's prophecy had been realised – the family would never have a daughter. After that, as the process of manufacturing Suwei dragged on, all he could do was accompany his wife to the 'experimental lifeform laboratory' (as he called it) and interminably repeat the brutish process of trying to cultivate life. Later on, their lovemaking started to resemble animal mating behaviour, and on countless occasions he glimpsed copious numbers of rabbits burrowing beneath their sheets, spinning in savage circles in a mindless, monotonous attempt to clone themselves.

Later still, when he thought of sex, he thought only of flinging away one test tube and syringe after another, then scrambling to pick them up again off the laboratory floor. The moment Suwei was born, he felt no fatherly joy at all. Filling his head were hopes that the boy could disrupt the heritage that had burdened every male in the family, since as far as he could see, all embryos cultivated in test tubes were inorganic. Suwei belonged completely to Mrs Luo, served as his wife's compensation for enduring prolonged pain: she said one day Suwei would be a dancer, a great one.

'Er . . . so you've been away at sea all these years?'

When Suwei finally spoke, Mrs Luo craned her neck to look at him, as if spellbound by this plot twist, as if the riddle of the 'disappearance' had at last been solved.

'I, uh . . . That's it, I was away at sea,' Mr Chen stammered, startled to have been seen through.

'I dream of you sometimes, out on the open sea, the breeze blowing, the waves lapping, and you, all alone, bobbing up and down.'

'Yes, out on the open sea, sometimes the waves are still, and sometimes there are storms.'

'But when I open my eyes, there's a hole in the sea. You're deep inside that hole, where I can't see, but I can hear you.'

*

Suwei once told his mother a story about the sea when they first took him to see his grandfather, although it was such a tiny tale that she had long forgotten what it was about. His grandfather, Chen Weiguo, made model boats out of pale wood, leaving them unpainted. As boats, they were completely useless. The smallest wave would sink them; in fact, they would not even float in the bathroom basin. Chen Weiguo was blind by the time Suwei arrived, so he could not see him at all. Instead, he reached out his wrinkly hands to feel the boy's face and arms. His grandson did not feel like the other Chen men. The Chens did not run to fat or grow especially tall, but they were not unpleasant to look at. In fact, there was nothing unusual about their appearance. They had round, boyish faces until they were thirty, and even after that, they still looked like boys. They never gave anyone the impression of being bad men, but it was clear that they would never be leaders either. Their faces lacked that craggy bone structure. But Suwei was different: he did not have a round face, and he did have lanky limbs. The boy approached his grandfather with the grace of one of those mysteriously melancholy actors Chen Weiguo had seen in Japanese films.

Chen Weiguo's wife had died ten years before; she never made it to the year 2000. He remembered how she used to go on about lasting into the new millennium and seeing her grandson, but she didn't hang around for either. His wife had been half a head taller than him, just the way his daughter-in-law and grandson were. It seemed like there was a pattern: women who married Chen men were tall and vigorous. His son had told him that his new wife was a dancer, a ballet dancer. In his view, the point of dancing was to illustrate the Chairman's revolutionary principles. Years ago, he and his wife would go to performances of the city art troupe, standing on tiptoes and craning their necks to see the stage. He vaguely remembered that his wife used to fasten her hair in a pigtail and then plait it. The way the dancers on stage did their hair, she told him.

When Mrs Luo married into their family as a young woman, his wife had not been happy. She said her daughter-in-law would be a terrible homemaker, with her clumsy way of doing things and her skinny haunches. Chen Weiguo said nothing. He was engrossed in a model mast, wondering if he should sand it a little more. He knew she was not expecting an answer; when women talked like this, it was because the pressure had built up, and they needed to let off steam. Times really had changed. When his wife secretly borrowed money to set their son up in business, he felt that the family was falling into a yawning abyss. In his lifetime, he had seen changes happen so fast that the thread of continuity with his ancestors – something to be proud of – was gone.

There had never been an official or a businessman in the family. His father and grandfather were village schoolteachers; he himself had joined the army when he was just twelve years old, not because he thought there was much in it for him, but because he believed they would look after him. And they did. He had a good brain and liked to tinker with engines, so he was sent to engineering school, after which they fixed him up with a wife. He was content with how things were. Before he married, his ambitions were no bigger than defending the patch of land where he had been born. He could not see anything wrong with that. But after they married, his wife was like a wall mirror that kept catching the light, irritating him with its flashes and flickers. The more she nagged him about everyone else 'going off to make their fortune', the less he wanted to go anywhere. Gradually, he reduced his world to trips between the factory and home. He did not feel that he had missed out on the numerous opportunities she talked about. The way she saw it, they would have taken him to Beijing, to success, to the top of the social ladder. It was not that he was ignorant of these opportunities, it was just that he felt they were like multiple-choice questions. He was afraid that they represented an enormous unknown that would make him forget all about his forebears.

The year before Chen Weiguo's father died, he suddenly stood up one day and stepped into a void. He found he had gone blind in both eyes. He said it was like being immersed in a freezing, dark sea. He told Chen Weiguo that it had been the same with his own father, all the Chen men lost their sight before they died, it was like a curse. And yet they had never done anything to hurt anyone, they had always been decent folk. There was no cure for the blindness. His wife searched high and low, forcing him to drink a tea of twenty goji berries every day, because they were good for the eyesight, supposedly. He learned the hard way that when a man married, he gave up all his rights. At home, the wife ruled the roost. In due course, it was Chen Weiguo's turn to lose his sight, and he felt like his whole body was floating. It turned out that eyes were not just for seeing, they were also a mechanism for balancing the human body. Being blind was like being a rudderless boat, waiting to be swallowed up by the waves at any moment.

So when he met his grandson Suwei for the first time, Chen Weiguo decided to bequeath the half-finished model boat to him. It was the one he had been working on when his eyes gave out, and seemed to embody his final days. He was getting old; he could smell the odour of death every day. When he closed his eyes, he was never sure if he would wake up again. Death stood outside, blowing at him through the cracks in the door. More and more, what had happened in the past invaded his dreams. He was not afraid of death. His wife was waiting for him on the other side of the door. He was not a restless soul as she had been, he had nothing to let go, but he was afraid of the dark, because it was the only thing that reminded him that his life had been completely useless. He already imagined that one day, his daughter-in-law and grandson would pack his model boats in brand-new cardboard boxes and chuck them down into the basement of their big Beijing house, where it was as cold and dark as the place he now found himself in.

What Chen Weiguo did not know was that on the first Grave-Sweeping Festival after his death, his grandson would put the half-finished model boat behind his glass window in the Martyrs Cemetery columbarium, and his son would add a miniature car, a house and a white wreath. Mr Chen did not bury his father in a large mountainside tomb. He felt that consigning him to the Martyrs Cemetery showed proper respect to his ancestors and was appropriate for a man whose name, Weiguo, meant Guard the Motherland.

It was on that occasion, on the plane back to Beijing, that Suwei first told his mother a story about the sea. She had no memory of how the story started or what happened in it. She only remembered Suwei gazing out of the porthole as the plane flung layers of clouds in its wake, and saying, 'Grandpa saw hope in the sea.' And that was probably how he ended the story.

17

Lɪ Wᴇɴ took the lift downstairs for the first time in a week. The fumes of the new plastic it was covered in smelled a bit like paint. As a child, whenever he caught the scent of paint, he just had to go and find what the source was, he couldn't help it. Not because it smelled good, but because he was curious. It would turn him into an idiot, his mother warned him, but he had to go looking anyway. He wanted to experiment, to see if it was true. Would it make his brain stupid? And if it did, would he get a halo and give off fumes himself?

The rubbish bins in the Youth Hostel compound now had a sign saying that Beijing was implementing a strict refuse classification system, with blue bins for recyclables and black bins for kitchen waste. He hoisted the black garbage bag, frowned, and tossed it all into the black bin. It had only been a week since he was last downstairs and suddenly the place was heaving with belligerent eco-warriors, feminists, and activists intent on fighting discrimination of one sort or another. So far, the hostel had been very comfortable, and he felt he had nothing to complain about. He especially liked the decor, which made him feel he was back in *The Sims*. (As long as you ticked a box on the screen, you got a newly decorated house. Action commands were triggered at the touch of a button, the next part of the game always instantly ready to launch at the twitch of a finger.)

He guessed that, of the building's residents, forty percent would choose 'elegant Scandinavian style' like him, another twenty percent would go for 'minimalist Chinese style', and another twenty percent, 'American country style'. The remaining twenty percent probably DIY'ed their décor. He could even guess whether the people who chose these different styles were single, living with a partner, married without children, or married with children. That was pretty much it, the city did not tell him anything more about its residents.

His first day at the hostel, he was still driving Mrs Luo's black Maybach. The night enveloped him in silence, and he spoke only to the security officer and the doorman who checked over the car and issued him with a parking permit. So he moved in. When he drove out of the compound gate the next day, he saw a big crowd waiting for buses that took them to the office blocks at East Third Ring Road. Under the lonely white bus sign, they looked like they adopted exactly the same postures day after day. There was a smartly-dressed woman who stood looking dazed, a man with a backpack hunched over his mobile phone, and a young student with headphones on, twitching her head in time to some inaudible music. He joined the queue of cars waiting for the parking bar to be lifted at the exit of the compound. The exit was so narrow that the drivers could not see the cars in front or behind them, and sat hemmed in by their car windows. This place was just like any other compound on the Fourth Ring Road, with people crowded together, queuing to leave their holes and go hunting, returning at dusk, their bellies full, or perhaps still hungry.

This was his new refuge, his lair, and it exuded the apocalyptic stink of a hyena's carrion. When he left GodSlayer's place, he had taken stock of his possessions and discovered that he had added little over the years – most of what he owned was just what his mother had packed for him when he went to M City University. He was good at marking his patch on other people's turf by means of cheap household items: bedsheets, a pair of much-washed chopsticks, the little pillows filled with buckwheat husks that his mother had made for him and toiletries in a plastic basket. He had taken all these things from his home to M City, then to Beijing, or wherever he was kipping down next.

The atmosphere was more tense here, however. As he went downstairs to take out the rubbish, he felt eyes levelled on him once more, peering at him through the maze of cracks. He seemed to see people in uniforms moving swiftly around the compound. They were dressed like the figures in his Stranger Danger handbook at primary school, though there were also blue uniforms like those he had seen at the underground station. Agitated, he tossed his phone aside. None of it had anything to do with him any more – celebrity sex scandals, missing persons and murders, international crises – he was too scared to look at the news. He found that as soon as he closed his eyes, he couldn't remember what any particular place actually looked like. Apart from their names, they were all the same. As soon as he fell asleep, he seemed to plummet into a black hole, where he could see nothing at all.

The game he used to play, Subway Surfing, had not been entirely pointless: it had allowed him to picture this city through the tangle of coloured lines and names. The red, green, yellow and blue writing on their white panels told him where people were. It was around this time that he began to imagine that he could be here making his own way, living in obscurity, submerged. He longed to be somewhere where no one could find him. Several times, he dreamed of the faraway house that still occupied most of his memories, though it seemed to evaporate with whatever wind blew in. In his dreams, he was always running, and as he ran, his home took on the shape of a funeral urn, ever more leaden and irrelevant. Ever since the day he brought back the Mutual Aid Society leaflet they had given him on the subway, threw it in the rubbish, then retrieved it again, dreams like this kept startling him awake, his chest so tight that he gasped for air.

In the villa compound (he could not now recall its proper name), the mother of his first student had opened the fridge and given him a carton of imported fruit juice, which beaded with droplets of water in the warm air. *Such kind people*, he had thought. Back then, he was sure that once he had left the fitness centre, he would be able to categorise these villa folk simply as good or bad. Then he realised that everyone in the house had their own cup. He was the only one who got a perfectly packaged drink handed to him by his smiling employer. He was an outsider to them, someone who didn't get a cup. The villas were as pin-neat and sparkling clean as a *Sims* house. The children and their mothers smiled and called him Mr Li, but he would never be one of them. The mothers had picked out his CV, in which he promised (by fair means or foul, and using all sorts of weasel words) to set their children off on a defined path to success, without deviating to one side or the other, however long it took. Yet once the children had had one or perhaps two summer holidays, they forgot about him. He never met his former pupils outside their villa home. It was as if they had whistled past him in a parallel universe.

He never saw GodSlayer again. He had given him a month's notice, as was the rule. (In fact, sometime before he left, he had found out that GodSlayer was not only his flatmate, he owned the house too.) Once, he caught a glimpse of GodSlayer on the TV screen on the subway that went north towards the villa area: he still had a long fringe that covered his eyes, and stood, arms crossed over his chest, with four young men who all had the same look in their eyes. Their names came up on the screen – they were a video games squad. Li Wen searched 'GodSlayer' on his phone and discovered that a professional gamer was a new type of competitive athlete. Someone who trained in a virtual world where night and day were reversed, and relied on reflexes, skill and frantic manual agility to slaughter his opponents. Li Wen felt GodSlayer had betrayed him, just as Shuisheng had. They went looking for him because they were lonely, then dropped him all on his own. They had never been together.

When he heard that M City University now offered a major in esports, he glanced at the tens of thousands of messages that popped up each day on their noticeboard. Nothing much had changed. Li

Wens, Big Brother Chens and Zheng Xiaoweis still skulked in the stinking alleys behind far-flung universities, sleepily gulping down bowls of hot soup in the morning, ignoring the rats that scurried unseen among the stacks of blue boxes of fizzy drinks in corner shops. His memories were permeated by the thrill those little white pills had given him. He really missed Zheng Xiaowei's skinny little body and her bursts of laughter as she undressed him.

At noon on the day he moved out of GodSlayer's house, just as he had done when he moved in, he had to check it was time to leave on his mobile phone (recently he had stopped checking the time, even electronically). In his perpetually dingy room, all light was concentrated in the light bulb on the ceiling. He felt like he was always in a state of panic about time. Apart from its seemingly inexorable advance on his mobile, there was nothing else in the room to tell him that time kept moving forward. Even his phone didn't show the time (the battery was dead and he had forgotten to charge it yesterday). He seemed to have managed to trick himself into believing, for an instant, that time had vanished. He suddenly felt sorry that he had not taken the watch off his mother's wrist and brought it with him. Or had he perhaps taken it off and left it lying somewhere in the road? Dying was like pressing a grey progress bar with the mouse until it filled up and jumped to a black screen, a great unknown, where he could only rely on smell and imagination to establish an intimate connection with someone he knew was dead, telling himself, *My mother was there.*

*

Mrs Luo was a firm believer that problems that could be solved with money were not problems, Li Wen knew. She could say this because she was rolling in it. A few of the villas in Mrs Luo's complex even had swimming pools in their gardens, though most of the time, they were filled with nothing but green caterpillars, yellowed leaves and the redoubtable North China dust. The dust did not bother him; after listening to Suwei's recording, he even tried turning into the wind and opening his eyes. Nothing went in, not coal cinders nor flying insects, though oddly enough, he did feel the weight of the dust. Once a certain amount of dust had built up in the pools, it was impossible to clean them properly; this place was no good for any outdoor facilities that needed to be kept clean. The topography was wrong, and so was the built environment. Almost half the families there were in the habit of spending a few months of the year elsewhere. They had a summer place to go in the summer and a winter place to go in the winter. They shut themselves away behind fortress-style walls, but had the whole world to play in. Only Mrs Luo and Suwei never went anywhere. Although their home did not travel, looked at another way, Suwei travelled every day in Diablo's world. Mrs Luo could not go with him – this was one problem she could not solve with money. Li Wen always envied Suwei his ability to travel, from the moment he saw him immersing himself in the world of Diablo. Li Wen did not give a damn for the future, no matter who promised it to him, he just wanted to get into that shell and become frozen in time, like Suwei.

After he moved out of GodSlayer's place, Li Wen discovered that shadows of the past lingered all around him. It seemed like this flat, so newly decorated it still smelled of paint, was teeming with the phantoms of people or things. From the moment he decided to use Suwei's memories to blackmail Mrs Luo, he had hoped to acquire complete independence and liberation, to disappear from their world without a sound. But now he found himself trapped in those memories. He had flashbacks, he heard his timid warning cries, and he felt a cold sweat trickling down his back. He suddenly saw himself as a cornered animal. He was no longer being controlled by marionette wires, but now Mrs Luo had found out where he came from. This place where he should have been free was actually his tomb.

So, like GodSlayer, he turned night and day upside down, and as he slept and woke and slept again, his chaotic body clock took him back once more to what he imagined had happened after his mother died, a period that he had shut himself off from. Sleep became a channel for everything he had managed to hide. Mrs Luo and his mother, Suwei and him, the four of them appeared repeatedly in his dreams. He was at school, running with Suwei on the shiny rubberized track, while Mrs Luo and his mother stood watching at the end.

A few days before, he had gone down to stretch his legs and stumbled over something at the foot of the stairs. It reminded him of how, in the first six months after his father died, his mother would take him for a stroll outside their compound after dinner. It took exactly half an hour to go out and back along the three streets. Once, he had stumbled the way he had just now, and his mother got upset. She kept telling him that big accidents happened as a result of small ones. People thought that only major accidents mattered, but it was the seemingly innocuous mishaps that were the deadliest. During those six months, his mother had acted ultra-cautious. It must have been the way his father died that brought home to her how unexpectedly death could happen, in a matter of seconds. Then, after six months, their after-dinner walks lapsed. He and his mother began to avoid each other's eyes. They had nothing to say to each other. Waves of heavy, solemn silence rolled off them. They could not express their closeness any more. Should he love her like the growing teenager that he was, or like an adult male? He had no idea. An invisible wall rose up between them.

No one had ever explained to him what love, or sexual desire, or death were. These dread topics were off-limits for his mother: love was unmentionable, sex was dirty, and talking about death was taboo, especially after the death of his father. She acted as though the very utterance of the word might bring catastrophe down on her and her Li Wen. She avoided buying him black clothes. She said that it made him look gloomy. It was as if the two of them were only kept alive by acting happy. She dinned into him that they were survivors.

*

In the morning, he updated the laptop. He would uninstall MSN Messenger – no one used the app these days. It occurred to him to open it before uninstalling it, and Shuisheng's profile picture flashed onto the screen. He had not replied to Shuisheng's last MSN message, and they had lost touch. It felt like a century ago. Li Wen clicked on Shuisheng's profile and scarcely noticed the 'ping' as he read:

Dear friends of Shuisheng. We are Shuisheng's parents, and we're posting here to everyone who's been in contact with him. At eight o'clock in the evening on 2 May, Shuisheng's car collided with a supermarket truck on a California freeway. The emergency services worked for three hours to rescue him, but he passed away. Shuisheng always said that he loved having his friends around him. We hope he finds another way of showing his love for you guys from heaven.

The world would never be the same again. Shuisheng had been his best friend.

But when Xiaorou told him in that saccharine voice that she loved him, all his problems were solved.

He knew he needed to do something to put a smile on his face, now that he had moved into a brand-new place like this. He opened the key box by the front door and felt around at the bottom for a piece of paper. It was something he had picked up in the doorway of the minimarket downstairs from GodSlayer's place and had kept in an old biscuit tin along with other odds and ends that might come in useful one day, like the Mutual Aid Society leaflets, clothes tags, and receipts for anything over two hundred yuan. Where exactly these garishly coloured scraps of paper were to be found seemed to be determined by the Beijing ring roads: most of them turned up where new and old housing developments merged, within the Third Ring Road, just about where the international apartments intersected with Sanfengli. The bits of paper lay on the ground as higgledy-piggledy as Lego blocks, around the countless minimarkets, hairdressers, fruit shops, and dimsum stalls. They did not usually turn up in the villa zones outside the Fifth Ring Road, areas which were too cut off and self-sufficient. Li Wen had never seen anything like them near the villa. He first read the phone number – 18952376655 – on the slip of paper three times, until he had memorised it. The more familiar it sounded, the more it felt cheap, dirty and sinful. It reminded him of when he was a teenager, escaping his mother's watchful eye to dream of women's bodies. He had always wanted to buy a girl's company, even just for one night. He put down the piece of paper and sat back on the living room sofa with its beige canvas cushions. It did not have the slippery feel of Mrs Luo's leather sofa, but it seemed to fit that phone number.

Every growing boy harboured many secrets that betrayed his mother. If the mothers did not die, those boys could never be free.

On his phone, Li Wen pressed the digits very deliberately, as if he wanted his mother, wherever she was, to know what he was doing. An hour later, Xiaorou pushed the intercom downstairs, and soon they were lying naked on the bare mattress in the bedroom. (The new sheets he had ordered online had not yet arrived.) Another hour passed, and this girl, with her Botox-puffed face and ridiculously long, false eyelashes, was telling him that she loved him. How cheap love and sex were, what vulgar disguises they used. He had stroked Mrs Luo's expensively youthful face. It had been beautiful, shining so brightly that it made him feel dark and small. Xiaorou's face was genuinely young, but it looked strangely old and wretchedly bloated, as if it was struggling to break out of a mask of age. After they finished, Li Wen knew that he would never call her again.

Looking at her skinny body and her face plastered with makeup, he suddenly felt guilty. He did not even have anything to cover her with. 'Xiaorou, how old are you?' he asked.

Xiaorou giggled. The punters always asked that.

'Twenty-five.'

Of course. It was the stock answer. She might be only eighteen, but had advanced the ageing process so she could stay in the city. Or she might be thirty, too old to ever go back to the small county town where she had grown up, even though there, she would not get called out like a delivery driver and have to find her way to a house she did not know and would not remember afterwards.

When Xiaorou was leaving, Li Wen stuffed an extra two hundred yuan into her hand. It was all the cash he had. No one used cash any more, people paid for things on their phones. But still he always kept a few hundred-yuan notes to hand, the way his mother used to keep some under the photo of the two of them when he was a child. *Just in case*, she said. He sent Xiaorou on her way and lay back on the mattress again. He was alone with the reek of her cheap perfume. He could tell instantly how much that perfume had cost. The cheaper the perfume, the more it made your head swim. He covered himself with a towel, and suddenly the room emptied. Even those shadowy figures that had haunted him were gone.

18

WHEN Mrs Luo went to Suwei's school to arrange for him to take time off, she bumped into Suwei's deskmate in the corridor, the half-Japanese girl with shiny black hair and a fringe. Leafy was rushing out of the toilet, pulling down the hem of her jacket, but stopped to glance shyly in her direction. The school head had arranged to see Mrs Luo during afternoon classes. She had only met Mr Hao once, when Mr Chen had invited him to a big dinner. She had been impressed. Mr Hao was short and precise, and looked like someone who had trained himself to conduct his business with care and propriety. He had regular, shiny teeth, as good as the ones she had seen in Dr Pei's display cabinet. In the empty corridor, Leafy seemed much shyer than normal today, and Mrs Luo supposed she must be on her period. At her age, every time she had her period, Mrs Luo would put on a sanitary towel, making sure it fitted snugly, and add a wad of crumpled toilet paper in her knickers. They were all too young to know about bellyaches or other period problems, and the teachers conducting rehearsals certainly never mentioned them. All they knew was that they could not miss a day's practice or another girl would hog the limelight instead of them, and there could only be one star on stage. No one wanted to miss the chance to be in the limelight. Later, when she arrived in Beijing, she found out that tampons made everything invisible, so none of the girls needed to waste a minute because of their period. The other thing that happened was that the dates of the girls' periods gradually grew closer together, so that eventually they were all menstruating in unison. Regardless of whether they normally came on at the beginning or end of the month, it seemed that, mysteriously, they all ended up bleeding on the same days mid-month, and when there was a heatwave in July and August (something that happened in Beijing every few years), the rehearsal room smelled distinctly fishy. Dancers were really hard on themselves, she thought.

'Is Suwei coming back to class, Auntie?'

Leafy turned to ask this question as she ran away. From where Mrs Luo was standing, the girl's eyes were shaped like two limpid drops of water. She looked earnest as she waited for an answer that she clearly expected Mrs Luo to provide. Children always think that all the questions in the world have correct answers. When they finally realise that most questions are either unanswerable or lead to more ambiguity, that is the day when they have arrived in the adult world.

'Suiwei's had an accident. He needs to make a proper recovery,' she said, hearing her voice warbling. 'He'll be back soon.'

'Great! My mum said he broke his leg dancing. I hope he's okay.'

'He'll be fine. Thank you for asking.'

Mrs Luo laid her hand on the girl's shoulder. It was soft and smooth to the touch. She hoped it would never have to bear the weight of the world's lies. Probably, in six months or so, Leafy's mother would tell her daughter that Suwei had transferred to another school. After that, as the girl grew up, Suwei would become no more than a distant satellite in the night sky, flickering ever more infrequently as the memories faded. She might feel sorry for her deskmate who had broken his leg, and along with this pity, she would remember the accident he had supposedly had. But soon, she would get another deskmate, and the new bond they would form would overlay that memory with many, many more, until Suwei was reduced to a name on an old calendar.

Leafy skipped away and went into a classroom on the left. Obviously she was not going to be punished for being five minutes late. Mrs Luo and Mr Chen had originally chosen this school because the headteacher espoused Westernised educational values. For them, and all the local villa folk, 'Westernisation' embodied all possible benefits and their hopes for the future. The children at the school were like mirror images of their parents. They rapidly, instinctively coalesced into a social class, an unbreakable alliance. But Suwei was a glass marble that could not find anything to rub up against. He did not belong, and that would destroy him.

The headteacher's office was up the stairs. The walls were covered in large crayon drawings showing children engaging in sports and arts activities: a boy in a white dobok doing taekwondo, a girl dancing in a pink ballet dress, more boys doing science experiments, ponytailed girls singing in a choir. The rays of the afternoon sun mottled the surface of the posters. Mrs Luo shielded her eyes with her hands, but the light leaked through her fingers anyway. With Leafy's disappearance, the corridor was deserted. The poster boys and girls looked as fresh as newly defrosted food, neatly defined and sorted. In that instant, it dawned on her how lonely Suwei must have felt.

The moment she saw the sign that read 'Head Teacher's Office', she almost forgot what she was going to do and what she should say. She almost blurted out, 'Surely Suwei can't be the only boy in the school doing ballet, can he?' In the first twenty years or so of her life, when she was still meek and docile, Mrs Luo had avoided rhetorical questions. And that had not changed during the last twenty years, even after she had become much more assertive. When she spoke, she avoided affirmative rhetorical questions (even though they were compulsory in her Chinese class) just as she avoided many similar language strategies. She had had little formal education, and this caused her constant anxiety. Although Mr Chen rarely talked to her about his own schooling, she knew that this was a lacuna that could not be filled in either of them. But in schools of art and dance, no one went around declaring themselves to be cultured in the literary sense. They spoke through their insteps, toes, necks, arms and hands. Their nerve endings embodied their language and emotions, and if they missed out on a day's rehearsals, they became rigid. There were often rumours in the group that such-and-such veteran dancer had injured herself so badly with a leap on the stage that she ended up paraplegic. Or that one of the dance teachers could not have children because dancing had displaced her womb. These tales were told with a kind of gleeful furtiveness – the way you might tell ghost stories – and seemed to have the same inevitability that the syncing of their menstrual periods had. A sort of nameless fear emanated from the listener and infected the teller too.

The male dancers had another fear, which they covered up by joining in the laughing and joking with the girls. At least one could always be found sitting in a circle with half a dozen girls in each corner of the practice room. As adolescents, the boys needed to cultivate this kind of pleasant, easy-going relationship with the girls in order to dampen their physiological responses when they danced with them; they needed to express all their language and emotion every time they stretched a part of their bodies, while at the same time stifling all the sensation in their nerve endings when their bodies touched their partner's. For them, the body was both an open and a closed thing. Other stories went around the dance troupe too, about boys staying until late at night in practice rooms and caressing each other, or naked assignations in the bathrooms. Mrs Luo always went red with embarrassment when she heard things like this. Obviously, they had nothing to do with her, yet she felt strangely ashamed.

'Good morning, Mrs Luo, please come in. Take a seat.'

Mr Hao, the headteacher, opened his office door and ushered her inside. His manner was measured, neither too enthusiastic (she was not here to accept any prizes Suwei had won) nor in any way slighting her (after all, she might enrol her son again).

He had lost weight since the first time she met him, maybe five or six pounds. The potbelly had gone, and his new slender profile made him look more like an upstanding academic, not dissimilar from Mr Chen's coterie of intellectual friends, that self-contained world from which she was excluded. And yet, strangely, when she and Mr Chen were at home alone, neither of them ever picked up a book, even though the study at the end of the corridor upstairs was stacked floor to ceiling with heavy tomes, all neatly arranged in alphabetical order. The mentor of a certain young architect from the southern countryside was one of their group, and he must have been a famous professor, the way the architect glowed with pride when he talked about him, as if his mentor's successes magically rubbed off on him simply by virtue of being repeated. According to the protégé, the most exciting thing was the annual gathering of his mentor and other scholars in different fields. They were a meeting of great minds, inhabiting a utopian realm, sharing their specialist knowledge freely with each other. Apparently, they had received generous donations from some nameless, culture-loving investor. Mrs Luo knew that this investor was her husband.

During the time when she was receiving fertility treatment (she felt like a laboratory mouse) and waiting for her eggs to be incubated and grow to life, her husband and his scholar friends were incubating grand dialogues about human knowledge. Mr Chen and the headteacher who had just invited her to sit down were alike in one respect: the more they tiptoed around the subject of her educational shortcomings, the more they hurt her. She felt stabs of distress that seemed to come out of nowhere. She knew it was her own problem and they were not at fault.

'How's Suwei getting along?' asked Mr Hao. He skirted the subject of what exactly had happened to Suwei, the way a moth in search of nectar circles around, creating the illusion that it is not interested, so that the target food will reveal itself of its own accord. Mr Hao was hinting that he would accept any publishable reason divulged to him by the boy's parents. After so many years in post, Mr Hao had seen students drop out (or the fees suddenly stop arriving) for a number of different reasons. In his experience, the higher up the social ladder the parents were, the more likely they were to obfuscate the truth.

'Suwei fell when he was dancing and broke his leg. The doctor we consulted says it will take a while for him to recover.'

The school had always instilled in parents and students alike complete trust in its staff, and Mrs Luo was immediately convinced that the head could see straight through her lie. She even had another answer ready, if need be. Now she simply stared Mr Hao down, her eyes wide. She was here to say goodbye, not to ask for an extended leave of absence.

'Suwei is the only dancer in the school. We encourage students to cultivate a number of different talents – and of course, it is a hard decision to become a professional dancer. I suggest, Mrs Luo, that we wait until Suwei is better and then see how he can make up the missed classes. But a child's bones recover quickly.'

'Thank you, Mr Hao, his leg is getting better quickly. But actually, after that, I want to send him to the high school attached to Beijing Dance Academy. The problem is that there are no other dancers here. He might benefit from having lots of dancing around him.'

'Mrs Luo, are you sure that's what he wants? Once boys become dancers, what future is there for them when they get older? I hear from his teacher that Suwei is very shy, almost . . . girly, would you say? Wouldn't it be better for him to do some sports?'

The windows of the head's office were open a crack, probably because it was July. The cries from outside were unbelievably loud, as if they were all following the lead of their inspirational head teacher, and their parents had chosen him so they could provide their children with a beautiful future. Mrs Luo felt she was up against it, but was not quite sure what 'it' was. When she was pregnant, Mr Chen had said he hoped their child would grow up to be a highly educated academic. But she always knew she wanted him to be a dancer. So now she looked up and spoke, though without answering the head's question: 'Suwei loves dancing, and he wants to go to the dance school. They've said he can go on to Los Angeles and take part in junior dance competitions. The English he's learned here will come in very useful, so we're very grateful to you.'

*

Mrs Zhao sensed that the boy she bathed in the tub once a week was like a small, silent animal with soft skin and sturdy bones. She had once worked for a family with a big, blonde, long-haired dog that was always jumping on her and smothering her in saliva. The husband was never home during the day, so the wife always asked Mrs Zhao for help bathing the big blonde dog – the wife too had dyed blonde hair, and each time she lathered up the dog, she patted it on the head, cooing, 'Mummy's going to bathe you now. Don't be afraid.' At times like these, Mrs Zhao would stand to the side, prepared at any moment to hand over a freshly dried, fluffy towel. She could tell it was imported from the feel of it, and she guessed it had cost about half her monthly salary. The first time she bathed Suwei, she was a bit taken aback, a bit incredulous that Mrs Luo had granted her this privilege. When she slathered the boy in bath gel, red welts broke out on his face, but his body remained translucent as a turnip. Suwei didn't raise his voice, and he didn't shake. He simply stewed in the water staring blankly, as if floating on air, and Mrs Zhao remembered what the last woman she worked for had said, 'Don't be afraid,' so she had said to him, in her involuntarily Anhui-inflected Mandarin, like a lullaby spewing gentle sea spray, 'Don't be afraid.'

Don't be afraid. The year Suwei turned one, Mrs Luo too would croon these words as she rocked him in the cradle. The boy had broad shoulders and long legs, like her, but he had inherited his eyes from Mr Chen. Even before he could speak, she would look into those eyes and glimpse an impenetrable world. She always sensed that Suwei must have been loitering within her for five years already by the time he was born, and the nurse who delivered him said he was the quietest baby she had ever seen. It seemed that to him, the world wasn't worth fussing over. Suwei didn't even cry when the sole link between them, the umbilical cord, was cut.

When the process of creating new life was deconstructed and dismantled into flesh-coloured fragments, life was surrounded by a sense of synthetic estrangement. By the time he was five, Mrs Luo had already exhaustively plumbed the boy's interior, getting the sense he was the creation of a laboratory rather than her womb. In fact, her probing was, to some extent, extremely zealous nit-picking: when she was pregnant, she played Bach and Mozart all day long on a loop, until Bach and Mozart became, for her, rote agony rather than inspiring music. After that, she put Suwei through a 'perfect pitch' test, assuming he must have been studying music all that time inside her womb. She would tell him all sorts of fairy tales and expect him to fill in the missing plot points, finishing the story before she did. She would toss paper and crayons into Suwei's room and peer in a few hours later to see whether he had created a masterpiece while she was away. Mrs Luo expected Suwei to exceed her and Mr Chen's limits absolutely; she hoped for this synthetic laboratory creation to transcend them in every way, bringing them to the brink of immortality.

One day, Mrs Luo sat beside Suwei in the back seat of a black limousine. As always, Suwei sat on the right, and Mrs Luo sat on the left. In two more years, when Suwei finished middle school, she would send him to the high school attached to Beijing Dance Academy, but first, she needed Mr Chen to take the director or headmaster of the academy to dinner. She was extremely confident in Suwei's innate dance abilities; she even indulged in repeated fantasies of his future dance instructors going wild with glee when they saw what he could do. Taking the headmaster to dinner was like seeing a feng shui master about her father's burial plot – perhaps primarily a placebo effect, but as Old Chen used to put it, it was important to 'work every angle'.

As they passed the row of villas nearest the main gate, Mrs Luo surreptitiously rolled down the driver's side window, convinced the driver, a boy named Zhang, had farted in the car. Anyway, it hadn't been her, and it hadn't been Suwei – surrounded by a cloud of flagrant opportunism, they were doomed to breathe in one another's ammonia, carbon dioxide, and methane within an impermeable space. She had to pretend nothing had happened, to roll down the window and safeguard the purity of their air. *Look, up ahead, the neighbourhood's most notorious swimming pool.* From time to time, a half-naked old man in red striped skivvies sat at the bottom, arse ensconced in a yellow plastic folding chair, wreathed by heaps of leaves that had been flung away by the branches of a nearby tree and yellowed in the span of a day, and all sorts of unidentified detritus that had been smothered by rushing time, taking on a deathly grey sheen. The old man and Mrs Wang were infamous as addled geriatrics. People whispered their names, as if they were the village witch and warlock, and their families kept them locked up like livestock in pens. Then, a little girl with countless small braids fastened with colourful rubber bands came prancing up. She was as tall as her grandpa, who was slumped in the plastic folding chair, and she squatted down beside him and glanced to where his desolate gaze was searching, at the distant, unseen house. There was the whizz of a sliding door, and a woman emerged onto the patio.

'A storm's coming,' she declared, promptly collaring the girl and the old man. Mrs Luo recalled suddenly that back when her father was alive, every Friday night, the only time of week he was ever sober, they would sit down and watch a TV show called *Treasures of a Vanished World* together. A portly host with round glasses would pick up some suspected fake vase, eyes wide like an opera singer, and shriek, 'Rubbish!', and the sound waves would shatter the vase.

Mrs Luo later reflected on countless occasions that if it hadn't rained that day, later events might have moved forward at a much slower pace.

She never fully pieced together the enigma of the boy the driver brought back that day: his arid body shook continually, and his head roared with heat like a giant bonfire heaped with lacerating flame. Until the driver left, he kept his lips pursed, refraining from saying a word, biting hard into his lower lip. Once the two of them were alone, the boy collapsed. A continual fever kept him overstimulated and covered in cold sweat. He kept repeating, 'Let me take a shower, let me take a shower.'

With a mighty effort, she half-carried, half-dragged Suwei to the soft bed, but he lashed out with his scorching limbs, absolutely refusing to be put to bed. Seemingly afraid of soiling the gleaming white sheets, Suwei simply kept repeating, 'Let me take a shower.' Several minutes before, on the phone, she had explained to Old Chen that they wouldn't be home for another half-hour. Mrs Luo peeled Suwei's clothes off, revealing a gaping black maw – his tights were wet between the legs, and the slowly bared skin of his inner loins was swollen and red. She began to shake, filling with fury, shame, and despair, combusting with the urge to retaliate. As flame singed her hairs, turning them to ash, she repeatedly wiped down Suwei's body with a wet towel, from top to bottom, from head to foot, from the furthest place to the nearest. She heard the sound of the hidden cord that connected them being cut, and then all there was was deathlike silence.

*

Beijing's blustering summer storms were always preceded by omens. As the air pressure plummeted, the compressed edges of limpid clouds flashed iridescent grey. At times like these, Suwei's body would begin pouring sweat, a child's sweat with the flavour of plain boiled water. The traffic report said it was the biggest storm in twelve years, a confounding colossus, and the motorway near the airport had flooded, leaving a dozen-odd cars stranded. Their driver had to go the long way around on the Fifth Ring Road. The droplets rammed the motorway like bits of meteorite, hewing deep crevasses. Mr Pan said he was taking Suwei to the office, where he could have some juice and wait safely for someone to come pick him up. Suwei simply sat, thinking Mr Pan rubbed his head because the large leap he had just taken had traced a lovely arc in the air, and stroked his hand so he wouldn't get bored while he waited. Mr Pan's hands began slithering all over him like snakes, and waves of intense revulsion and resistance welled up from his gut. He curled up into a small ball, shrinking as far into the chair back as he could, but there was no escape.

'Don't be afraid.'

Mr Pan's hair was soaked through with sweat, and his steamy breath was all-encompassing. At that moment, Suwei hated the fact that he couldn't control his entire body as precisely as he could calculate the height of his jumps, and he sensed that some sickness had transfixed his entire system, continually corroding and debasing him. At the final moment when his back and the chair seemed stuck fast, he suddenly pounced, bit hard into Mr Pan's extended hand, and set off at top speed for the main door of the big building with the training room. Bathing in the shadows on the rooftop, he simply couldn't stop trembling. He hugged himself, but grew colder by the minute. Much, much later, his entire body was sodden with rain. By the time the driver came to take him home, he revelled in the shadows, a creature of the cold and dark.

After that, whenever he found himself in shadow and stillness, Suwei tried to staunch the flow of that uncontrollable viscous fluid within him, that current that electrified him to the tips of his hairs, wiping his memory clean. For a long time, he did without any linguistic faculties, until, in the pitch darkness, his fever broke, and he regained his health. Mrs Luo remained by the bedside while his father sailed the seas. Every inkling of their presence plunged him more deeply into despair; every time he closed his eyes, terrifying apparitions swirled, and he kept saying, 'I'm cold.' He wanted to cover up with a thicker blanket, to wall himself off from the filthy roving hands that slithered over him continually.

The day after the incident, Mrs Luo fired the driver, Zhang, sending him away with a generous payment, enough to go home and forget about that storm-blasted summer night. Suwei was a marionette with the wires severed, an addled degenerate like the neighbourhood warlock and witch. They all knew that there was a black room inside the house, and inside that room lurked a strange hermit boy who only talked to people in video games. There were true secrets buried within the strange boy; from then on, his mother told people a different story.

19

THE twentieth time he attacked Diablo, Suwei decided to play as the Necromancer. After his attacks pierced the secret veil over death, the skeletal warrior Starlight and blue will-o'-the-wisps came gushing out. They had once been the fearless warriors and whirling demons of the wasted continent. After beating the game for the first time, players could uncover secret portals hidden beneath the models, take part in endless ferocious battles apart from the main questline, and if they won, gain extraordinary strength outside of ordinary experience levels. These hidden portals ceaselessly shifted position depending on the number of times the player had beaten the game, and this reasonless, endless drifting convinced Suwei that Diablo's world was not built completely of data models – it was alive.

Li Wen did not appear until the day Mrs Zhao came to bathe him. They wrongly assumed that he didn't remember which day or which week it was, but he in fact remembered everything, though not in accordance with a redundant cycle of millions of circulating numbers. With his innate mammalian sense of smell, he sussed out the colour of each day, and he observed the heat emitted by the body language and gaze of his mother and the others, determining on this basis which day it was. When Mr Chen appeared downstairs, he caught a strong whiff of honey.

He realised that in fact, though still wallowing in stagnant water, he had gained physical stability – when the capacity of his limbs weakened, his vision strengthened to compensate; when the black holes overtook his vision, his sense of smell became extraordinarily sharp; when all his senses declined, his memory gleamed in an ultimate burst of terminal lucidity. Because of the black holes in Suwei's eyes, Mr Chen first appeared near, then far, like a facula swallowed by the sun's surface, until he had no idea how far this man, whom his mother had declared disappeared, really was from him. He concentrated momentarily, until the fust of decaying wood in his memory covered over the scent of honey, and he remembered the immobile model boat his grandfather had given him as he lay dying. Now, Suwei put everybody – his vanished father, his dead grandfather, and the missing Li Wen – into the wooden boat. A red river flowed before the skeleton altar that housed Diablo's soulstone. The river ran with the blood of the warriors who had searched for the soulstone, and Suwei could only reach the altar by having the Old Man of the Void ferry him across aboard the Boat of Time. By the time the black holes in his eyes swallowed up the faces of these characters, they had changed to different faces amid the snarls his memory – the Old Man of the Void had his grandfather's face, the warriors flanking the old man had the face of his father, and the face of the Soul Demon guarding the altar belonged to Li Wen. These illusions were like light beams leaking ceaselessly from stagnating memories, bridging the gap between two model worlds, the flourishing world within the screen and the gasping, flailing world outside it.

It seemed to Suwei that his father had been lurking with the Old Man of the Void in a desolate, completely transparent cavern. But because it was transparent, no one could see them. So when he saw his father appear, he asked, 'So you've been away at sea all these years?', fully prepared to accept this as the entire reason for his father's disappearance, as if the argument his parents had had while he was in bed with fever on the day in question had nothing to do with it. While arguing ferociously, the adults raised fingers to their lips and went 'shh'. They were like children working a misery whip, one looking offended, the other looking misunderstood, jerking back and forth. The silent Suwei was the fuse that lit the keg, and 'Old Chen' was merely a flagman signalling offence and counter-offence.

Now, his father had reappeared beside his bloated, luminescent mother, like a black obelisk. Joined by Dr Pei and Dr Zhong (who had pronounced, 'The problem is that his amygdala has dislocated from the cranial nerve.'), they ringed the circular, ice-cold dining table in the kitchen. Suwei disliked the table, which Mrs Zhao scrubbed until it glared, leaving behind a whiff of lemon-scented cleaner. All cleaning agents were the same: the more corrosive the chemicals involved, the harder the chemists worked to formulate distracting aromas to cover them over. He disliked Dr Pei, suspecting the dentist was the only one capable of penetrating his secrets without the aid of the recording device. Dr Pei had perfectly straight gleaming teeth, and Suwei glimpsed in his gaze the same pity, delight and indifference that had been in Mr Song's eyes on first returning with his father many years ago. He never told his mum about this, and when his father returned with Mr Song that day, she wasn't there. Mr Song, in fact, never came in, simply lingered outside the doorway.

Now, they were talking in front of him about whether he would go or stay, as if he were a mute house pet. A room away, in the sitting room, Mrs Zhao scrubbed the floor; the thick soundproofing panels walled off the droning debate from the sound of Mrs Zhao humming while she worked. Nobody could hear what anybody else was doing on the other side. Just as the floor of the sitting room was on the verge of being scrubbed spotless with lemon-scented cleaning agent, the adults at the table were wandering into a labyrinth of fruitless possibilities. Mrs Luo looked up, then dropped her gaze again. Dr Wen was warning her to be aware of habitual daily movements: having more than fifty careless daily habits could leave lines on your face, and not even new collagen produced under light stimulation could repair the damage. But Mrs Luo immediately buried her head in her hands as if to say she didn't care, lips wrenched into a contemptuous grimace.

At first, Mr Chen simply sat to the side listening – listening as Dr Pei analysed whether Suwei's eyes could be operated on, whether, if operated on, they could be fully fixed, and whether he might have a relapse, speculating as to the success rate and relapse rate; listening as Dr Zhong analysed whether, in Suwei's condition, he was fit to travel or undergo surgery at all, whether all this might have a negative psychological impact, driving him deeper inside himself – what was the likelihood of that? In the beginning, it definitely made them all feel better to bandy about concrete figures. Statistical analysis made excellent medicine, and mathematical clarity greatly reduced their anxiety over unknown consequences. The process of calculating probabilities kneaded the unknown into a more pleasant shape, but soon all this seemingly definitive data winked out of existence, and he was staring up at the dreamlike miniaturised landscape reflected in the glass ceiling, listening to the voice of his father, Chen Weiguo, issuing over and over from the pitch-black cavern, along with his repetitive deathbed incantation against blindness. 'I'm dead set on getting Suwei a new set of eyes,' Mr Chen said to himself.

Dr Pei and the others finally settled on getting Suwei a pair of new crystal eyeballs with artificial corneas. The surgery had a risk of complications, and the likelihood of Suwei losing his sight entirely was between thirty to ninety percent. Mrs Luo had no way to discern the probability that the operation would free Suwei from his predestined blindness, hearing only one thing amid these extended monologues and calculations: Suwei might suffer a mental shutdown due to changes in the environment and the condition of his eyes, and at worst, he might retreat into a hermetically sealed space. What this meant was that, regardless of whether his eyes could be fixed, the incurable black holes in his mind were the greatest risk he faced.

'I really don't think you know how to care for Suwei,' she said to Mr Chen. 'This is his home. Here with me, he's safe.'

'I'm dead set on getting Suwei a new pair of eyes.' Mr Chen

repeated the same sentence, forcefully spitting out each syllable. It wasn't Mrs Luo's stubbornness, but her selfishness that had ignited the rage he now struggled to quash. At the same time, Mr Chen himself couldn't determine whether his determination to replace his son's eyes originated from rigid opposition to the family's hereditary predicament, or his dread of finally going blind himself.

While Mr Chen and Dr Pei wrangled with wispy threads of possibilities, Mrs Luo sat dumbly, as if in a trance. In fact, she had never before felt such assurance, and she was fully convinced Suwei would be safe as long as her eyes were on him. She suddenly stood and went upstairs, but this time, she didn't knock. She pushed open the bedroom door and went inside. In the glistening blackness, she tightly embraced the immobile Suwei.

She said, 'We're not going anywhere.'

That evening, Suwei didn't turn on his gaming monitor. Following Li Wen's disappearance, he had in fact spent several days surveying the hidden missions. He had known Li Wen would never touch this game on his own, and that was why he had had Li Wen play as the Priest of Light, but most of the time, he had gone ahead and slaughtered the demon without waiting for the priest to bless him. Moments before, when his mother had come upstairs to look for him, he had already half-finished his recording, saying he would definitely play the priest character himself next time.

This time, the battered Diablo had become a shard of mutilated flame lodged in his eyeball, but when he closed his eyes, everybody, even Diablo, was whole again. He closed his eyes and opened them, opened them and closed them, again and again, squinting at two worlds, both patchworks of jagged and intact bits, struggling to make out the difference. At nightfall, a frightening silence fell upon the estate. Their home especially, with its thick soundproof panelling, was almost completely walled off from sound, but Suwei thought he heard a stir. It wasn't his father's aeroplane shrieking through the sky, but the sound of someone climbing the crabapple tree outside the window. That someone was now crouched on the extremity of a branch, just metres away, staring straight into the pale-yellow house.

He turned his head to look, but there was nothing there. Only when he closed his eyes did he see Li Wen sitting in the tree. Both of them had lost bits of their memories. Suwei had made his mind up: they weren't going anywhere.

*

Li Wen peered through the slit in the curtains. The man in the police uniform was there again. It had been four days, maybe more, and he was still pacing back and forth in the courtyard. Li Wen hadn't been downstairs to take the rubbish out for days, and he didn't dare open the window. A stifling reek filled the room. Just two cups of instant noodles remained – he supposed he could make it for two more days. Hopefully, by then, the officer would be gone.

'He's here to haul me away.'

Li Wen flipped every device with a screen on its face. He sensed the entire world was screaming that he had killed his mother, the accusing cries emanating from the sky and the earth, accompanied by the image he had glimpsed countless times in the blackness, his mother's body sprawled on the floor, completely intact, immune to decay. He could even make out the fine hairs sprouting from her pores.

Immersed in a cloud of nameless dread, Li Wen didn't move a muscle. He had nowhere left to go. Each day, he had a few cans of Yanjing Beer delivered from the corner store. In this way he was able to silence his thoughts. Once, on the verge of sleep, he had a vision, seeing himself, Mrs Luo and Suwei together again, and he watched himself shimmy like a monkey up the neatly manicured crabapple tree outside the villa – no one would find him there. He didn't need a cushion or a sofa. He simply sat on the floor in the sitting room, keeping a lamp lit day and night, as if waiting resolutely for the policeman to beat down the door and drag him to his Last Judgement.

Someone was knocking on the door, rapping out a repetitious cycle. Li Wen held a cup of noodles in his hands – he had just eaten two mouthfuls – and waited for the knocking to stop. He didn't dare go near the peephole, fearing the person on the other side would see him. He huddled breathlessly behind the door, clinging to a tenuous hope: maybe the person on the other side had gone away. He wasn't sure how long he remained there, the noodles turning to mush, until he released a hasty exhalation, seeming to blow himself over. A wave of vertigo washed over him. The knocking started again.

'Hello? I know you're in there.'

He was sure he had heard that voice, with its Beijing accent, somewhere before. Li Wen realised he was shivering uncontrollably, but he didn't feel at all cold. Like the time Big Brother Chen rammed the small white tablet down his throat, his guts were churning. Where was the knife? Where had he stashed it before rushing for the train? Was there still blood on it? Damn it, it didn't matter any more. He put the cup of noodles back down on the tea table, went straight to the kitchen, spun in two circles and grabbed a pair of plastic-handled scissors. His head was clouded. He sensed invisible hands were dragging him down.

Holding his breath again, he opened up the door. The officer was old, perhaps sixty. He recognised not just the voice, but the face, though he wasn't sure where he knew him from.

One of the officer's shoulders was lifted higher than the other, and the buttons on his uniform intensified his general aura of uncomfortable compression. The officer leisurely sized Li Wen up, seemingly in no hurry to slap handcuffs on him. Li Wen saw no hint of hostility in his eyes. The officer pulled out a newspaper.

'What's your name, Son?'

He couldn't read what was on the paper, but he knew that it must be levelling heinous accusations at him. Who had tipped off the officer? Did everybody know where he was? He was struck by the urge to snatch the paper away, so he could see what a putrid son of a bitch they were making him out to be. He stayed almost completely motionless. He didn't shake his head, and he didn't nod.

The old officer folded the paper back up, poked his head through the door and asked in a strangely soft voice, 'Are you Li Wen?'

It was all over. He knew that now, when people said the name 'Li Wen', they weren't talking about the 'Li Wen' on the fake ID card.

My mum is dead. I killed her. A roaring sound filled his cranium, but his mouth wouldn't work, and he didn't move.

The officer saw the cup of instant noodles on the table.

'Oh, pardon me for barging in while you were having dinner. The noodles must be getting mushy. Don't mind me, carry on.'

Li Wen watched himself shuffle to the table, and he watched the old officer sit down beside him on the sofa. It was the first time he had ever sat on that sofa with someone else. Unlike the sofa in Mrs Luo's house, pressed beneath the weight of two people, the springs sank in on themselves and didn't spring back up.

It seemed the officer was in a state of intense awareness, the fine hairs on his body attuned to the slightest stir. Li Wen swiftly set the scissors down on the tea table and chewed at the noodles, which had turned into a gloopy mess, the roar in his brain growing louder. He took another glance at the officer, wondering to himself, what has he got it in his head to do? Letting him have his last supper, was that it? Damn it all to hell, his thoughts were a muddle. He had to sober up.

Li Wen shoved the half-finished cup of noodles to the edge of the table, stood up, and said, 'Would it be alright if I had a beer?'

The old officer nodded, edging his rear end toward the door.

'I imagine it would be.'

Li Wen grabbed two bottles of beer, pried open the caps with the scissors, and handed one to the old officer. When the beer washed down his throat, his head felt clearer. Silence filled the room like cheap air freshener, the kind that came in solid blocks, the kind they used in the toilet at the fitness centre. He despised the deathlike, oily odour. The officer eyed the bottle for a long while before accepting it, tipping his head back, and taking a gulp. Something about the officer's body language revived a memory – his maternal grandfather taking swigs of liquor. He said that when people got old, they became crabby in every way, brusquely flinging liquor down their grumpy gullets. Li Wen's spirit was sinking lower. He even began to wish that this officer was an old friend of his, like Shuisheng; he wanted to keep drinking with the old man until darkness covered everything.

'Can I get you another?'

It was the first time he had ever had a proper chat with a police officer. The two people sitting on the sofa seemed to have known each other for decades. They each took sips from their bottles. Neither of them said anything, and neither planned on saying anything.

The old officer took another swig, and said slowly, without looking at Li Wen, 'Li Jianxin, that's your mother's name?'

Li Wen suddenly saw his heart thud to the floor. His entire body was utterly hollow, as if it were propped up now not by bones, but the white ghosts in the video game.

Then, he listened to what seemed like some sort of fantasy story. It wasn't too long or too short, and it was hard to tell where it started and ended.

*

Li Wen heard the old officer say, call me Officer Wang. He explained that he was the assistant chief constable of the local station, and he had been here the week before, too. Someone in the Youth Hostel complex had reported their neighbour was running an illicit still, and Officer Wang had gone to investigate. As it turned out, the owner of the home had accepted crates of liquor in payment for a debt, so many they were stacked nearly to the ceiling. The suspected still operator had given him several boxes to take back with him, and he had passed around the bottles of baijiu at the station, keeping the beer for himself. There were a few cases like this each year, and he had a well-stocked home bar. As long as he had enough to drink, he didn't get greedy.

For the last several days, though, he had been hearing the mother's cries echoing in his brain again, even in his dreams. She was harried, incoherent, but Officer Wang believed what she said. According to their neighbours, someone in the complex had seen Li Wen. He had to come get this Li Wen. In fact, he absolutely had to haul this Li Wen away. Beijing was a vast slaughterhouse where everyone under thirty-five seemed to be suddenly dropping dead, committing suicide, falling prey to accidents, or suddenly, mysteriously disappearing. Like Officer Wang when he was young, their heads were stuffed with grandiose ideals, yet, ground down by the lethargic solitude of everyday life, they turned to infants again: wrinkled all over, wailing piteously for food, screeching monotonously and repetitively, as if to remind everyone, *I'm still alive.*

There was a swig of beer left in the bottom of Officer Wang's bottle, and he said he would leave the last bit, as custom dictated, to be a polite guest. Li Wen drained his bottle and felt more sober than ever. He was so clear-headed that he concluded he could completely trust the old officer, and anyway, he couldn't get away. The thought sent currents of excitement coursing through him: he was prepared to put himself completely in Officer Wang's hands. He thought suddenly of Suwei's portable recorder, and he knew the full truth would eventually come to light. Li Wen let out a long exhalation. Everything was ending. He said, seemingly to no one but himself, 'I killed my mother.'

Officer Wang slapped his knee and, eyes wide, reached out and grabbed Li Wen's arm. 'What do you mean, you killed your mum?' Without waiting for Li Wen to look up, Officer Wang pulled out the newspaper, pointed to a headline reading 'University Student Flees from Family', and said, 'Son, it's about time for you to get back to your family. You know what they say, a mother is always beautiful in her son's eyes. You can't hate your mum, no matter what!'

That hum filled his head again. Officer Wang's words seemed to hover in a dreamlike haze: last year, his mother had gone to look for him in Beijing Station, but she seemed to have suffered some sort of head injury, walking in circles for hours, blundering about ineptly, struggling to make her legs obey her, almost falling flat on the floor. Officer Wang had helped her up, made contact with her family, and then bought her a ticket home, promising her that he would get her son back to her before he retired.

Li Wen longed to lean in closer, but in an instant, his entire body turned thin and flat, as if syphoned away by a vacuum bag. He vaguely, repeatedly mumbled, 'Did Mum make it home?'

Only after many repetitions did Officer Wang manage to make out the whole sentence. He folded the paper further, revealing a photo of Li Wen's mother and the headline in extra-large print: 'Mother Seeks Son Who Mysteriously Disappeared Before Graduating'.

Every breath was hastier than the one before. The black and white photo began to quiver, so he abruptly snatched the paper. He heard himself loudly bleat something that might have been the word 'mum' or 'me'. His mother's body was buried in rumpled grey newsprint, her back curved like a bow, eyes staring straight ahead – no, straight at him. Li Wen tried to rub his eyes, which had misted over (they both itched and stung), but his hand landed on his mother's eyes instead and began massaging gently. He couldn't tell if he was deep in despair or wild with glee, but either way, he had reached a dead end.

*

He had never before taken a train in the daytime. The scalding sun pierced the railway car, bathing the indelible greasy blobs on the sheets and chair backs in glistening radiance as the screaming train hurled them toward the final destination, before flinging them back to the starting point. He seemed to have fallen asleep, but at the same time, he was fully awake. The hard sleeper carriage appeared absolutely deserted, as if only he had managed to shove his way through the boisterous crowd and onto the train. He rummaged through the red plastic bag Officer Wang had given him, finding inside a cup of instant noodles, eggs boiled in tea, sausages wrapped in plastic and two cans of beer. The officer had insisted on seeing him off, making him promise to go straight back to his mum. It wouldn't take long – he would be home before the evening was out.

Eventually, a woman in a cream-coloured silk shirt came aboard. Her sleeves were rolled up to the elbows, revealing an old-fashioned wristwatch with a steel bracelet. Li Wen turned onto his side, trying to get a clear look at the woman's face, but the scalding sunlight intervened, and all he saw were jumbled features in a blinding flash. But he did make out a look of strange pity on the woman's face, like the expression his mother had worn a lifetime ago while boiling eggs for him in the morning.

A conductor in a blue uniform came to inspect his ticket, and after raking every conceivable crevice, he discovered, in the left inner pocket of his track jacket, the train ticket that would deliver him home in just twelve hours. The conductor expressionlessly punched the ticket – this meant he had passed muster, been deemed a properly ticketed passenger. They all underwent the same scrutiny, heads cocked to the sides, as if they might lose focus if they stared straight ahead instead.

Once the conductor walked away, Li Wen extracted a boiled egg from the plastic bag and cracked it open on the table top, immediately exposing the mottled brown egg white. Officer Wang had boiled it himself, he said, and since Beijingers liked salty foods, he had poured extra soy sauce into the pot. After eating the egg, he started to feel sick. He hated eating on trains. As the train tottered along the rails, he felt as if his stomach contents were clanging together like drab, tasteless rocks. He dozed off to the swaying of the carriage and briefly napped. When he woke, the sunlight remained piping hot and piercing. The train seemed to have gained a new passenger, a man in a black cloak who walked without making a sound, like one of Suwei's favourite characters, the Necromancer. The man said hello, and Li Wen got a glimpse of his face. He started. The man looked exactly like Suwei, or to be more exact, what he imagined Suwei would look like as an adult.

It was then that he began to worry he might not find his way home: What was the name of the street again? Was it Longhe East Street Number Two, or South Street Number Five? He remembered there was a hole-in-the-wall dumpling shop behind their place. His mother wouldn't let him eat any food with filling outside the home, so the only way to satisfy his craving was to steal into the shop and buy a dumpling or two. He loved the raw bloody taste, the meat paste oozing out and clinging to his fingers. Just moments ago, in the dream, he had watched himself half-carry, half-drag his mother to the bed and tuck her in, just as she had put him to bed when he was little; her body had turned transparent, and there were no bloodstains anywhere on her. She was alive. For just a second, perhaps ten seconds, she entered that state of mystical suffocation, her body light as air, every bit of weight concentrated in her pursed lips, which were pressed more tightly than ever and exuded an unprecedented sacred aura.

The train roared to a halt at a white platform. There were no fields, and no mountains, only emptiness, as if the scenery had come untethered and floated away. Once again, the conductor approached, explaining to Li Wen that the train had gone the wrong direction, and they needed to go west to get back on course. Momentarily, they pulled away from the white platform, heading west. It wasn't long before Li Wen drifted into a doze. At first, he clearly remembered which direction they were headed, but the train and the rails collided so often that amid the pitching oblivion, he couldn't tell any more which end was the front of the train and which was the back. Finally, the sky began to darken. The atmospheric pressure was very low, and the earth's energy gradually seethed up through the gaps in the rails, until both the earth and the sun turned to vapour.

There was another burst of sound, and the train halted completely. He watched through the window as a crush of people erupted onto the platform. He heard them saying that his mother was on the platform waiting for him, and he ran over to take a look, and saw her. The first woman to board the train and the man who had boarded afterwards disembarked, and he took the beer from the plastic bag and stuffed it into his black backpack. Now, he was the only person in the entire compartment. He took several steps backward, away from the door, as if the backpack on his back weighed him down so heavily he couldn't move.

He heard a little boy's shrill voice crying out, 'Mummy, mummy, wait! I'm coming!'

He followed the voice to the recesses of the platform and found his mother there, curled into a small ball atop a black wheelchair. He shoved his way through the crowd, breaking into a sprint, his feet growing heavier. At last, he took his mother's hand in his, and as if he were a baby, climbed up onto her lap. Everything had gone quiet.

Author's Note

Postscripts, afterwords, and descriptions of the writing process written by authors after completing works should be approached with suspicion. Words tacked onto the ends and beginnings of books are like product instruction manuals, serving to make the author appear sincere, which seems to be the criterion by which contemporary readers judge literature – putting the focus on the author instead of the work.

I was awaiting the publication of my first novel, *Novel Noir*, when images and characters from *Diablo's Boys* began surging into my mind, beginning with an old man and a model ship. I spent a long time adjusting the perspective between the two, until 'near' and 'far' were in balance, both driven onward and endlessly obstructed by a mist of gathering mystery. I bought a metre-long whiteboard, the kind used in after-school English classes. I wrote countless names on the board, then wiped them away. The book wasn't going anywhere. About half a year passed, and the coronavirus outbreak forced us to rapidly retreat into our homes. The whiteboard sat dead in the middle of my living room, sequestered for months, looking out on a deserted boulevard and a Ming dynasty observatory. Everything around me, and the world itself, seemed to be advancing at a crawl – time was moving forward, while the times regressed.

Thus, the entire story of *Diablo's Boys* originates with a model ship and an old man. Though confined to several inconspicuous corners in the last half of the book, they provided the impetus and the uncertainty that motivated me to write. Even before this, the world was heaping information on us, decimating our ability to cope. What surprised me most was that, as the fate of two boys, Li Wen and Suwei, mysteriously intertwined with my own daily life, I realised I could not banish their struggle from my sight, yet the silhouettes of the old man and the model ship lurked in the background, reducing the possibility of a return home to a slight thread of warm hope. This assured me that there was a soul at the core of the novel. Yes, the story was a part of this, and the characters were another, and on top of that, the novel was unfolding of its own accord.

Li Wen, Suwei, and Mrs Luo are all beguiling, untrustworthy narrators. Like us, they live in a young age, and this brings particular risks and difficulties to the narrative – the social, moral message may promptly detach from the story, trumpeting 'reality' or 'truth'. To think that a story can clearly sort out everything about a person or a time period is an illusion. Yet the fate of people does not change with the changing times. Even in a virtual world, we find survival, destruction, evil, passion, compassion, desire, resistance, denial, weakness, everything that ought to be there.

Yang Hao

Monday, 1 March 2021
Beijing